RAVE REVIEWS FOR
JENNIFER ARCHER!

ONCE UPON A DREAM

"Wildly entertaining. Wonderfully unique. Jennifer Archer gives readers another one for the keeper shelf."
—Ronda Thompson, Author of *Scandalous*

"Guaranteed to keep a reader turning pages long past bedtime!"
—*Under the Covers Book Reviews*

BODY & SOUL

"A charmer of a debut and a MUST for fans who love humor that makes you laugh out loud. Sassy dialogue and sizzling sensuality. Jennifer Archer is definitely an author to watch."
—Dia Hunter, Author of *The Beholding*

"*Body and Soul,* Jennifer Archer's first book . . . promises readers new and exciting things in the future from this gifted author."
—*Calico Trails*

"I think I'll add Ms.Archer to my 'Get Next Book' list. . . . I can't wait to see what she'll come up with next."
—*Romance Novel Central*

"*Body and Soul* is a fun, fast read that's going to please a lot of readers. It's easy to recommend this one!"
—*The Romance Reader*

Other *Love Spell* books by Jennifer Archer:
BODY & SOUL

FRIEND OR FOE?

"What's your name, Gambler? I prefer to know the identity of my enemies."

Meeting her steady gaze, Alex touched the tip of his sword to her chest and slid it ever so gently between her breasts and down her belly, knowing full well that the slightest pressure might tear the delicate fabric of her dress. "Don't make me your enemy," he said quietly. "I want to be your friend. A very good friend . . . if you'll let me."

Her eyes heated, darkened. "The sheriff . . . ," she said, her voice breathless. "He said to be wary of you. . . . He said you've a way with the ladies. Is that true?"

Alex placed the sword on the table beside her hat. Stepping forward, he drew her up from the chair into his arms. I'll let you be the judge of that."

Her head tilted back, her hair spilled across his hands, down his arms. It smelled as fresh and sweet as rain. Her stormy, dark eyes defied him one moment, dared him the next. With one hand at her waist, the other cradling her neck, Alex lowered his mouth, looked into her eyes and grinned the crooked grin that had captured the virginity of more than one proper Miss from his past. Then, ignoring the whistles and jeers all around them, he crushed the lady against him . . . and kissed her thoroughly. . . .

Once Upon A Dream

Jennifer Archer

LOVE SPELL   ◆   NEW YORK CITY

*This book is dedicated to
my nephew, Andy,
and my sons, Ryan and Jason.
Your lively imaginations and love of fun
inspired this story.*

A LOVE SPELL BOOK®

January 2001

Published by

Dorchester Publishing Co., Inc.
276 Fifth Avenue
New York, NY 10001

Cover art by John Ennis.
www.ennisart.com

ISBN 0-505-52418-X

The name "Love Spell" and its logo are trademarks of Dorchester Publishing Co., Inc.

Printed in the United States of America.

Visit us on the web at www.dorchesterpub.com.

ACKNOWLEDGMENTS

Many thanks to my Thursday night critique group: Karen Smith, DeWanna Pace, Jodi Koumalats, Bruce Edwards, Kim Cambell and Judy Andrew. Each week you challenge me, encourage me and teach me something new.

Thanks also to Ronda Thompson, Kimberly Willis Holt and Charlotte Goebel for giving me their time, suggestions and friendship.

And, as always, to Jeff for making it possible for me to chase a dream.

Once Upon A Dream

An ancient superstition holds that the
soul, or a part of it, can escape a
person's body if the mouth isn't covered
when yawning or sneezing....

In the folklore of many cultures,
butterflies have the ability to capture wandering souls....

And what is a dream if not a soul's
whispered secret? A revelation of one's
deepest fear or desire?

Chapter One

"TGIF, America!" the radio blared. "This is Doctor Dave, The Voice of Reason, coming to you live via KRLA Talk Radio from Big D, otherwise known as Dallas, Texas, on this sultry May night. What's on your minds this evening? Give me a call at 800-555-6676, and we'll talk about it."

Alex Simon tapped the earpiece of his glasses with his pencil while squinting at the crossword puzzle on the folded newspaper in his lap. *Thirteen down. Miserably inadequate. Eight letters.* Frowning, he tilted the paper so that it was better illuminated by the backyard light. *P, a, blank, blank, e, t, blank, blank.* "Hmmm."

As a caller relayed to Doctor Dave every sordid, embarrassing detail of the events leading up to his messy divorce, Alex only half-listened. The man's ex ruined his credit, humiliated him in front of his parents and slept with his best friend. Still, the caller continued to bend over backward to please her. He couldn't stop loving her.

Alex shook his head. Poor, pathetic prat. He imagined the bloke sitting home alone on this Friday night, a bottle of beer at his side, his fingers clutched tightly about the telephone receiver while he revealed his most private thoughts to a voice across the line. Not to mention every stranger in the nation who cared to listen in.

With a noisy sigh, Alex stretched, repositioned himself in the lawn chair, glanced around the shadowed backyard, then returned his attention to the crossword puzzle. Without looking up, he reached for the pint that sat on the picnic table alongside the radio. His hand skimmed over his cordless phone and the paperback Western he'd checked out yesterday at the library, then settled on the beer.

Before moving to the States and the small university town of Canyon, Texas, six months ago, he'd spirited a set of pint glasses away from his favorite pub. They provided a touch of familiarity on nights like tonight when he suffered a bout of homesickness.

A light came on upstairs in the house next door to Alex's, spoiling his concentration. Sampling the local brew, he glanced up and peered through the branches of the oak tree in his neighbor's side yard.

Her blinds weren't drawn. He could clearly see inside her window. He could see her, too—the back of her, anyway. She stepped onto a treadmill and started to walk.

Waving distractedly at a butterfly that fluttered past his face, Alex returned the pint to the table and forced his attention back to the puzzle. *Thirteen down. Miserably inadequate.* He considered the word *pitiful,* realized there weren't enough letters, then kept pondering.

His eyes strayed again to the window. Since moving into his house last week, he'd yet to meet the woman who lived next door. As he watched, she began to trot, her dark braid bouncing against her shoulders with each stride.

The butterfly returned. Scowling, Alex shooed it away and continued to contemplate his jogging neighbor.

Late this afternoon, he'd spotted her in a wide-brimmed straw hat, gardening across the hedge separating their yards. Because she'd seemed preoccupied, he hadn't bothered her. But he'd been close enough to notice the baggy overalls rolled up to her knees. He'd noticed her bare feet, too, and the pale purple polish on her toenails. A tiny silver ring adorned her second left toe, and she wore a matching silver ankle bracelet. Most definitely a loony. Purple toenails and foot jewelry! Ridiculous. She had a nice little bum, though. The skintight exercise clothes she wore tonight displayed it quite well. Alex adjusted his glasses and squinted. Quite well, indeed.

In his experience, women always looked best when walking—or in this case, jogging—away. His final glimpse of his ex-fiancée had been a lovely, bittersweet sight. Alex still cherished that blink in time just before the door slammed shut on her backside, that last flash of tempting misery . . . there one moment, gone the next.

Women. He hadn't the foggiest notion how to please them. Leigh, the ex, had made his reformation her personal pet project. His clothes weren't fashionable enough; his hairstyle was much too long, shaggy and outdated; she didn't like his eyeglasses. He was too analytical, too introspective, too cautious; overly picky about some things, not picky enough about others. If only he'd change just a bit. Be a bit more socially aware, more spontaneous, more polished. Then he'd be perfect.

The trouble was, Alex decided he didn't particularly want to be perfect. So eventually he quit trying, and Leigh became annoyed and gave up. Poor Leigh. Her project had failed miserably.

Miserably. Alex lowered the pencil and his gaze to the newspaper. *Miserably inadequate.* A perfect description of him, he guessed, as far as women were concerned.

Bored with the puzzle, he set it aside and reached for the paperback Western, *Amigo's Justice.* Not exactly his usual type of reading material but he'd been in the mood for something different. After scanning the back blurb, he'd thought it sounded like a fun escape from reality. And he'd been right. Zorro in a Stetson, with a gun instead of a sword. Though if it were Alex in the mask, he thought he'd prefer the sword.

Alex supposed if he were more like Johnny Amigo, the novel's macho main character, Leigh would have been extremely pleased with him. Johnny Amigo would never be found sitting alone in the dark spying on his curvy-bummed neighbor like a perverted peeping Tom.

He studied the masked hero on the book's cover. Unfortunately, the only thing he and Johnny Amigo had in common was a head of black, wavy hair. But while Johnny's curls somehow added to his machismo, Alex's simply looked like an unruly mess.

Lowering the book to his lap, Alex glanced up to see his neighbor progress from a trot to a run. Meanwhile, on the radio, Doctor Dave offered a final word of advice to the poor lovelorn bloke before breaking the connection.

"Who's next?" the doctor asked. "We're discussing relationships gone sour. Confused about your love life? Give me a call. 800-555-6676."

Confused? Alex reached for his beer, took a drink, set it down again. A bloody understatement. He tried to imagine calling the radio program, but couldn't. How could anyone—doctor or otherwise—offer relevant advice after conversing with a "patient" for a brief few minutes? Impossible.

Still . . . talking to someone about his concerns might be a relief. He felt more than a bit lonely tonight.

Alex's hand drifted toward the cordless phone on the picnic table but, just before he touched it, he jerked back like he'd been grazed by one of Amigo's bullets. Bloody hell. What was he doing?

The doctor made another plea for a call. Alex wavered. He'd thought he was long over his breakup with Leigh. But, lately, he found himself dwelling on their time together, wondering if she might have had a point. Perhaps he *was* in denial when it came to his own shortcomings. After all, he was his father's son. And Pop had never succeeded at pleasing his mum.

Again, Alex reached for the phone.

Again, he pulled back.

He should ring his sister, not some stranger . . . a voice on the airwaves. But his sister would only pity and pamper him. Alex loathed such attention, which was why he shied away from discussing personal problems with family and close friends.

Alex took another swig of beer. His ex had often accused him of being too cautious, of over-analyzing everything. She claimed a bit of spontaneity would enrich the quality of his life, make him less boring. Perhaps now was the perfect opportunity to test her theory. What could one phone call hurt?

Before he could analyze his reasons further or change his mind, Alex grabbed the phone and rang up the good doctor. After several tense seconds, an operator put him through.

"Welcome to the program! This is Doctor Dave. What would you like to talk about tonight?"

"Hello? I . . . uh . . ."

When Alex heard his own voice echoing from the radio at his side, the beer in his stomach threatened to come back up. *Pathetic. That's you, Alex old boy.* His gaze darted to the newspaper on the table. *Pathetic. Eight letters. Thirteen down. Voila!*

"Would you turn off your radio?" Doctor Dave asked. "I'm getting some feedback here."

Alex did as he was told. Then, with his eyes fixed on the woman in the window, he stood, toppling the lawn chair on its side as he hurried toward the back of his house. When he reached the door, he switched off the yard light. Confident he couldn't be seen now should she turn around, Alex leaned against the door, exhaled a breath of pure relief, then filled his lungs with rain-scented air.

"Hello? Are you there, Caller? Who am I speaking with?" Doctor Dave asked.

The stench of panic suddenly overpowered him. This was a dreadful mistake. What if one of his students listened and recognized his voice? Or one of his colleagues? He'd never live this down. Alex's heart did a perfect pole vault—up to his throat, down to his stomach in one smooth leap. Better try to lose the English accent, he decided.

"I—ah—anonymous," he stammered.

"Okay, Anonymous," the doctor said, chuckling, "Can I at least ask where you're calling from?"

His gaze skipped to the book on the picnic table. "West Texas," he drawled. "I'm a Panhandle boy, born and bred."

"Okay, we have Anonymous on the line from deep in the heart of cattle country. What's on your mind, Anonymous?"

Cringing, Alex glanced from the window, to the hedge, to every shadow surrounding his yard, then back to the window again. "I'm having a bit—" He caught himself. "I don't trust women," Alex blurted, this time sounding as pure Texan as chicken-fried steak. Raindrops started falling around him. He barely noticed.

Doctor Dave laughed. "You and the rest of the male population."

"I've never understood 'em. Whenever I get too close, they always end up tryin' to change me. And *I* always end up doin' my best to please 'em. At least at first."

"Go on."

"I've about decided I don't have what it takes

for a committed relationship. Maybe if I just don't get too involved, just keep it friendly, I can deal with women. You know, without havin' to try to be something I'm not."

Robin slowed her pace on the treadmill as she listened to the conversation on the radio between Doctor Dave and a male caller. She glanced from the radio to the phone. Poor man. He sounded like a down-to-earth, down-home kind of guy. A really nice person who'd been made to feel un-lovable. Now he was questioning himself, devel-oping a fear of getting close to the opposite sex. Well, if anyone could sympathize with him, she could.

Switching off the treadmill, Robin slowed to a stop. She walked to her bedside table, picked up a glass of water and gulped down half the con-tents. Then, as Doctor Dave counseled the caller on accepting himself, facing fears and learning to use positive aggression, she slipped on her glasses, grabbed the phone and punched in the radio program's number.

Facing fears. She'd heard her share of psycho-babble on that one. It hadn't helped. The caller didn't need a lecture. He needed to know he wasn't alone. He also needed to know that if he chose isolation, a lonely life stretched ahead of him. She hated the thought of anyone else ending up in her situation.

While she waited to be put through, her gaze

drifted to the bedroom window. She'd left it open just a crack. She would have liked to raise it higher, but she needed to buy new screens. Soon, the Texas heat would prevent her from enjoying the fresh night air, and she'd be forced to resort to twenty-four-hour-a-day air conditioning. Until then, though, she liked leaving the windows open and the blinds up. She liked seeing her yard and the old, giant oak that reigned over it. A full, silver moon peeked through the stately branches, highlighting the flutter of leaves on twisted limbs.

Sympathy for the anonymous caller wasn't the only reason Robin had reached for the phone. A part of her longed to tell her tale, to let Doctor Dave's soothing voice wash over her in waves of reassurance. Though she doubted he could, she yearned for him to dismantle her fears, to explain away her cursed heritage and set her free.

Tapping the receiver with an impatient forefinger, Robin stared outside at the dark silhouette of the oak tree against the circle of the moon. A sudden strong breeze swayed the branches, tossing the leaves into a flickering frenzy and blowing the smell of rain into the room. When the phone line clicked, Robin jumped.

"We have another caller on the line. Welcome to the program. Who am I speaking to?"

"I—" Robin lowered the volume on her radio. "I'd rather not say."

Doctor Dave laughed. "So . . . another Anonymous, I gather? Female, this time. Fair enough. What's your story?"

She toyed with the amulet that hung from a chain around her neck. The ankh, a symbol of long life and immortality, was a gift from Uncle Ethan, her mother's brother. Ethan and Millie, her mother's best friend, had both raised her. And they'd both be mortified, though for different reasons, if they knew she was about to reveal her hexed legacy over the airwaves.

Better disguise my voice, Robin decided, *just in case one of them might be listening.* Ethan and Millie would know it was her just from the story, but no one else would. That might make them a little less annoyed with her. "I just wanted to tell the last caller that I understand what he's going through," Robin said, deepening her voice to a husky pitch. "But I wish he wouldn't shut himself off from people. If he starts, before he knows it his life could change in ways he can't even imagine. Terrible ways." She drew a breath. "I know what I'm talking about. I know what it's like to be afraid of closeness. In fact, fear is one of my few close relationships. We're very old acquaintances, fear and I."

"Are you implying you harbor other fears, too?"

"You might say that." She thought of Millie. "I know of one person who thinks so, anyway."

"Tell me about it."

Robin took a breath. "My great-great-grandmother died between her twenty-ninth and thirtieth birthdays."

"And?"

"It was deemed an accident. A runaway stagecoach."

"Nothing odd about that. At least not during the time your great-great-grandmother must've lived in."

Robin released the amulet to reach for the braid that lay over her left shoulder. She twirled it round and round her finger—a nervous habit. "I suppose not. But I'm not so sure it was an accident."

"I see," Doctor Dave said slowly, drawing out the words. "You think she was murdered?"

"I'm not sure what I think." Robin tightened her grip on the receiver. "I only know that years later, one month before my *great-grandmother's* thirtieth birthday, she died, too. She was struck by a stray bullet during a bank robbery."

"That's an incredible coincidence, both mother and daughter suffering such unusual deaths at the same young age. But that's all it is . . . a coincidence."

Robin sighed. "There's more. My grandmother died, too. One week before her thirtieth birthday. It was a hit-and-run car accident. At least they called it an accident. The car came right up onto the sidewalk alongside her house and ran her down. The driver was never caught."

When Doctor Dave didn't immediately respond, Robin continued, "And finally there's my mother. The day before she would've turned thirty, she walked under a ladder my dad was standing on while painting our house. A full gallon of paint fell off the ladder and struck her on the head. White semigloss enamel. She died immediately. I was two months old."

The silence following her words lasted only seconds but seemed far longer. The wind sighed . . . a cloud passed over the moon . . . raindrops tapped on the roof. Robin waited. Then, Doctor Dave began.

As he rattled off a monologue about the psychology behind superstitious beliefs, even going so far as to quote supposedly renowned studies Robin had never heard of, she listened with a hopeful ear. But nothing he said comforted or convinced her. It was easy for him to be skeptical. It wasn't his legacy under discussion. *He* didn't face his thirtieth birthday in two weeks with the deck of fate stacked against him.

Robin broke the connection midsentence. After turning up her radio, she removed her glasses, switched off the lamp and reclined on the bed. She stared out the window into the darkness beyond her yard, into a world she feared as much as she feared never stepping into it again. She was afraid—afraid of suffering an accident that wasn't an accident at all. Yet if the women in her family were truly cursed, if she was destined to die before turning thirty, confining herself to her home wouldn't save her. Still . . . the mere thought of leaving her property caused her heart to hammer and her skin to break out in a cold, clammy sweat.

Robin hugged her pillow and listened to the people who called in to Doctor Dave's program to discuss their views on the topics of coincidence, curses and superstitions. Tinker, her schnauzer, jumped onto the bed and cuddled up next to her. Before the program went off the air, Robin was half-asleep, too groggy to shut the window or change into pajamas.

Must be comforting to be so secure about your beliefs and about life, she thought as Doctor Dave's contentions sifted through her mind. Up until the past year, she, too, had sneered at superstition . . . or at least pretended to do so. She'd refused to listen to Uncle Ethan's warnings, had scorned his stories of the cryptic affliction that had felled four generations of women in her family. But the day after she turned twenty-nine, all of that changed. Since then, to trust in logic was a luxury she couldn't afford.

Doctor Dave's soothing tone wove its way through her consciousness like a black satin ribbon . . . so smooth, so elegant, so strong. She wanted to believe all he said, to feel his steadfast assurance, to put this curse business behind her and get on with living her life. She thought of Anonymous and wondered if he felt as alone and uncertain as she did. As defenseless.

Robin stroked Tinker's fur, her eyelids heavy.

The truth was, she'd been a prisoner of fear far longer than the year she'd shut herself away. The curse had been in the back of her mind all her life, taunting her. She wondered what it would be like to be brave. To face fears like Doctor Dave advised instead of hiding from them. If she could do that, she'd trace the origins of this curse all the way back to where it started and end it before it began. Back to her great-great-grandmother's time . . .

Beyond the window, the rain fell faster. Beneath the old oak tree, wind stirred a few scattered leaves in the grass then sent them scampering across the brick path that ran from the house to the alley. Through the open window a butterfly blew into the house. It rose above the breeze, then hovered in place for a moment before gliding toward the bed.

Robin felt the brush of something soft against her cheek, like the mother's kiss she'd imagined hundreds of times but couldn't remember . . . or maybe the flutter of a feather. She yawned, covering her mouth as Uncle Ethan had warned her always, always to do. *Gotta keep your trap covered when you yawn or sneeze, or your soul could slip right out, slick as a whistle*, he'd told her a thousand times.

When the feather tickled again, Robin blinked her heavy eyelids and squinted. *A butterfly.* She closed her eyes, grateful she'd followed Uncle Ethan's advice about the yawn. He'd taught her, too, that butterflies could capture wandering souls.

The butterfly settled on the pillow beside her. Ignoring it, Robin's thoughts returned to the curse. As she drifted off to sleep, she yawned a second time, but was too far gone to heed her uncle's warning.

Chapter Two

Alex began his usual bedtime ritual: floss three minutes, brush two, gargle one. Then he told himself Johnny Amigo wouldn't preoccupy himself with such finicky grooming habits. So, disgusted by his own tendencies, he turned his back on his dental floss and went to bed.

But the beer he'd consumed tasted stale in his mouth, and he couldn't sleep. So, ten minutes after turning out the light, he rose again and resigned himself to resuming the habitual routine.

He still couldn't sleep.

For the second time, Alex got up. He opened the window wider, hoping fresh air and the sounds of the summer rain shower would do the trick. He couldn't quit thinking about the caller who'd followed him on Doctor Dave's radio program. Finally . . . a woman who claimed to understand him, and he'd never know who she was. Just his luck.

Her fears were as illogical as his own. More so. As an academic, a professor of both botany and entomology, Alex didn't believe in curses and other such superstitions. Still, he could understand how a woman, even an intelligent one, with the caller's family history might become obsessed with such beliefs, logical or not. Although she was a stranger, for some reason, he wished he could help, that he could convince her the so-called curse could only hurt her if she believed in it.

Giving up on sleep, Alex switched on the bedside lamp and sat up. He reached for *Amigo's Justice,* the second book in the Johnny Amigo trilogy. The first in the series had been checked out, so he had yet to read it. If Alex couldn't rescue the damsel in distress on the radio, he guessed he might as well see how Johnny fared with his damsel.

After readjusting and plumping the pillows beneath his shoulders, Alex slipped on his glasses and started to read. Fifteen minutes later, his eyes drifted shut. *Amigo's Justice* slipped from his fingers, slid down his bare stomach, then toppled to the floor.

A breeze rippled the bedroom curtains, but Alex was unaware. He didn't see the blue butter-fly flutter into the room through the tiny hole in the window screen. At first the butterfly settled on the pillow beside Alex's head. But after a moment, it perched atop his nose, causing a tickle and making him sneeze.

And Alex dreamed . . .

The Crazy Ace Saloon hadn't been this rowdy since they'd toasted in the new year of 1888 four months back. Laughter, whoops and hollers filled the big, crowded room. Slick, the piano player, pounded out a boot-tappin' tune. Bottles clinked against glasses, and the cloying smell of cheap perfume tainted the smoky air.

Cowhands from the Double Z Ranch were back home after a long trail drive. The boys had arrived for their night on the town thirsty as the West Texas prairie, horny as a two-peckered billy goat and with plenty of cash in their pockets.

Alex always looked forward to the boys' return. He relished the challenge of winning their hard-earned money fair and square.

He shifted in his chair. Ruby had put on a few extra pounds since the last time she sat on his lap. He didn't have the heart to ask her to get up. Ruby was a good ol' gal. Besides that, he'd ruin his image as a lady's man if he admitted his left leg had gone to sleep, and his foot was tingling.

Staring across Ruby's red satin-covered bosom at the cards in his hand, Alex narrowed his eyes. He suspected the young cowhand on the other side of the table was trying to pull a fast one on

31

him. Alex was biding his time 'til he caught the kid red-handed. Then he'd call him on it.

The piano music stopped abruptly. A hush fell over the room. Alex looked up.

She stood just this side of the double swinging doors, an auburn-haired lady with a lacy yellow parasol and a matching yellow hat. A fancy lady. Not fancy like Ruby with her berry-stained lips and curve-huggin' red satin. Fancy in a refined sort of way. Like the women who went to school back East when they came of age. This lady didn't belong in the Crazy Ace, that was for damn sure. She looked delicate and out of place . . . like a dewy yellow rose standing alone in a field of sagebrush and prickly pear cactus.

The fancy lady didn't seem to know that, though. Or didn't care. Holding her head high, she gazed straight across the room at Alex with her thick-lashed brown eyes.

"Can I have a word with you, Gambler?"

Her voice defied her delicate appearance. It was husky, sultry and sure, making Alex think of slick, satin sheets and hot, sweaty nights.

With his eyes held steady on the lady, he leaned toward Ruby, whispered a promise in her ear, then gave her a pat on her shapely rump.

Batting her eyelashes at him, Ruby smiled, then turned a scowl on the woman in the doorway before standing and walking behind the bar.

Alex stood, too. He staggered a little when his numb leg took his weight. He gave it a shake to restart the circulation. As was his habit, he automatically touched one hand to the Colt on his left hip, the other to the sword on his right. Then, glancing at Slick, he nodded.

The piano player turned and kicked the jukebox in the corner, and Willie Nelson instantly crooned "Of All The Girls I've Loved Before."

Alex scratched behind his ear and frowned as he made his way past tables of whispering, snickering cowhands. Something didn't seem quite right about that song . . . or that jukebox. . . .

When he reached the fancy lady's side, he tipped the brim of his black Stetson. "Ma'am."

"I'm told you're the best detective this side of the Mississippi," she said in her husky voice.

"You're told wrong."

She tilted her head to one side. "Oh?"

Alex flashed her a smile. "I'm the best detective this side of the North Atlantic. Best gambler, too." He motioned toward the door. "This is no place for a lady. We can talk outside."

Her gaze traveled slowly around the gaudy saloon. Then, just as slowly, she closed her parasol and pointed it toward the only empty table in the house. "I could use a drink."

Alex felt his smile waver. She didn't seem the type to indulge. But her habits were none of his business, so he snapped his fingers, and the bartender appeared at his side.

"Perrier with a lemon twist," the lady said without blinking.

*Alex blinked enough for them both as he fol-
lowed her to the table, his eyes riveted on her
bustle and the hypnotic way it moved left then
right with each step she took. He pulled in his
eyeballs and pulled out her chair when they
reached their destination. Then he moved to sit
across from her. "So . . . how did you find me?"*

*"The sheriff said to look for a man in a mask."
She glanced around the room, then shrugged.
"You're the only one who fits the description. If
you don't mind my asking, why do you wear it?"*

*Frowning, Alex touched the black cloth that
covered the upper half of his face. Why did he
wear it? He hadn't read the first book in the series yet, so he wasn't real sure. With a shrug of
his own, he drawled, "Good question. Now, I've
got one for you. Why do you need a detective?"*

*"Someone's trying to kill my great-great-
grandmother," she blurted, then paused, her big,
soulful eyes shifting to the tabletop before meeting his again. Her look of quiet determination
nudged his heart. "And me. They're trying to kill
me, too."*

*Alex reached across the table to squeeze her
hand. "Your great-great-grandmother? Why
would anyone want to kill an old woman?"*

*"That's what I want you to help me find out.
But she's really not so old. She's about to turn
thirty."*

*"Thirty?" Alex frowned again. "And how old
are you?"*

"I'm about to turn thirty, too."

Before he had time to ponder that one, a commotion drew Alex's attention. He heard Ruby's scream as if it came from far away . . . saw the saloon doors swing open as if in slow motion. From the shadows beyond, a knife sailed into the room. It turned end over end, aimed right toward the fancy lady's throat. Alex dove across the table and knocked her to the floor while, at the same time, he reached up to grab the airborne weapon. He caught it by the handle, dropped it on the floor, then, in one swift move, stood and drew his gun with one hand, his sword with the other.

"Stay put," he shouted over his shoulder as he ran toward the doors. "I'll handle this."

When he reached the exit, it had somehow changed. Instead of swinging wooden doors, it now contained a revolving glass one. Pointing the gun with his left hand, he used his sword hand to push through the revolving door. He walked a half circle and came out on the other side . . . into his own backyard. No knife-wielding culprits here. Only shadows, his picnic table, the hedge and, beyond, his neighbor's yard with the big oak tree.

He went back inside the saloon. The lady's yellow hat sat on the table; he guessed he'd knocked it off when he dived on top of her. Her hair hung loose about her shoulders in long, dark, shiny waves. Beside her hat lay the knife. Only it wasn't a knife anymore, it was a sword. His sword. Alex *looked down at his right hand and found it empty. He walked to the table and picked up the sword. "This is mine."*

"Then maybe it's you I'm after. What's your name, Gambler?" She reached for her parasol, but it had transformed into a pair of gardening shears. The lady didn't seem to notice. She picked them up and pointed them at him, clicking the blades open and closed like the snapping jaw of an irate dog. "I prefer to know the identity of my enemies." After a moment, she quit clicking the shears and stared at him, her eyes narrowed.

Meeting her steady gaze, Alex touched the tip of his sword to her chest and slid it ever so gently between her breasts and down to her belly, knowing full well that the slightest pressure might tear the delicate fabric of her dress. "Don't make me your enemy," he said quietly. "I want to be your friend. A very good friend . . . if you'll let me."

Her eyes heated, darkened. Slowly, she lowered the shears to the table. "The sheriff . . ." she said, her voice breathless. "He said to be wary of you . . . he said you've a way with the ladies. Is that true?"

Alex placed the sword on the table beside her hat and the shears. Stepping forward, he drew her up from the chair into his arms. "I'll let you be the judge of that, Lady."

Her head tilted back, her hair spilled across his hands, down his arms. It smelled as fresh and sweet as rain. Her stormy, dark eyes defied him

*one moment, dared him the next. With one hand
at her waist, the other cradling her neck, Alex
lowered his mouth, hesitated only a breath away
from hers, then lowered it further.*

*The first touch of their lips was soft as a spring
breeze, gentle and sweet. She made a quiet sound
in her throat that told him she was as astonished
as he by the power of that simple, brief contact.*

*Alex pulled back, looked into her eyes and
grinned the crooked grin that had captured the
virginity of more than one proper Miss from his
past. Then, ignoring the whistles and jeers all
around them, he crushed the lady against him . . .
and kissed her thoroughly. . . .*

Robin drew back a hand, then let it fly.

Tinker yelped.

Robin's eyes popped open. She sat up abruptly
and reached for the lamp, switching it on. Tinker
cowered on the floor looking up at her.

"Oh, baby!" Scooping the dog into her arms,
Robin leaned against the headboard, her heart
pounding. "You licked my face, didn't you? I'm
sorry I hit you. I thought . . ."

She touched her lips with her fingertips. They
felt swollen, tingly. As if . . .

"It was only a dream," Robin whispered, closing her eyes. Crazy as it was, it had seemed so
real. She could still smell the scent of bay rum
on his skin, could still taste the whiskey on his
lips and feel the powerful pull of his arms as he

drew her against him. His voice . . . it had sounded like the caller on the radio.

Holding Tinker in her arms, Robin stood and walked to the window. She stared through the drizzling rain past the big oak tree to a dim glowing light. It shone from within the dark shadow of her neighbor's house.

Blinking away sleep, Alex leaned down and snatched *Amigo's Justice* off the floor. For several seconds, he studied the masked image of Johnny Amigo on the cover. Finally, shaking his head and chuckling, he placed the book on the bedside table, slipped off his glasses and turned off the light. He chuckled again, deciding he'd suffered the side effects of indulging in too much escapist fiction.

Sprawled on his back, he stared at the ceiling and listened to the rain. The fresh, sweet smell of it permeated the room, bringing memories of the scent of her hair. Alex closed his eyes. "It was just a silly dream," he said aloud. "Get a grip, old boy."

Sheeba, his Siamese cat, hopped up onto the bed and brushed against his feet before settling atop them.

Silly dream or not, Alex passed the rest of the night without sleeping, recalling the feel of her slender body pressed against his and laughing at himself. He thought about the woman on the radio who believed she was cursed and about the neighbor he'd spotted in her garden just that afternoon. The vision in yellow he had conjured in a dream was an odd combination of the two. And both the dream . . . and the woman in it . . . seemed far too real.

Chapter Three

Tinker's yelp drew Robin's attention away from her roses. On her knees, wrist-deep in mulch, she sat back on her heels and scanned the yard.

Her new next-door neighbor wore an odd-looking white bonnet with a mesh mask that covered his face. Holding Tinker by the scruff of the neck with one hand and a long sword with the other, he lifted the dog over the low hedge separating Robin's backyard from his.

"Home you go." Tapping the schnauzer's bottom with the flat edge of the sword, he leaned down and deposited the dog in the grass. Tinker landed with a whimper. "Now, stay put," the man said sternly, his accent distinctly British. He pointed the end of his sword at Tinker's upturned face. "Or I'll chop you up into little pieces and use you for cat food."

Robin slapped a dirty gloved hand atop her straw hat. Grabbing her gardening shears, she sprang to her bare feet. She stepped around a bag of fertilizer and started toward him. "Just what do you think you're doing?" Scooping Tinker into the crook of her arm, she checked for injuries before turning to glare at her neighbor. "You could've hurt him, dumping him on the ground like that. And you hit him with your sword." She pointed the gardening shears at him. "I saw you."

He stepped back, trampling a well-tended bed of pansies in the process.

Robin summed him up through the lenses of her glasses. Lanky and broad-shouldered. Tall. Six feet, at least. He wore running shoes, jeans that had seen better days, a too-short T-shirt with Oxford University printed across the front. Because of the mask covering his face, she couldn't make out his features, but his reaction told her she'd startled him, that he hadn't noticed her working in the garden when he'd taken the liberty of raising a weapon to her puppy.

"Uh . . . that tap on the tail end was just to make an impression," he said.

"You threatened to chop Tinker up into little pieces." Robin jabbed the shears at him for emphasis.

He chuckled unconvincingly. "Just a bit of a

41

joke, I assure you. I'm afraid your dog is taunting Sheeba." He stooped, picked up a large Siamese cat. "I'd hate for Tinker to get his eyes scratched out."

The cat looked at Tinker with a piercing blue gaze and hissed.

Robin narrowed her eyes. "Is that another threat?"

"Are you asking Sheeba or me?" Chuckling again, he lowered the cat to the ground.

Unamused by his sorry attempt at a joke, Robin bristled. "What are you doing out here with a sword, anyway?"

"It was my father's. Fencing was a hobby of his." After a moment's hesitation, he stepped closer to the hedge again, apparently unaware of the suffering flowers beneath his feet. "We haven't met."

He extended his hand, then abruptly drew it back. The sword stabbed the hedge and lashed sideways through the air before he managed to pull off his glove. Finally, he offered his hand again. "I'm—"

Robin didn't hear his name. The flailing sword had caused panic to rear its ugly head. Maybe the joke was on her, she thought. Hoping to avoid a fatal accident, she'd secluded herself on her own property this past year. But maybe the unknown danger she dreaded was as close as her own backyard.

Leaving her glove on, her arm at her side,

Robin glanced at his outstretched hand. It was large, strong-looking, callused. His fingers were long and tan, the nails clipped short. A very nice, masculine hand. Too bad it belonged to a moron. "Would you get rid of that thing?"

He lowered his arm. "Pardon?"

"The sword. Don't you think it's dangerous, waving it around in people's faces . . . and at animals?"

"Well . . . I . . ." He lifted the end of the sword to eye level. "It's a saber. See, here? It isn't sharp."

Sword, saber. As far as Robin was concerned, they were one and the same. She glanced down. The weapon's tip was blunt. Her heartbeat slowed.

He placed the saber on the ground at his feet. "I apologize. I haven't practiced for years. Not since my father died when I was a lad. But I assure you, fencing's perfectly safe if it's done correctly. Perhaps you'd like a demonstration. It's really quite interesting." He gestured toward an open place in the hedge where a bush had died and never been replaced. It offered a passage from her yard to his. "Here," he said. "I'll help you through."

Shaking her head, Robin stumbled backward. Her heart stumbled, too, at the prospect of venturing beyond the confines of her property . . . of stepping outside her own yard. "I-I'm really not interested in that sort of thing," she stammered, hating the anxiety in her voice but unable to control it. She drew Tinker closer, her mouth dry as dust. Though she couldn't see the man's eyes, Robin knew he was staring at her . . . knew he noticed her trembling body and wondered at her overreaction. At least her hat shielded her blushing face.

"In the future," she said, managing to sound more piqued now than apprehensive, "if Tinker needs disciplining, Mr. . . ."

"Simon."

She lifted her chin. "Mr. Simon, I'd appreciate it if you'd tell me rather than taking on the responsibility yourself."

"I . . . uh . . . I'm . . ." He wrung his glove like a dishrag, twisting it unmercifully between both hands.

Cradling Tinker against her chest, Robin started for the house. "I'll make sure my dog stays away from your cat," she said over her shoulder.

Tinker gazed up at Robin with love-filled eyes.

Alex stepped away from the hedge. *Daft woman.* Scowling down at the pansies in his yard—the ones he'd demolished—he pondered her baffling reaction to him. Angry at first, then nervous, then indignant. She hadn't introduced herself; Alex didn't even know her name. *Daft, cheeky woman.* Her precious Trinket or Tinker, or whatever the dog's name was, had been in the wrong, not him.

Annoyed with himself nonetheless, Alex

stooped to pick up his saber. Suddenly he realized he'd left his mask on throughout their entire conversation. His face heated. She must've thought him a complete prat.

Alex stood, shook off his embarrassment. He bloody well wouldn't concern himself with her opinion. Johnny Amigo certainly wouldn't. In fact, if Johnny Amigo were confronted by such a woman, he wouldn't stammer and stumble around, either. Never would the tough, virile, Old West seeker of justice allow some frisky-tempered female to get the best of him while he fumbled like an awkward teenager; trampling flowers beneath his big, clumsy feet, getting all but tangled up with his own saber. Johnny, in his black Stetson and black half-mask, would swiftly and suavely set the filly straight . . . then leave her swooning.

Alex cringed at his own absurd musings. Johnny Amigo was becoming a bit of a nuisance, invading his dreams, slipping into his thoughts with disturbing frequency throughout the morning. It was the dream about the paperback hero being his alter ego that had brought to mind the long-neglected fencing equipment. Earlier, he'd searched the boxes stashed in his attic until he found the mask and saber.

Returning to the center of the yard, Alex resumed his fencing stance. But as he parried the incoming thrust of a nonexistent opponent, his thoughts returned again and again to the previous confrontation with his neighbor. Something about it bothered him. Something more than her curt attitude and insinuations.

Alex executed a counterattack, the riposte. Of course. The gardening shears! The way she'd pointed them at him! The gesture seemed familiar, as though she'd confronted him with the tool before. Certain that wasn't the case, he lowered the saber and tugged off his mask. Fencing had lost its appeal. The morning sun was too hot for it, anyway. Perhaps he'd get back to it later.

The back door opened, and his nephew stepped out of the house.

"Ty! Just in time to save me from my own ineptness." He crossed the yard. "Where's your mum?"

"Shopping." Ty's rust-colored hair shimmered in the sunlight. He scratched his freckled nose. "She dropped me off."

"What do you say we do a bit of shopping ourselves? We need to pick up a few things at the auto shop if we're ever to get started restoring the Mustang."

"Sure." Ty lifted a shoulder. "Whatever."

Alex didn't take his nephew's lack of enthusiasm personally. His sister assured him that, lately, the fifteen-year-old lad considered one-word sentences to be the height of conversation.

As they started into the house, he glanced across at the rosebushes surrounding his neighbor's yard. Too bad for her she hadn't been more

46

friendly. He could tell her a thing or two about those roses. He noted the black spots on the foliage beneath the tender yellow blooms and frowned. Too bad, indeed.

That evening, Robin stood at the windows that stretched across her living room wall looking out into her large side yard. Tinker had found a shady spot in the grass and was sleeping soundly. The hedge beside him moved slightly. From within the greenery, a tiny, dark paw darted out, swiped at Tinker's ear then disappeared.

Tinker's head came up. He looked around, stretched, rolled to his back and resumed his nap.

"So . . . what do you think?" Millie asked from across the room.

"I think my neighbor's cat is a sneaky, conniving little—"

"About this painting," Millie interrupted. "Do you think you'll finish it soon? The city block party is next month. There'll be a lot of foot traffic through my stores. You'd get some good exposure."

Robin kept her eyes on Tinker. Millie owned two businesses in the nearby city of Amarillo, just a twenty-minute drive from the house. Her antique shop and clothing boutique stood side-by-side in a renovated downtown building. In both, she displayed and sold the work of Texas artists— Robin included. Robin's line of silver jewelry and hand-beaded purses, which she made in a studio

47

she'd assembled in a spare bedroom of her house, was a hot seller at Millie's Boutique. And, in the past year, several other stores in Texas, as well as outside the state, had picked up the line.

In between jewelry pieces, Robin dabbled in painting. Whenever she finished a piece, Millie displayed it in her antique shop.

This latest painting, the one Millie spoke of, was giving Robin trouble. An Old West scene inspired by Ethan's stories of her great-great-grandmother, Hannah Sann, it was far different from her usual, more contemporary work.

"Come over here, Millie," Robin said quietly. "I want a witness." When Millie moved up beside her, Robin caught a familiar whiff of the older woman's spicy perfume.

"A witness to what, sweetie?"

"Look over there." Robin pointed. "At the edge of the yard."

The Siamese cat's head peeked out from the hedge. "That cat is deliberately badgering Tinker. Now I know why he keeps going over there. I never had a problem with him leaving the yard before *they* moved in."

"Someone finally moved in next door?"

"Yeah, and he's about to get a surprise when I set him straight about who's bothering whom."

"He?"

Recognizing the curiosity in Millie's voice, Robin met her gaze. "An eccentric nerd by the name of Simon."

Millie pursed her red lips. Her pencil-darkened brows arched with interest. "First or last?"

Robin frowned at the question.

"Simon," Millie explained, tapping her leather sandal against the carpet. "Is it his first name or last?"

"Last."

"What's his first name?"

"Mr."

Millie gave an exasperated sigh. "Since when do you have a problem with eccentrics? You were raised by the master." She smoothed a hand down her cream-colored knit pantsuit. A silver-studded brown leather belt cinched her tiny waist, accentuating an hourglass figure. "Simon's a very noble name. And don't knock nerds. They make the best husbands."

"How would you know? You never married a nerd."

"Exactly. And all my exes were lazy, untrustworthy, good-for-nothing losers. I bet if you quizzed Mrs. Gates on the subject, she wouldn't have those same complaints about Bill."

"No, but she'd have others. All wives do."

"Maybe. Still, we might be wise to give computer hackers, school band directors and scientists a closer look." Millie faced the window again. "Speaking of wives, is there a Mrs. Simon?"

"I don't know. We only talked for a minute. We didn't exchange résumés." Robin returned her attention to the hedge in time to see the cat take

49

another lightning-quick swipe at Tinker's ear.

"Hmmm." Millie crossed her arms, lifted one hand to her mouth, tapped her lower lip with a glossy red fingernail. "What does this new neighbor of yours look like?"

"I don't know that, either."

"If you haven't seen the man, then how do you know he's a nerd?"

"Oh, I've seen him. But he was wearing a fencing mask."

"Fencing?"

"As in dueling swords. Mr. Simon turned his on Tinker because Tinker ventured beyond the hedge after that cat . . . or so he said."

"Did he skewer the dog?"

Robin noticed Millie didn't sound the least bit concerned one way or the other. "Just his pride."

"Well, then . . . the mongrel probably deserved what he got."

Frowning, Robin faced her. As usual, Millie looked flawless; her stylishly layered blond hair free of gray, her makeup sparse and precise. Anyone would swear she was a decade younger than her sixty years.

"That eccentric British lout whacked my dog on the butt and made threats just because Tinker was a little curious about his stupid old cat."

"British?" Millie's eyes widened. "You didn't tell me he was British."

"What kind of wacko gets all decked out to battle an invisible opponent in the backyard anyway?" Robin drew a quick breath. She wouldn't admit to Millie she'd liked the guy's accent. There was something sweet and . . . well . . . sexy about it. Too bad she couldn't say the same for his fencing mask.

"That cat is getting a big kick out of tormenting Tinker," Robin continued. "You saw her with your own eyes. You just hate dogs. Admit it."

"Or maybe *you* hate *cats.*"

"So? They're creepy." A shudder skittered up her spine. "Dangerous, too."

Millie scowled. "Why do you say that?"

"I've heard stories. They've been known to . . . um . . . smother people." Heat climbed the back of her neck. Wishing she'd refrained from blurting out that particular tidbit of information, Robin averted her eyes. She was well aware how ridiculous she sounded.

"What? Says who?" Before Robin could answer, Millie held up a hand. "No, don't tell me, let me guess. Ethan."

Not bothering to confirm or deny Millie's suspicion, Robin moved to the easel and studied the watercolor of a dusty Texas town from long ago.

"That man," Millie seethed. "Sometimes I really think your uncle is a raving lunatic."

She joined Robin and eyed the canvas critically. "It's missing something."

"No kidding. It's not half-finished."

Tilting her head, Millie said, "It isn't you."

"I know that." Robin covered her mouth and

yawned. "For some reason, I feel compelled to paint it anyway." She yawned again.

Millie turned and studied her as if she were seeing her for the first time. "It's four o'clock in the afternoon and you look like you just climbed out of bed."

"I've been gardening all day." Robin glanced down at her robe. "I just took a shower. Besides, I didn't sleep well last night."

A vision flashed to mind . . . a man in a black mask, his dark hair curling from beneath a black Stetson. A man who knew how to handle a sword without mutilating himself. A man who knew how to handle other things, too. Robin's heartbeat increased its rate, and she silently chided herself for being so affected by a dream.

"Why aren't you sleeping, sweetie?" Millie's eyes darkened with worry. "The last time I came over, you were wearing pajamas. Do you ever get dressed anymore?"

"I told you . . . I just took a shower."

"When was the last time you made up your face?"

Robin shrugged. "Why bother?"

"And your hair . . . every time I see you lately, it's braided. You need a haircut. And when did you stop wearing contacts?"

When Robin didn't respond, Millie walked to the sofa and sat on the arm. "I'm sorry. I don't mean to harp." Crossing her legs, she leaned forward. "I heard about a new clinical psychologist who has an office near my building." Her voice sounded more concerned now than critical. "I'd like you to see him. You don't have to do a thing. I'll make the appointment and take you myself."

"I don't need a shrink." Folding her arms across her chest, Robin lifted her chin and scowled at Millie. They'd been over this subject before. More than once. She'd thought she had already made her feelings on the matter perfectly clear.

"I won't leave your side for a second. Please, Robin. For me, if not for yourself. This has gone on too long. It's been a year."

Ashamed of her own weakness, Robin shifted her gaze to the window so she wouldn't have to contend with the troubled look on Millie's face. She couldn't stand knowing she was the cause of that look.

"I told you . . . I don't need a psychologist. I know what's wrong with me."

"I know what's wrong with you, too." Millie leaned back. "Damn that man!" she hissed. "I'd like nothing better than to wring his beefy red neck."

Robin couldn't stop the corner of her mouth from twitching. "Stick around, and you'll get your chance. Uncle E's bringing dinner tonight."

Millie lifted her chin. "When? I want to be long gone before he arrives."

"Please don't leave. It's been a while since the three of us were together." Robin wiggled her brows. "He's bringing his famous barbecue with all the fixings. When was the last time you tasted anything half as good as Uncle E's barbecue?" She grinned. "Your mouth's watering. I can tell."

When Millie didn't waver, Robin added, "What if I said I'd consider seeing your psycho doctor if you stay?"

Millie slid Robin a sidelong look. "Don't tease me."

"I'm serious. I'd consider it." When Millie's eyes brightened, she added, "Mind you, I said consider."

Millie tapped her forefinger against her upper arm. "Barbecue?"

"And beans."

"From that nasty bowling alley cafe of his, I guess."

"Yeah. That nasty cafe that was written up in *Texas Monthly* last March."

"Well, fine." Millie lifted her hands into the air then lowered them, slapping her thighs. "But don't get angry if I give that man a piece of my mind while he's here."

"I look forward to the entertainment."

Satisfied that she'd finally have her family together under one roof for at least one evening, Robin headed for the kitchen. "Now, let's get some stuff from the garden for a salad."

She found a large plastic bowl, then led Millie out the back door. "You're in luck," she said, keeping her voice low. "There's my new neighbor now. Since you're so interested in him, you might make a point of meeting him while we're out here."

Her neighbor stood in the center of his yard wearing his fencing mask. He positioned himself sideways, his left arm bent at the elbow, fist up at his side. His other hand held the saber upright in front of his body.

"Fascinating," Millie murmured. "Nice ass for a nerd."

Robin lowered her gaze. Millie had a point. She guessed she'd been too irritated with Mr. Simon to notice his backside before. Grinning, she reached up to twist her braid.

He lunged forward, thrust the sword straight out in the air, and staggered a little as he tried to hold the pose.

"Touché," Robin whispered, giggling.

She and Millie slipped quietly around to the opposite side of her yard where her vegetable garden grew. Nice ass or not, the guy was a klutz. No wonder she was so affected by the skillful rogue in her dream. Look what reality had to offer.

Chapter Four

Alex looked down. "Bloody hell!" Some dog had mistaken his yard for a loo.

Lifting his soiled foot, he tried to use the saber like a makeshift cane to steady himself as he hopped toward the hedge. It didn't work. The blade bowed beneath his weight.

Bloody schnauzer! When I find him, I'll . . .

Blowing out a frustrated breath, Alex stopped to wipe his shoe in the grass. While he cleaned, he struggled to fight down his temper. It would do him no good to strangle the dog. He'd only get himself in a deeper pile of . . .

Alex glanced back at the mess he'd stepped into. He needed to find the dog's owner, not the dog. And this time, he wouldn't falter if she tried to turn the tables on him. After all, he was staring now at proof of her precious Tickle's trespass into his yard. Alex wrinkled his nose and sniffed. He was smelling it, too. How could the woman argue with that?

When he'd done all he could for his shoe, Alex laid his saber in the grass and resumed his course toward the hedge. He intended to knock on his neighbor's back door, explain the situation, accept her apology, then offer a simple solution or two. A leash, perhaps, attached somehow to the house, long enough to allow the dog roaming room while still remaining confined to the yard. Or, better yet, she might fence off an area for the animal. Her property was certainly large enough to do so. It would require only a small investment and would be money well spent.

Alex squeezed through open space in the hedge and stepped onto his neighbor's lawn. A menacing growl stopped him short. He lowered his gaze to the ground.

The schnauzer stood at his feet staring up at him, teeth bared, ready to pounce.

"I don't intend to hurt you," Alex crooned softly, peering down through the mesh of his mask. "Be a good fellow and let me pass." Cautiously, he lifted his foot.

The dog lunged. Teeth tore into the fabric of Alex's trousers, missing the skin of his ankle by a hair.

He shook his leg frantically, but the schnauzer held tight. "Bugger off! Do you hear?" Through the dog's growling and his own shouted curses, he heard a woman's shriek.

"What do you think you're doing?"

Alex didn't glance up to answer the question. He kept his foot in motion and his eyes on the snarling mongrel, afraid at any second the teeth ripping his trousers would slice into him. After a moment, ten pale purple toenails came into his line of vision, and the dog was suddenly snatched up, tearing his trousers to the knee.

Relieved, Alex staggered back against the hedge and concentrated on catching his breath.

"I said, what do you think you're doing?"

He looked up. His neighbor held the schnauzer in one hand, a plastic bowl in the other. Panting, Alex glanced from her to the immaculate woman beside her. If the old girl wasn't near the same age as his own mum, he'd swear she was taking stock of his crotch. Growing hot beneath the collar, he turned back to the younger of the two. "What am *I* doing? Surely you're joking?"

"You were kicking my dog!"

"Your dog took a fancy to my leg. Attached himself like a blood-sucking leech."

"Only because you came into our yard. Tinker was just protecting my property from prowlers, as any good watchdog would."

"He—I—" Alex drew a deep breath, released it, then drew another. His chest rose and fell with the effort. The young woman's lovely mouth looked as ready to snap at him as her dog. Alex drew another breath. This time, he would not let her get the best of him. He shifted to her companion. The old girl openly ogled him. Refusing to squirm, he turned back to his neighbor and pulled off his mask. "Miss—"

She gasped. It was so quick and slight a sound, Alex might have missed it if he'd stood an inch farther away. "I'm sorry." He ran a hand through his disheveled hair, puzzled by her sudden change of behavior. "Is it Mrs.? We haven't been formally introduced."

She stepped back. "No. No, it's um . . . it's Miss."

She hugged the dog closer, and Alex saw for the first time that she wore a robe. Pale pink and flimsy, it did little to hide the outline of her slender body with the sun shining down on her.

"Wise," she said quietly, handing the bowl to her companion, then nibbling her lower lip as if self-conscious. "My name's Robin Wise."

He softened like heated butter. Never had he met anyone so peculiar, aggravating and alluring all at once. "Splendid to meet you. I'm Alex. Alex Simon." He pulled off his glove and offered his hand, but drew it back quickly when her dog growled. "Now that we're chums . . ." He paused to smile. "Perhaps we can discuss this matter more rationally."

She didn't respond, just stood and stared at him. Alex wondered what he'd missed. Something had obviously occurred to render the woman speechless. And as for him, he couldn't seem to pull his gaze from her mouth. He wasn't certain why . . . maybe it was simply because her eyes were hard to read behind her glasses, or maybe because he could so vividly imagine how her lips would taste, how they'd feel against his own.

Flustered by an eerie sense of déjà vu, Alex blinked. That mouth of hers was playing bloody havoc with his senses.

"If you'll take a look at my yard," he continued, forcing himself to focus on her glasses, "you'll see that your Tinkle—"

"Tinker," she corrected.

"Yes, well, Tinker has been over again for a visit. Not that I dislike visitors, mind you. It's just that I'd prefer they flush." He smiled. "I was hoping the two of us might put our heads together and come up with a solution to the problem."

The blonde stepped immediately to the hedge and peered over. "Oh, my." Lifting a hand to her mouth, she snickered. "Robin, he's right. Who'd have thought such a little dog could make such a great big mess?"

Scowling, Robin moved up to the hedge for a look.

The older woman turned to Alex. "Mr. Simon," she said, still laughing, "I'm Millie McCutcheon. You might say I'm Robin's mother."

"Lovely to meet you." Alex took her hand, then cleared his throat. "Are you?" he asked, baffled by her statement but not certain if it was appropriate to ask such a question.

"Robin's mother?" She squeezed his hand, then released it. "I don't guess you'd believe me if I said I'm her younger sister, would you?"

Alex smiled.

"I was afraid I couldn't get away with that," she said. "To answer your question, I'm not exactly Robin's mother, but I'm close."

"I see." Alex didn't have the foggiest notion what the woman meant.

"Are you and your family new to Canyon?" she asked with a flirtatious tilt of her head. "Or just to this neighborhood?"

"There's only me," Alex told her. "I moved here from England six months ago, but I rented a flat until a couple of weeks back when I found this house. I'm a professor of botany and entomology at the university."

"A scientist." Millie's mouth curled up at one corner. She cut a glance in Robin's direction. "How interesting."

When Robin cleared her throat, Alex had the uncomfortable feeling he was the brunt of a private joke. He squeezed his glove. "I'm on summer break at the moment, though I tutor a couple of students in my home."

Robin covered her mouth and yawned.

"Sorry to be such a bore," Alex said.

She lowered her hand. "Oh . . . you're not. I didn't get much sleep last night."

The yawn was contagious. Alex yawned, too. "Nor did I." Memories of the sexy, slow swing of a frilly, yellow bustle had kept him awake half the night.

He followed Robin's gaze skyward where a butterfly darted and dipped like a miniature stunt plane.

"Seems no one can sleep around here," Millie murmured. "Must be something in the air."

"Sorry about your shoe." Robin looked down at his leg, then up again. "If it's ruined, I'll pay to replace it. Your pants, too." She lifted her chin. "I'll send someone to clean up your yard. But, I hope you realize your cat is luring Tinker over there."

"Sheeba?"

"She's—" Before she could finish the sentence, a man's booming voice bellowed Robin's name from within her house. "Uncle E's here," she said.

For the first time since she'd come outside, Millie McCutcheon's eager smile faded. Scowling, she tried to cross her arms, but the bowl she held got in the way.

The man inside the house bellowed Robin's name again.

"We'll have to finish this discussion later, Mr. Simon," Robin said.

"I'll look forward to it." Again, he offered his hand. Again, the schnauzer growled at him.

Robin started for the house. "I'll have my uncle

come over to your place in a while to clean up after Tinker."

"Don't trouble him. I'll tend to it."

Millie seemed to perk up again. "Ethan won't mind. Believe me, he'll be in his element. He's always been full of—"

"Millie!"

Robin sounded appalled. But when she looked over her shoulder, Alex spied a hint of a smile.

"Fill the bowl, would you?" she said firmly, nodding toward a garden at the far side of the yard. "You know the way. Talk to you later, Mr. Simon."

"Please, call me—" The door slammed. "Alex," he finished, lifting a brow.

"I have an idea," Millie said.

Alex turned to her. She stared at him, the corners of her mouth curved up, a glint of mischief in her eyes. The look she gave him made him self-conscious. Despite that, Alex was curious. He smiled back at her. "I'm all ears."

When Millie came through the back door with a bowlful of lettuce, Robin looked up from the corn she'd just placed on the stovetop to steam. "What took you so long?"

Millie smiled, averting her eyes when Robin met her gaze. "Just looking for the best leaves."

"There're tomatoes in the fridge," Robin told her. Wondering over Millie's sudden shiftiness, she placed a lid on the pot. "You can make the salad."

Ethan came around the corner into the kitchen carrying an ice chest he'd just brought in from the car. "Throw some onions in, too. Onions and lettuce help ya sleep." Looking across the counter that separated the kitchen from the living room, he settled his gaze on Millie. He grinned. "Guess you heard our Robin's not sleepin' good these days."

"Hello, Ethan." Millie's own smile was considerably cooler than his. She crossed to the counter, then placed the bowl atop it.

"You're lookin' good, Mil. That's an interesting new shade of hair color. Covers the gray better, I guess."

Millie walked around the counter, slid open a drawer, then pulled out a cutting board and a knife. "My hairdresser would be happy to sell you a bottle." She eyed the top of Ethan's head and sniffed. "But I see you no longer have enough hair to bother. What a shame. Perhaps for your eyebrows."

Robin opened the oven door. The spicy aroma of barbecue sauce drifted out on a warm waft of air. "I realize it's been a while, but could you try not to act so happy to see each other? All this gushing is making me sick." She placed a loaf of foil-wrapped bread on the rack above the warming barbecue beef.

From the chest he'd brought in, Ethan unloaded

two bowls, a sack of pecans and a string of garlic bulbs. "I brought you some pecans from my trees, sugar," he said to Robin, Millie's comment apparently already forgotten. "They're from last year's crop. I froze 'em in the shell 'cause I didn't have time to mess with them. No use letting good pecans go to waste. If you'll tackle that chore sometime, I'll make you a pie."

After Millie took the tomatoes from the refrigerator, he placed the bowls inside. Carrying the garlic into the living room, he hung the string of bulbs on the Christmas stocking hook beneath Robin's mantel.

"I won't even ask," Millie mumbled tersely. The diamonds on her fingers flashed in the light as she diced.

Ethan's cowboy boots clicked against the Saltillo tile floor as he returned to the kitchen. "No need for you to ask. I'll flat out tell you. Garlic on the mantel brings good luck." He tugged Robin's braid. "What with the big three-o just two weeks away, you need all the luck you can get, don't ya, sugar?"

"You haven't changed, Ethan," Millie said, chopping more forcefully with each word she spoke.

"Well, I don't know about that." Grinning, he patted his belly. "I have gained a few extra pounds since the last time I saw you."

"And lost a few more brain cells, if that's possible. You're scaring Robin to death with this curse nonsense." Millie's fingers stilled. She'd chopped the tomatoes to mush. "You should be ashamed of yourself, Ethan Yarborough. You've taken an intelligent, outgoing, vibrant young woman and turned her into a skittish recluse. Robin has nothing to fea—"

"You're right about that," Ethan interrupted with a snort. " 'Cause I'm gonna break the curse before it can hurt her. I've been studying up on it. I think I know what to do."

Millie dropped the knife on top of the cutting board. Tomato juice spattered across the counter. "Would you listen to yourself? You sound like—"

Robin whistled. When the bickering stopped, she pulled her fingers from her mouth. "Hey, you two! Enough! Quit talking about me like I'm not in the room." She opened the cupboard. "Now . . . let's have a nice dinner. Just the three of us."

"Four," Millie muttered, wiping her hands on a dish towel as a knock sounded at the back door.

Robin turned, her hand resting on a stack of plates in the cabinet. "You *didn't.*"

Millie looked smug as she started around the counter. "Set four places at the table." She glanced over her shoulder. "And take off your glasses, Robin."

Ignoring Millie's order, Robin ran from the room to change out of her robe.

Chapter Five

Alex had never seen such a feast for only four people. They dined on barbecued beef, potato salad, corn, pinto beans and more.

From serving the food to selecting the background music, Ethan Yarborough acted as host. The barbecue seemed typical of Robin's robust, redneck uncle. But Alex was a bit surprised by his choice of dinner music. Alex was no symphony buff. He didn't know if the selection was Bach, Beethoven or Mozart. But no matter which composer wrote the piece, it seemed at odds with Ethan's coarse personality.

Throughout dinner, Ethan shoveled in food and talked nonstop.

Millie alternately scowled at Ethan and grinned at Alex.

While Ethan talked and Millie scowled and grinned, Robin picked at her food, her eyes focused on him. Alex felt her gaze even when he wasn't looking her way. She studied him—his hair, his glasses, his face. Certainly not in the same way Millie did—as if she wanted to sample him for dessert. And not in the way Leigh used to size him up as though she saw promise in him . . . if only . . .

Robin's look was a searching one, a look of perplexed recollection. Alex sensed, though, that she couldn't get a firm grasp on why he seemed familiar. He sensed, too, that she liked what she saw, but didn't *like* that she liked it. That possibility astonished him. More astounding was the fact that when he looked at her he, too, liked what he saw.

Robin Wise definitely wasn't his type. Less polished and tailored than Leigh, she had a somewhat earthy, somewhat trendy appearance; no makeup, wisps of hair curling free of her braid, tiny modish eyeglasses.

Striving to concentrate on Ethan's chatter instead of Ethan's niece, Alex made use of his napkin, then leaned back in his chair. "That was by far the finest meal I've had since coming to the States."

Ethan slapped him on the back. "Stop by the cafe at the Ten Pin sometime. I make a mean chicken fry, too."

"The Ten Pin?"

"My bowling alley. Owned it for twenty-five years."

Robin lowered her fork to the table. "Uncle E's cafe is famous statewide."

Millie almost choked on a bite of bread.

When the coughing stopped, Robin sent the older woman a smug look. "The Ten Pin Cafe was written up in a recent issue of *Texas Monthly*."

"Sure enough," Ethan said. "They called me a time-tested Texas tradition." He winked at Robin. " 'Course, I'm not one to brag."

Though everyone else at the table had finished eating, Ethan helped himself to the last ear of corn. With a knife, he slathered on butter while humming along with the dignified strains of music floating throughout the room.

"My mama was one quarter Cherokee," he finally said. "She died when I was five years old, so I don't recall much about her; just a flash of shiny black hair, a soft laugh, a story or two she'd tell." He lowered the knife. "One of those stories, about how corn came to be on this earth, was passed down to her from my grandma who'd heard it from her mama."

Millie drummed her fingers restlessly atop the table, her gaze lifted to the ceiling. "Here we go," she muttered.

Oblivious, Ethan held the cob lengthwise between the index fingers of his huge hands and stared down at it. "My great-grandma was a white woman, you see, but she had a child by a Cherokee warrior who died in a battle soon after. Great-grandma was shunned by the whites when she escaped the tribe and went home. A crazy woman who dabbled in potions and herbs took in my great-grandma and her baby, who was my grandma, you see. Anyhow, that's neither here nor there where this story's concerned."

He paused for a breath. "Seems the Indians my great-grandma had lived with believed a beautiful young yellow-haired maiden was being chased down by a fierce river god one sunny afternoon. The maiden was alone and afraid, so she hid out in a field of tall weeds and, to save her, the Great Spirit turned her into a stalk of corn."

Millie groaned.

Ethan took a bite, chewed it, swallowed. "The Indians didn't abide by wasting corn. Said those who did were doomed to wander the earth, alone and hungry like that pretty young maiden." He took another bite.

Alex couldn't fathom why that tale would scatter goose bumps up his arms, but it did.

"Well, thank the Great Spirit we're all finished with the fascinating tidbits of Ethan's family folklore." Millie turned to Alex, her eyes brightening. "What brings you to the States, Alex?"

Alex always hated hearing this question. He didn't care to recall the two painful incidents that had brought him here. Memories of his failed engagement were bad enough, but remembering his brother-in-law's death was far worse.

Crossing his arms, Alex rubbed the goose bumps away. In truth, his breakup with Leigh had only played a minor part in his decision to move. True, the incident had depressed him. His life had suddenly stalled out. He'd felt like a failure. But, in the end, the split had been the best thing for them both.

Alex decided not to bore them with the doleful details of his love life. "My sister, Carin, lives here. She's a nurse. She went to college in the States, then moved here permanently more than fifteen years ago after marrying a Yank." He winced at his unfortunate word choice. "No offense intended."

Ethan chuckled. "Son," he said, sprinkling salt onto a radish then pinching up some of the grains that spilled onto the table. "An American's not a Yankee 'less he's born north of the Mason-Dixon Line." He tossed the salt over his left shoulder.

Relieved by the man's light tone, Alex grinned. "I've still a lot to learn, I guess." He shifted his attention to Robin. "Anyway, Carin's recently widowed. She wanted to be closer to family after her husband's death, but didn't want to uproot her teenaged son." He shrugged. "She and my nephew, Ty, needed family, and I needed a change of scenery. Carin told me of an opening in the Department of Science at the university. I looked into it, and here I am."

"What did you say your specialty is?" Millie asked. "Botany?"

He nodded. "And entomology."

"Which means?"

"Plants and insects."

"Hmmm," Millie said. "Maybe you can help Robin with her roses. They've contracted some sort of disease."

Robin sat back and sighed. "It's not a disease. I've got rose bugs, that's all."

"Black spot," Alex blurted.

She blinked. "What?"

"Your roses may well have chafers, or rose bugs as you called them, but they only eat parts of the foliage and stem. I stopped for a look at your plants when I came over. The leaves are yellow and spotty. They're dropping off. My guess is you've contracted the black spot."

"And what exactly is black spot?"

"A fungus. It's possible to control it through regular use of a fungicide spray. I'd be happy to write down the ingredients you'll need." He smiled. "For the rose bugs as well as the fungus."

"Okay," Robin said, lifting a shoulder. "I guess it's worth a try." With her elbow propped on the arm of her chair, she nibbled the nail of her little finger and resumed her appraisal of him. "How long did you say you've lived in Canyon?"

"Six months."

"Strange. You seem familiar. I get the sense we've met before."

"I feel the same way. Perhaps we've passed each other at the market or some other such place."

She glanced at Millie, then Ethan, then down at her lap, and Alex sensed a distinct and disarming rise of tension in the room.

"I don't think so," Robin said quietly.

Millie quickly leaned forward. "Get Alex some paper and a pencil, Robin, so he can write down the formula to save your roses."

"Okay." Robin pushed away from the table and stood.

As she started for the kitchen, Alex said, "You might bring a rubber, too, just in case I cock up."

She paused, turning to face him. Alex was taken aback by the startled look in her eyes, by the sudden stunned silence of everyone in the room. The only audible sound was the lilting music on the stereo. As it reached a crescendo, Alex glanced around the table.

Millie snickered.

"I've—uh—been known to do so from time to time when under pressure," Alex stammered.

"Watch your mouth, son," Ethan muttered, his voice a low rumble. "That's my little girl you're talking to."

Millie clasped her hands to her stomach and laughed. "Well, at least he's honest. That's an unusual trait in a man." She laughed again. "Honesty, that is."

Heat climbed the back of Alex's neck. He felt

baffled and strangely defensive. "Compounding these multipurpose remedies can be tricky business. The ingredients must be compatible." He returned his gaze to Robin.

She licked her lips, lifted a hand to touch the corner of her glasses, lowered it. "Well . . . you certainly are passionate about your work."

Alex scratched his head. "Did I say something wrong?" When no one answered, he rewound their conversation in his mind. Cymbals crashed from the stereo. Alex's heart crashed, too, as he realized his mistake. "I—I'm afraid I've made an unfortunate blunder." He issued a fragmented laugh. "What I believe you Americans refer to as an eraser, we Limey's call a . . . um, rubber."

Millie shrieked.

Ethan looked skeptical. "But you said—"

"Cock up," Alex finished, hurrying to add, "As in 'make a mistake.' Or, as I believe you Americans often put it, 'screw up.' "

To Alex's relief, Robin laughed. Then they all joined in until, finally, Robin pulled off her glasses and wiped the tears from her eyes.

"I'll get that rubber now," she said. "Try not to cock up until I get back."

Alex watched her walk away. He liked the sound of her laughter. Hearing it now, he realized something he hadn't before. She always seemed worried—on edge. Even yesterday, when he'd first spotted her gardening, she'd seemed tense, so preoccupied she didn't notice his presence. Instinctively, he'd held back from disturbing her thoughts.

Moments later, Robin returned with a tray containing not only paper, pencil and rubber, but four long-stemmed glasses and a corkscrew. "I thought we'd pop open that bottle of wine you brought, Alex."

"Splendid idea," he said as she set the tray on the table.

He took the paper and pencil and began scribbling while she poured the wine. "You should be able to find all of this at a nursery with no difficulty," he said. Finished, he handed her the paper and took the glass she offered in return.

Robin read what he'd written. "Thanks."

"My pleasure."

She looked up at him, and Alex felt a tug of attraction so strong it staggered him.

Blushing, she glanced down at the paper. "No need for the rubber, I see."

Alex found himself wishing she were wrong about that—at least if she referred to the American version.

Millie clapped her hands. "Have a seat, Robin. Let's make a toast."

After a moment's hesitation, Robin sat across the table from Alex.

Millie raised her glass. "To being neighborly. Despite taunting cats and snarling dogs."

Lifting his glass, too, Alex looked again into Robin's warm brown eyes. "Peace," he said.

She touched her glass to his. "Peace."

Wine sloshed over the glasses and onto their fingertips.

"I'm sorry." Robin drew back her hand but couldn't break her connection with Alex's blue eyes. "I—I guess I clinked too hard."

"No need to apologize. It was my fault." He reached for his napkin while continuing to hold her gaze.

"Don't wipe that up!" Ethan grabbed Alex's wrist. "They say fermented grape juice contains a spirit."

Millie exhaled noisily. "And I'll turn into a pumpkin when the clock strikes twelve."

"Spilled wine is supposedly the spirit's way of warnin' of danger," Ethan said, ignoring her sarcasm.

Robin watched Alex warily. He seemed more interested than repelled by her uncle's unorthodox beliefs.

Ethan released Alex's wrist. "To counter the danger, the spiller has to rub a drop of the wine behind the spillee's ear."

"Well, what do you know?" Millie propped an elbow on the table and leaned in, her focus on Ethan, her chin in the palm of her hand. "For once you've come up with some superstitious nonsense I find both appealing and worthwhile. Do tell us more."

Robin's cheeks burned. She fidgeted in her chair. "I'm sure Alex has better things to do than—"

"—No, no, not at all." Alex surprised her with his eager tone of voice. "I'm all for avoiding danger." The corner of his lip twitched when he looked at her. "But we were both the spillers as well as the spillees, were we not?"

"Yes!" Sitting straighter, Millie looked from one to the other. "Yes, you were. That must mean you'll each have to put wine behind the other's ear. Isn't that right, Ethan?"

"Well . . . to tell you the truth, I don't—*ouch!*" Ethan jumped and reached under the table. He grimaced at Millie. "I guess it does mean that. Won't hurt, anyhow. Just to be safe."

Robin narrowed her eyes as she glanced from her uncle to Millie.

Millie rubbed her palms together. "Let's get started."

Instructed by Ethan, Alex dipped the middle finger of his right hand into the wine puddle and touched it to a spot behind Robin's ear. Their eyes met, and she suddenly found it difficult to think. Everything intensified. The pungent scent of wine. Alex's steady blue stare. The warmth of his touch. Strains of a concerto stirred the air, the music swirling, weaving through her senses. It seemed each trembling note, every breathtaking beat, took place within her own body.

Too much time had passed since she'd allowed

77

herself to feel anything for a man. But as she followed Alex's lead—dipping her own fingertip into the wine, sliding her hand through his curling hair to the spot behind his ear—she knew she'd never felt anything like *this* . . . this powerful awareness, this all-consuming need.

The music paused. The resulting silence was as startling as a slap.

Flinching, Alex quickly lowered his hand.

Robin had the sickening suspicion that what she'd interpreted as desire in his eyes was truly alarm. She pulled back in humiliation and chanced a quick glance at her uncle and Millie.

"I—uh . . ." Alex took off his glasses, then put them on again. He licked his lips and blinked. "Now that the danger's been diverted, I guess I can safely start home."

"Oh, there's no hurry." Millie snatched up the wine bottle and poured more into his glass.

He glanced at his watch. "It's getting late. I have papers to grade. I'll help you clean up, then be on my way."

"It's Saturday night." Millie lowered the bottle, lifted her glass and sipped. "Surely, the papers can wait."

"Millie . . ." Frowning, Robin wiped the spilled wine with a napkin. "If he has to go, he has to go. No need to help us, Alex. We three can handle it."

"It's been a lovely evening." Alex scooted back his chair, almost toppling it over. "Thank you for saving me from that wine spirit, Ethan."

Chuckling, Ethan stood, too. "Anytime, son. Drop by the Ten Pin sometime, and I'll feed you lunch."

Aware of Millie's foot tapping beneath the table, Robin busied herself gathering dishes and flatware.

Alex started for the door.

"Robin will walk you out," Millie blurted.

He paused, turned to them. "Thank you, but I wouldn't want to trouble her."

"He knows the way home, Millie," Robin said quietly as she continued to clear the table.

Millie hurried to the door and offered Alex her arm. "I'd be delighted to walk you out. Between the two of us, maybe we can dodge any land mines Robin's dog might've planted."

Alex laughed. "I'd appreciate the help."

He paused, and in that brief moment of silence, Robin glanced up.

"I'll be seeing you, Robin," he said.

A fork slipped through her fingers and clattered on the floor. She felt the intensity of his gaze— felt it as surely as if he were touching her. Looking irresistibly rumpled, from his messy dark hair to his wrinkled khaki pants, he stood with one hand on the doorknob, the other on Millie's arm.

Robin moistened her dry lips. "Thanks for the advice about the black spot."

He nodded. "I hope your roses benefit." The

corner of his mouth twitched. "Give my regards to Tigger."

Robin started to correct him but decided against it. "And mine to Sheeba." She smiled. "Tell her to behave."

"I'll do that." Turning, he twisted the knob.

"Don't open that door!" Ethan boomed.

Alex jerked back his hand.

When Millie protested, Ethan snapped, "Don't move!" Moving slowly . . . cautiously, he started toward them.

Robin held her breath, wondering what could be wrong. A tarantula in Millie's hair? A prowler outside? A mouse?

Midway across the room, Ethan pointed over-head. Alex and Millie glanced up. Robin did, too. A butterfly hovered above them in the doorway.

"Ethan Yarborough," Millie hissed, "you scared the life out of me over a harmless little butterfly."

"Not only harmless . . ." Going still, Ethan poised one hand in midair, as if to catch the winged creature, and whispered, "Down right valuable, too."

"Uncle E says if you trap a butterfly in your house," Robin explained, "it'll bring you good luck."

"The hell it will." In one rapid move, Millie reached around Alex and opened the door.

"No!" Ethan lunged. The butterfly escaped. "Damn you, woman!" His ruddy face turned a deeper shade of red. "I ought to strangle the life out of you!"

Noting the bulging vein at her uncle's temple, Robin moved quickly to stand between him and Millie. "Now, Uncle E—"

Millie lifted her hands, curled her fingers like claws. "Just try it, you big galoot. I had my nails done yesterday. They're nice and sharp, and I'm just waiting for an excuse to scratch your eyes out."

As Millie and Ethan continued their verbal sparring, Robin glanced over her shoulder at Alex. "Thanks so much for joining my family in a quiet evening at home."

He stepped backward through the doorway, his eyes wide behind his glasses. "Yes . . . it's been . . . delightful."

Over the bickering, Robin heard a tiny, menacing growl. She and Alex looked down at the same time.

Tinker tugged at the hem of Alex's slacks with bared teeth.

Chapter Six

Robin stood in her dark bedroom and stared across at Alex's house. Light glowed dimly from a single window. She guessed he must be grading papers.

Twisting her braid around her finger, she frowned. He'd said he was on his summer break from teaching, that he only tutored a student or two. Surely a couple of students wouldn't generate many papers. Or any, for that matter. He was tutoring, not teaching.

As understanding dawned, Robin scoffed at herself. He'd only used the papers as an excuse to leave. She'd scared him away by cooperating with Millie's matchmaking and Ethan's silly ritual, by looking at him like a simpering, love-hungry fool.

Humiliated, Robin closed her eyes. How foolish she'd been to think she might risk entertaining a flirtation. What did she—a walking bag of nerves, a basket case with an uncertain future—have to offer any man? She was almost thirty years old. By all outward accounts an intelligent woman. She held degrees in art and art history, had her own successful line of accessories. Yet, she half believed in a curse, a date with destiny in two weeks. Robin opened her eyes and sighed. Dear God! She more than half believed it! Though her rational mind insisted such ideas were ignorant, she couldn't seem to laugh off her legacy.

The past year of seclusion must have finally taken its toll. She stood here, alone in the dark, obsessed by thoughts of Alex Simon. Alex, with his outdated glasses and bumbling, hesitant manner. Still, what she would consider shortcomings in any other man only bolstered Alex's sex appeal. She couldn't explain it. Maybe it was his sharp blue gaze—the way he took everything in at once, the way his eyes softened when they settled on her. Or maybe his humor—the way he made her laugh. Or his off-kilter smile, so warm and quick and relaxed. Or his hands . . .

Robin wondered how a professor of botany and entomology got calluses on his hands. Wondered how those hands would feel on her body. Wondered if his occasional awkward hesitance would fade in bed. Something about the way he'd looked

at her ... *something,* had made her believe it
would, had made her want to believe.

Robin stood a moment longer at the window
and gazed at Alex's light. A breeze lifted the cur-
tain, escorting a butterfly into the room. A blue
butterfly. She nibbled her lower lip. Blue butterflies certainly were abundant lately.

As the butterfly disappeared inside the room,
she started to shut the window to trap it inside for
good luck; then, disgusted by her impulse, she
shoved the window wider. Men like Alex Simon—
curious, highly intelligent, sensitive men—
weren't interested in women who allowed superstition to guide their lives. They wanted rational
women. Independent women. Women who tack-
led problems head-on instead of hiding from
them.

Outside, lightning flashed, followed seconds
later by a slow roll of thunder. Yawning, Robin
turned from the window, unbraided her hair, then
joined Tinker on the bed. More than anything, she
wished she could be all the things she wasn't ...
daring, dauntless, aggressive.

She fell asleep wishing.

Pencil in hand, Alex sat propped up in bed, a
crossword puzzle in his lap, Sheeba purring at his
feet. Draped across a nearby easy chair were the
second pair of his trousers to be ripped in one day
by the neighbor's bloody schnauzer.

At Robin's, he'd restrained himself from neutering the dog with his bare hands. And he'd waited until he stood in his own house with the door closed behind him before snarling a string of curses at the mongrel.

A gust of wind rattled the window. Alex looked up. A blue butterfly sailed into the room.

"You again," Alex muttered, though he told himself this most likely was a different specimen from the one at dinner. "You caused quite a dither this evening."

The butterfly settled on the puzzle. *Twenty-two across. Six letters. A person who lacks courage in facing danger, pain, etc.* Alex didn't shoo the insect away. Concentrating on the clues seemed impossible tonight, anyway. Besides, according to Robin, butterflies brought good luck, and he could certainly use a bit of that lately. Not that he'd suffered any bad luck, exactly. Other than his recent run-ins with Robin's precious canine, he couldn't complain.

Alex tapped the earpiece of his glasses with the pencil. The butterfly didn't budge. In fact, the insect wasn't the least bit affected by his movements. Perplexed, Alex leaned closer and squinted. Nothing exceptional. An ordinary enough specimen.

As he studied the butterfly's blue and yellow wings, thoughts of Robin Wise whispered again through his mind. Yes, other than her Tinker, his luck was simply . . . indifferent. Not good, not bad. Boring.

Alex grinned. Dinner tonight had most definitely not been boring. Dinner tonight had amused him, intrigued him . . . scared him. Robin and her makeshift family made quite a colorful group. Though obviously at odds about most issues, Ethan and Millie seemed united in acting as Robin's parents. Alex wondered about her real parents. He wondered about other things, too. In fact, when it came to his neighbor, he suddenly found himself extremely curious about everything.

The butterfly moved from *twenty-two across* to the edge of the newspaper. Alex glanced down. *Six letters. A person who lacks courage in facing danger, pain, etc.* Lowering the pencil to the puzzle, he wrote the word *coward,* then sighed. *That's you, old boy.*

The second he'd recognized the dreamy look in Robin's eyes, the instant he'd experienced a spark of attraction, he'd turned tail and run.

Alex huffed. Spark of attraction! *Bollocks!* More like a flash fire! And why shouldn't he be afraid? He didn't relish the prospect of adding fuel to the flames, then getting burned again. Who would?

The butterfly lifted off the paper and flitted about his face. Alex yawned as he shooed the insect away. He watched it drift toward the window. An hour ago, he'd peeked across the way and found Robin's house dark. She certainly wasn't losing any sleep over him.

Alex traded the puzzle for *Amigo's Justice*. Perhaps Johnny's adventures would take his mind off his neighbor. Perhaps he'd learn something, too. Amigo was an expert at love 'em and leave 'em—no looking back.

Glancing at the masked hero on the book's cover, Alex chuckled. He could definitely use a lesson or two in the love-'em-and-leave-'em attitude. He opened *Amigo's Justice* and read for a few minutes, then fell asleep to the rumble of thunder. . . .

Hoofbeats shook the earth, stirred the prairie dirt into a choking brown cloud.

Alex leaned low in the saddle and spurred Thunder on. He'd cut off a band of outlaws half a mile back. He wasn't sure what they were after, but he could guess. At the side of the road, he'd spotted a red Honda Civic with smoke pouring from the hood. A lacy yellow parasol lay propped against one of its windows.

A bullet whizzed past his left ear. Drawing his gun, Alex squinted over his shoulder through the fog of dust and shot off a round. He faced forward again, hoping to catch sight of the fancy lady from the saloon. She was up ahead somewhere on foot and in a heap of trouble; he'd bet his sword on it. He had to lengthen his lead if he wanted to reach her and get her to safety before the varmints behind him caught up.

As he gained ground, the dust cloud cleared,

and lightning fractured the sky. At the edge of a cornfield, Alex spied a quick flash of yellow. But it quickly disappeared within the tall, sturdy stalks.

He reached the field and reigned Thunder in, guiding the stallion through towering rows of corn. "Ma'am!" he called out.

The hammer of hooves grew louder. Alex turned Thunder toward the road and climbed down. After a quick word of instruction and a slap to the rump, he sent the horse off again in the direction they'd previously been heading.

Dropping to his hands and knees, he crawled through the corn, rustling the stalks as he moved from row to row. "Show yourself, ma'am! Trouble's comin'."

Alex turned a corner and almost collided with a lacy yellow blur. He lunged, grabbed her around the knees, pulled her feet out from under her. She landed on her bustle with a startled gasp. He fell facedown on top of her, pinning her to the ground. She squirmed and twisted beneath him as the outlaws drummed past, no doubt following Thunder's trail, as Alex had planned.

The lady pummelled his shoulders with her fists. "Let me go!"

Keeping his face close to her ear, Alex snapped, "Be still!"

She shrieked again.

He pressed his hand over her mouth.

She kneed him in the groin, knocking the breath from his lungs in a strangled grunt.

Rolling to his side, Alex clutched his crotch and lifted his knees to his chest. In his peripheral vision, he saw her crouched amid the cornstalks, eyes wide and fierce, yellow hat askew. Strands of tangled auburn hair tumbled to her shoulders, a smear of dirt smudged her cheek. She pointed something at him . . . a tiny black cylinder attached to a dangling ring of keys. Mace.

"Stay back!" The keys jingled as she jabbed the cylinder at him. Her index finger was poised and ready to spray.

By sheer force of will, Alex lifted his head and looked at her.

"You!" she hissed. Her gaze settled on the mask. "I should've guessed!"

The noise of the riders subsided. "Quiet!" Alex hissed.

"Don't you tell me—"

He grabbed her wrist and sent the cylinder flying. The hat tumbled from her head as she twisted to sit on the ground. Wincing with pain, Alex shifted to his knees and leaned over her. "Quiet!" He slid his gun from the holster at his side then added, "Please."

With a look of disgust and a noisy sigh, she settled back on her elbows.

Alex held his gun at the ready. He scanned the field around them and listened. Wind whispered through the cornstalks. A crow cawed overhead.

Somewhere nearby, one mouse answered the squeak of another. Satisfied he and the lady were alone, Alex gave the gun a twirl. It went off mid-rotation, startling an expletive from him and wounding the scarecrow that hung on a post five yards away.

Hoping she'd think the shot was intentional, Alex risked a sly glance at the lady, blew on the barrel then holstered his gun. "Bingo," he said with a sniff and a lazy roll of his shoulders.

The corner of the lady's mouth twitched. She arched a shapely brow. "When you ran into me, Gambler, why didn't you just say who you were and ask me to sit down? It would've been a lot easier." Shifting on her bustle, she frowned. "A sight less painful, too."

"But not near as much fun," Alex drawled. Grinning, he swept up her hat, plopped it atop her head, then stretched out beside her, propping himself on one elbow. "You sought out my services, ma'am. I'm only trying to oblige."

"As I recall, Gambler," she said in her husky voice, "we never sealed the deal."

Alex touched the corner of her mouth, brushed a stray strand of hair from her face. "I seem to remember a kiss."

"And I remember a slap." She met his gaze, her brown eyes steady. "That kiss was no contract, Gambler. It was a warning for you to steer clear of me. I need a cunning detective, not some

show-off playboy who'll only bring more danger into my life."

"If you're referrin' to that knife the other night, it was aimed at your throat, not mine. And as for those riders, it isn't my hide they're after." He lowered his gaze to the tempting swell of her bosom, arched his brows and slowly met her eyes. "I may be a danger to you, ma'am, but not in the way you imply."

She didn't tense or hesitate; her attention never wavered. "Is that a threat, Gambler?"

Her sultry voice shoved a spear of heat through Alex's gut straight to the lower regions of his body. He was suddenly much too aware of her smooth, soft curves, each finely molded feature of her face; her high, strong cheekbones . . . her pert nose . . . those luscious pink lips, moist as dew.

She shifted restlessly. "Well? Is it a threat, or isn't it?"

"I'm tryin' to decide."

"While you're pondering," she said sassily, "since the outlaws are gone, can you think of any reason for me to remain flat on my back in the middle of this field?"

"Only one." Alex slid her his crooked grin. "But thanks to the quick reflexes of your knee, I don't think it's an option." He winced. "Not today anyway."

Easing to his feet, he reached down to give her a hand up.

When the lady was standing, she adjusted her

hat and dusted off her bustle. Retrieving her keys, she dropped them between her breasts with a saucy smile.

"Those riders," Alex said. "Why were they after you?"

"They're betting I'll lead them to my great-great-grandmother. They must've mistaken me for her in the saloon. Otherwise they wouldn't have tried to kill me. She's first on their hit list. I come later."

He lifted his Stetson, scratched his head. "How could anybody get you confused with an old woman?"

"As I've told you before, my great-great—"

Alex's sigh was heavy with frustration. "Pardon me, ma'am, but does your granny have a name?"

"Of course. Hannah Sann. And as I was saying, she's only twenty-nine. I've been told she lives out here somewhere on the edge of town with her baby and some crazy woman who fancies herself a healer. I thought I saw her running toward this field, but I've looked everywhere. She disappeared. It's as if she turned into one of these stalks of corn."

She lowered her gaze to the ground, her lip trembling. "The outlaws . . . what if they get to her first? What if I'm too late?"

A blood-red sunset seeped through the rows of corn, casting shadows across the field. "Don't give up hope," Alex said quietly. He placed a

*finger beneath her chin, tilted her face up, wiped
a tear from her cheek. "Let me help you."*

*When her arms encircled his neck he pulled
her to him and pressed his hands against the
small of her back. And then she kissed him . . .
kissed him as if she craved his taste, clung to
his body as if she feared letting go. A symphony surged around them. Violins wept. Cymbals
crashed. He skimmed his hands over her body. The
rise of her breasts . . . the curve of her waist . . .
her soft, round hips. His palms moved lower, beneath the jut of her bustle.*

*He drew back to look at her, but when he
opened his eyes, the music stopped . . . and she
was gone. The cornfield had blossomed into a
meadow filled with thousands of yellow roses. The
leaves beneath the blooms were spotty and dropping off. Faster and faster they fell, scattering in
the wind, swirling about his feet.*

*Alex looked down. In his hand lay one perfect
yellow long-stemmed rose, the tightly bound petals fresh with dew. As he lifted it to his face, the
wind stopped. The air grew still. All around him,
leaves fell from the dying flowers and sprinkled
the ground like raindrops.*

*"I won't let it happen to you," he whispered.
"I won't let anything hurt you. . . ."*

"I won't—!" Alex woke abruptly to the sound of
his own voice. Raindrops pattered on the roof. He
blinked away sleep.

Jennifer Archer

Untangling himself from the sheet twisted about his legs, he tried to get comfortable, tried to calm the rapid pace of his heartbeat.

The mind was a clever thing. The events of the day—Robin's sick roses, Ethan's story about the Indian maiden, Johnny Amigo—all had woven themselves into a dream.

But something else nagged at him, something he couldn't explain, something he needed to understand. The woman in his dream tonight was the same woman he'd dreamed of last night. And that woman was very much like Robin in appearance. She had the same build, the same wide brown eyes and shiny auburn highlights in her hair.

Yet, before this morning, he'd only seen Robin from a distance—at night through the window of her house while she exercised, and then again in her garden yesterday morning wearing a hat that shadowed her face. How could he have dreamed her so precisely last night? How could he have known the size and color of her eyes? The shape of her face and nose? The exact shade of her hair?

One house away, Robin contemplated the same questions. She'd awakened with tears on her cheeks and an acute sense of longing. The gambler looked a lot like Alex Simon. A more polished Alex. Alex with a Texas drawl. Alex with the sexual finesse, the physical agility and skill of an Old West James Bond.

94

How could that be? Until this evening, she'd never laid eyes on her neighbor's face or hair. But last night the gambler had been in her dream and he'd looked exactly the same. She must have seen Alex somewhere before. Maybe she'd caught a glimpse of him entering his house or driving by in his car.

Groaning, Robin buried her face in a pillow. *I must be losing my mind!* She would swear in a court of law that he'd really had his hands on her body. She could still feel their heat on her breasts, at the small of her back, on her hips and bottom. She would swear, too, that he'd really kissed her and that it hadn't been the first time. But most insane of all, she would swear that, just when things were getting good between them, really, really good, she'd turned into a rose.

Robin laughed aloud, muffling the sound in her pillow. Oh, if Millie could only hear this! God, how she'd love it! But Robin wasn't stupid enough to tell her. Millie would make more of the dream than what it was: a byproduct of a long-starved libido. Millie would instantly start scheming to get Alex Simon into Robin's bed for real. Robin nibbled her lip and sighed. Right now, that didn't sound half bad.

She glanced at the clock. It was well past midnight.

No way would she share her dream with Millie. In Alex's eyes she probably already looked like a fool after last night's dinner. She didn't need Millie to help in that department.

Listening to the rain, Robin pulled the covers under her chin and tried to sleep again. She tried to recapture the dream, tried to return to that place in her mind where she was a bold and arrogant lady. Where the gambler waited with skillful hands, a crooked grin and an irresistible twinkle in his sexy blue eyes.

Chapter Seven

The red '68 Mustang sat on the far side of Alex's double garage, a reminder of a promise to Ty. A promise Alex would keep because his nephew's father couldn't.

Since moving in and towing the automobile home, Alex never set foot inside the garage without that car nagging at him. So he'd made up his mind right off not to postpone the project. At the bookstore, he found a manual on restoring classic vehicles, then read and studied, calculated and recalculated the necessary specifications. Now, with Ty beside him and his trusty manual close by, he was ready for the task.

Together, they had removed the engine from the chassis. It now sat on a worktable.

"Why so glum?" Alex asked when he saw the

worried expression on his nephew's freckled face. "Rebuilding an automobile engine is a bit like working on a puzzle. It's all a matter of detail."

Ty stared skeptically at the engine while scratching his head. "Yeah, if you get one piece in the wrong place the whole thing's screwed up. You sure it's a good idea for us to tear this thing apart, Uncle Alex? Maybe we should take it to a real mechanic."

"No fun in that," Alex said.

Ty took a drink of soda, then set the can aside. "Whatever you say."

The lad's voice was as deep as his own—the voice of a man. Though he'd noticed the change before now, Alex marveled over it as he chose a torque wrench from Ray's stash of equipment. It seemed that, overnight, Ty had caught up to him in height. He'd grown into a fine-looking lad. The image of his father.

Thoughts of his late brother-in-law, Ray, brought a bittersweet sadness. Carin's husband would never know this grown-up young man beside him. And though Alex wished it could be otherwise, he felt privileged to be standing in for Ray on this long-planned project with his son.

Ray Mitchell had worked as a mechanic to put himself through college. He'd saved all of his tools, which now belonged to Ty. The Mustang, Ray's first car, belonged to Ty now, too. Alex was determined that when the lad turned sixteen, he'd be driving a Mustang shiny as a new penny and with a purr like Sheeba's. Restored by Ty's own hands—and Alex's.

Alex passed the boy the wrench. He picked up one for himself, then instructed Ty on beginning disassembly. As they worked side by side, he pondered how to start the lad talking. Usually effusive and rambunctious, Ty had withdrawn since his father's death last August.

Taking a shot, Alex asked, "So . . . what are your plans for the summer?"

Ty frowned. "I don't know. This town sucks." He sniffed. "There's nothing to do here unless you can drive."

"Come now. Surely there must be something. What did you do last night?"

Ty kept his eyes on his hands. "Went to a dance."

"With school out for the summer?"

"It was at church."

"Ah . . ." Alex said, picking up a note of aversion in the lad's tone. "Sounds like something your mum might've suggested."

"More like demanded," Ty said with a huff. He glanced up. "How'd you know?"

"Didn't much like dances myself when I was fifteen. Church either, for that matter." Alex winked. "Still don't, if the truth be known. But don't tell your mum I said so."

A hint of a smile passed over Ty's face before he resumed work on the engine. A minute passed in silence. Then two.

"So, how was it?" Alex prodded.

"What?"

"The dance."

Ty's shoulders lifted in a shrug. "It sucked."

"Ah . . . too bad. Boogying down's not your thing, I gather."

Ty rolled his eyes at the antiquated expression, exactly as Alex had hoped. Any reaction was preferable to the indifference the lad often displayed these days.

"I danced a couple a times."

"That's good."

"It sucked. I felt like a loser."

Alex suppressed a grin. "Dancing will do that to a man. At least you gave it a go. Same lass both times?"

Ty shot him a quick look, his freckled face splotching red. "Yeah."

"Fancy her, do you?" Alex nudged him in the ribs with an elbow.

"She's okay."

Relieved to hear the girl didn't suck, Alex decided to pursue a different track of conversation. This one seemed doomed to a string of grunted one-liners.

He returned his attention to the engine. "We'll clean all these parts with a steamer once they're out; then we'll coat the surfaces with a light film of oil so they won't corrode."

He had hoped that might generate a comment from Ty, maybe a question or two. When it didn't, he continued, "The internal combustion engine is quite an amazing thing. It produces power by transforming the chemical energy of fuel into mechanical energy that rotates the vehicle's wheels. Torque—that's what the power is called. Torque or horse—"

"—What's with girls?"

The sudden shift of subject threw Alex off guard. "Pardon?"

"Girls. I don't get 'em."

"I'm afraid that's the plight of most men, Ty."

"How come one day they act like they like you, and the next day they don't even know your name?"

"Are you referring to the lass at the dance?"

"Not really. There was this other one. Back during the school year."

"I see." Alex laid his wrench aside. "And you're afraid this new lass will treat you the same?"

Ty flushed. "Well . . . yeah, I guess so. I mean, why bother calling her if I'm gonna end up looking like a loser?"

"Well . . ." Stalling for time, Alex cleared his throat. Ty wanted his opinion, his advice. This was progress; he'd bloody well better come through. No lectures, he decided. If he sounded like the teacher he was, Ty would only tune him out.

"Well," Alex said again. "The way I see it, sometimes a chap has to forget about the past and take a gamble on the future. A slim chance is better than none. And I'd wager you have better odds than that."

"Yeah, but if I don't gamble, there's no chance I'll look like a loser."

"And no chance you'll win, either."

Ty busied himself with the engine again. He squinted. A muscle worked along the edge of his jaw.

Alex shifted his focus back to the machine, too. He feared he had failed the boy. Feeling frustrated, he sighed. Rejection was a frightful prospect. How could he convince Ty that facing it from time to time was an inevitable part of life? A fact the boy couldn't escape? Nurturing his fear of rejection would only make Ty what he most dreaded being—a loser.

"Who's to say this lass is like the other?" Alex asked. "By assuming so, you're not being fair to her, Ty. Or to yourself. She might be wishing you'd ring her up. And even if she doesn't become your girl, she might become your friend. No loss there." Pleased with himself for coming up with that bit of wisdom, Alex added, "Just be yourself. If she likes you, you'll know soon enough. If not, well, chalk it up as her misfortune."

They worked in silence for a while. Alex mulled over the advice he'd given his nephew and slowly realized he was a bloody hypocrite. How could he expect a lad of fifteen to do what he himself was terrified to do? Only last night, he'd run from Robin Wise and the feelings she'd stirred in him. His relationship with Leigh had injured his pride, made him feel like a loser, as Ty would say. Now Alex was afraid of getting close to another woman and risking failure again.

Inside the house, the phone rang. Alex excused himself and started off to answer it as Ty laid his wrench aside for another drink of soda.

When Alex reached the door, Ty belched.

Alex glanced back at his nephew. "You remember what I said about being yourself with this young lady you fancy?"

"Yeah?"

"I'm not certain that was wise advice." Alex grinned.

When Robin entered the kitchen, she was surprised to find Millie on the phone.

"Okay now, Alex, let me read this back to you so Robin and I will be sure to get everything we need to spray her roses."

"What are you doing?" Robin whispered harshly, hurrying to Millie's side.

"Let's see here . . ." Ignoring her, Millie lifted the paper Alex had written on the night before. "DDT and lindane for the rose bugs, then for the black spot . . ."

Crossing her arms, Robin tapped her foot and glared as she listened to the rest of the conversation.

"Thanks so much, Alex. I really enjoyed dinner last night." With a scowl, Millie added, "Well, most of it, anyway. Ethan can be such a bore. Nonetheless, it was wonderful getting to know you. Robin's thrilled to have you for a neighbor." She met Robin's glare with a coy smile. "She told me so. Perhaps you could help her spray her roses later so she doesn't cock up." After a long, lusty laugh, Millie ended the conversation by saying, "Well, we're off to run our errands now. See you soon."

She hung up, handing Robin the list as she moved to the easel by the living room window. "Such a nice man. I was right about nerds. This one definitely merits your attention. Did you take a good look at him last night?"

"Millie—"

"The man's not only sweet as pie, he's hung like a Brahman bull."

"For crying out loud, Millie!" Robin snickered despite herself.

"Well, he is."

Groaning, Robin glanced toward the window. "How could you possibly know such a thing about him?"

Millie arched a brow. "Oh, believe me, sweetie, I can tell these things about a man."

Shaking her head, Robin laughed again as Millie eyed the painting.

"I see you've been working this morning."

Robin walked up beside her. "A little." She'd

added a blood-red sunset to the background of the Old West town.

"Nice colors." Dismissing the canvas, Millie walked off toward the kitchen again. "Now where do you suppose I put my purse?"

"I don't have a clue. Just like I don't have a clue where I'm headed with this painting." Crossing her arms, Robin studied it. "I just show up at the easel, lift my brush and see what happens."

"I swear." Millie sounded distracted as she continued to look for her purse. "I'd forget my head if it weren't attached to my shoulders."

"Are you sure about what you said?"

"About losing my head?"

"No, silly." Robin met Millie's gaze. "About what Alex Simon has in common with a bull."

Millie stopped looking for her purse and grinned. "Now, that's my girl. I like that gleam in your eye. I believe you are getting better." She laughed. "Rather than asking me that question, why don't you find out for yourself? Sounds like fun, doesn't it? You could use some fun."

Heat rose to Robin's cheeks. She glanced back at the painting.

"I have another question for you," Millie said. "One you won't mind answering. Are you sure you're ready to go out?"

"I'm sure."

"Maybe your first excursion should be to that psychologist you said you'd consider seeing."

"Let me give these errands a try."

Robin felt Millie's concern in the long pause that followed.

"Well, look at that," Millie said. "There's my purse. Right in front of my nose." She scooped it up from one of the kitchen bar stools, then slipped the strap over her shoulder. Turning to Robin, she reached out her hand. "Ready?"

Robin crossed the room and took Millie's hand. She gave it a gentle squeeze.

Millie smiled and squeezed back. "I'm proud of you, sweetie."

As they started for the front door, Millie talked nonstop. Robin knew by the sound of her voice that she was nervous, too.

"So," Millie said, "to the nursery first for the gardening supplies, then where?"

They neared the door. Robin's heart lurched. All at once she felt dizzy and cold. She drew a deep breath, then blew it out slowly. "To the library," she said, her voice jittery. "I—I want to get some books."

"Good idea." Millie reached for the doorknob with her free hand. Her other hand gripped Robin's sweaty palm tighter. "I remember when you were just a tiny thing, not more than five years old. I'd take you to the library, and you'd browse the shelves for an hour without getting bored. You'd end up with a stack of books as tall as you were and want to take them all home."

Millie opened the door. Sunlight poured into

the entryway. Robin's entire body broke out in a cold, clammy sweat. She hesitated.

One step at a time. Lift your foot over the threshold and onto the porch. That's all you have to do.

She took a deep breath but couldn't lift her foot.

"I'm right here, sweetie," Millie said calmly.

Robin barely heard her over the rushing sound in her ears.

"I won't let go of you. I promise."

She tried to swallow. Her mouth was dry as cotton. Robin closed her eyes. Her breath exited her mouth in small, jerky gasps. Her muscles jumped.

When she opened her eyes again, the yard beyond her porch looked hazy and blurred.

She couldn't breathe.

Later that afternoon, Alex looked up Robin's number and gave her a ring. The suggestions he'd made to his nephew about dealing with the fairer sex had troubled him all day. Not that they weren't good suggestions. But, like Ty, he was leery of them. And that bothered him. Alex didn't fancy being a loser any more than Ty did.

"Hello, Robin!" he said cheerfully when she answered. "Alex Simon here. I see you're back from your errands." He paused, wincing. Nothing like stating the obvious. "I—uh wondered if I might drop by and help you spray your roses?"

"It's nice of you to offer, Alex, but I'm afraid something came up. Millie and I didn't make it to the nursery."

"Oh. Sorry to hear it."

He tried to think of something else to say, another excuse to see her. He hated to step up to the plate only to strike out. But maybe it was best not to push his luck right now. She sounded fatigued, perhaps even a bit upset. "I hope Sheeba's behaved herself with Tinkle today," he said.

"It's Tinker."

Alex winced again. Why did the bloody dog's name always escape him? "Has there been a problem? I haven't heard any commotion."

"No. No problem as far as I know."

"That's good. I only asked because you sound a bit—"

"—I've had a trying day, that's all. I'm sorry if I sound cranky. It's not your fault."

Relieved, Alex said, "I understand. Anything I can do? Bring you dinner, perhaps?"

"I already ate, but thanks for asking."

"You're welcome. Take care of yourself. We'll talk again soon."

Feeling deflated, he hung up and reached for one of the chocolate biscuits Carin had brought by when she picked up Ty. Cookies, Alex reminded himself as he took a bite. In the States, biscuits were called cookies, Ty had informed him. He took another bite. Nothing like Carin's cookies to lift the spirit. Munching, he recalled how depressed Robin had sounded on the phone.

Alex smiled and glanced at his watch. Four-thirty. Still time. Time to take another swing.

Chapter Eight

Alex stood on Robin's front porch with a Green Thumb Nursery sack in one hand, a foil-covered plate in the other. She had been half asleep when the doorbell rang, half tuned in to some mind-numbing program on the television—a funny home video thing that wasn't particularly funny.

Robin shoved fingers through her tangled hair, then tightened the belt of her robe. When Tinker growled, she scooped the dog into her arms. "I'm sorry. I don't know what his problem is when it comes to you. He's always friendly to strangers."

"Yes, well . . ." Alex drew the plate back slightly when Tinker sniffed it. "I can't explain it, either. Usually animals are quite fond of me."

"I guess Tinker doesn't take kindly to being threatened at sword-point."

His brows drew together, furrowing the space between them. "I brought the chemicals for your roses." He lifted the sack. "I'll just leave them and be on my way."

The last thing she needed was for Alex Simon to see her at her worst. But, damn it, she was lonely and sick of her own company. Summoning a smile, Robin opened the door wider. "Would you like to come in?"

Hesitating, he glanced at Tinker.

"I was teasing about the sword." She watched Alex's gaze move from her loose hair to her robe down to her bare toes and was glad she'd applied fresh polish earlier. Her toenails were pale pink now instead of the trendy purple she'd recently given a try.

"I don't want to intrude," Alex said.

"I wish you would. These are my pity-party clothes, and this particular pity party is long past dull. I could use the company." She stepped back. "Enter at your own risk."

The corner of Alex's mouth twitched. He stepped inside. "I made it to the nursery just before it closed."

"You didn't have to go to so much trouble. I would've gotten around to it sooner or later."

"Later might be too late, I'm afraid. Your leaves are dropping fast."

Their eyes met suddenly. In the silent moments that followed, an image flashed into Robin's mind—the gambler standing in a field of yellow roses, leaves falling at his feet.

Robin looked away first. Alex's eyes . . . they were an unusual shade of blue, as soft and faded as his jeans. Sometime during the wee hours of the morning, she'd stared into eyes the exact same color. Eyes surrounded by a mask.

Lowering Tinker to the floor, she closed the door, then took the sack from Alex. "Well, thanks. It was nice of you to think of me. Could we wait until morning to spray, though? I'm not up to it now."

"Of course."

Trying not to think about the passionate kisses of a ridiculous macho dream man, she led Alex into the living room, her hands trembling. She told herself it was silly to overreact. Her recent dreams had definitely messed up her mind. They could mess up other things, too, if she let them. Having someone other than Millie and Uncle E visit from time to time would be a welcome change of routine. But Alex would be scared off again if she got dizzy and doe-eyed every time she looked at him.

"I brought something else." Alex nodded at the plate he held, his mouth curving up at one side. "Are cookies allowed at a pity party? I'm afraid I've never attended such an event."

Robin deposited the sack of chemicals on the kitchen counter. "Are they chocolate?"

He nodded. "My sister's specialty."

"Anything chocolate's allowed. But they have to be eaten in the right way and with the right frame of mind."

"You'll have to explain that one. I wouldn't want to break any rules."

"Well, you have to overindulge . . . make yourself sick you eat so many. And it's crucial that you *know* you're making yourself sick but that you just don't give a damn."

One brow arched above the wire rim of his glasses. "I see. Interesting." He peeled back the foil. "With these, there's no need to gorge. One bite and you'll forget all your troubles. Come see for yourself."

"Oh, but troubles are the mainstay of any good pity party." Robin crossed to where he stood, then lifted a cookie from the plate. She took a bite and continued to speak with her mouth full. "Troubles and complaints. Whining's good, too. Mmmm." She closed her eyes and sighed. "These are sinful. Your sister is my kind of woman."

"I'm certain I could coax the recipe from her."

"Promise you'll share if you do." Taking the plate from him, she set it on the coffee table, then gestured toward the sofa. "Make yourself comfortable."

While Alex settled in, she went to the stereo and shuffled through her CDs. "Country-and-western music is always played at the best pity parties." She slid a disc into the player. "You know . . . my sister's sleepin' with my husband,

113

and I'm stuck here in prison for shootin' my lover's wife."

A steel guitar twanged. Alex laughed.

"A little crying-in-your-beer music to set the mood. We Texans love to cry in our beer. But since I don't have any, how about some milk?"

"Sounds delicious."

She rounded the bar into the kitchen. "So," she called out from behind the refrigerator door, "what would you like to complain about?"

"I can't think of a single thing. I have a lovely new home, a lovely new neighbor and it's a lovely evening. What could be more—"

"—Lovely?" she asked, rounding the corner into the living room with a stack of napkins, and a glass of milk in each hand.

He grinned. "Exactly."

When Robin gave him his glass she noticed he had a cut on one finger and that his hand looked surprisingly strong. Out of nowhere, Millie's comment about Alex and a bull sprang to mind. Her gaze shifted beneath his belt.

"So, what do you think—"

Robin jumped. Milk splashed out of the glass. "About what?" she blurted.

Alex eyed her with curiosity, a puzzled look on his face. "About the rain showers we've had the past couple of nights."

"Oh, that." Embarrassed, Robin moved to the opposite end of the sofa and sat. She slid him a sidelong look. "They sure are . . . um . . . wet."

Lifting her glass, she sipped. "The showers, I mean."

Alex blinked at her over the rim of his glass, then took a slow drink of milk. "I'm not certain why," he said when he finished, "but I'd assumed this part of Texas would be drier."

Silently damning Millie for painting lewd pictures in her mind, Robin wiped off her glass with a napkin. "Sometimes we're dry, sometimes we're wet. Sometimes cold, sometimes hot. This time of year you never know what you're gonna get." Wondering if she could possibly sound any dumber, she lifted both shoulders and made a face that was half sheepish grin, half humiliated wince. "Our weather's unpredictable."

"I see." Alex put his milk on the table. He leaned back, adjusted his glasses, glanced around the room.

Robin wished she could turn into a rose like she had last night in her dream. Then she could wither and disappear. Had she really been holed up in this house for so long that she couldn't think of a single interesting thing to discuss? They were down to mindless babble about the weather. It couldn't get much worse.

"Miss McCutcheon told me you make jewelry," Alex suddenly blurted.

"Yes. I have a studio here in the house."

"I'd like to see it sometime."

"Remind me to give you the tour later."

He nodded, reached for his glass, took another sip.

Robin sipped, too, then placed her glass on the coffee table. She heard the kitchen clock ticking, a gust of wind at the window, the buzz of a housefly. All at once, she was much too conscious of her naked body beneath her threadbare robe. She reached for the amulet that hung between her breasts and stroked the ankh with the pad of her thumb, hoping it might give her courage.

"You do well with it, do you?"

She glanced across at him. "What's that?"

"Your line of accessories."

"Oh . . . yes. It's selling very well. But I'm lucky. My mother left me a trust fund. I live comfortably off of it, so I was able to pursue my creative interests full time even when I didn't make a living at it."

"So, your parents have passed on?"

"My mother has. I'm not sure about my father. He left after she died."

"I'm sorry."

She shrugged. "I was a baby. I never knew them at all. Besides, I couldn't have asked for better parents than Millie and Uncle E."

He nodded. "They're delightful people."

She continued to stroke the ankh.

"Is that one of your pieces?"

"This?" she asked, following his gaze down to the amulet in her hand.

"Yes. It's very unusual."

She drew the edges of her robe together. "Thanks, but it's not my design. It's an ankh; a gift from Uncle E for good luck. He's extremely superstitious."

He seemed amused by that comment. "I noticed."

"Hey," she said, hoping to steer the conversation to talk of his life instead of hers, "you're going to get kicked out of this party if you're not careful. Surely you can come up with something to gripe about."

He set aside his glass, tapped his chin. "Well, let's see. I'm blind as a bat. That's a bit of a nuisance at times."

"Just a bit?"

"Well . . ." He sat forward. "No. It's bloody annoying. Always has been. Why, when I was a lad trying for my first kiss, my eyeglasses bumped up against the eyeglasses of the lass I was kissing. I was too humiliated to follow through. Believe me, there's nothing more ego-bruising to the teenaged male than making an ass of himself while trying to impress a young lady."

She laughed. "I can imagine. What else?"

"Well . . . to be honest, I'm tired of being told I need an update."

"An update?"

"Seems my hair's too long and my clothes, as well as everything else about me, could use a bit of a polish."

Robin glanced from his head to his feet, liking

what she saw: messy, dark curls; curious eyes; broad shoulders above a long, lean body. The cuffs of his wrinkled denim shirt were rolled up to just beneath the elbow, exposing tanned forearms dusted with dark hair. "Who told you that?"

"My sister, Carin, for one and . . ." he paused. "It doesn't matter."

"Well, just because Carin's a great cook doesn't mean she's an expert at everything." Robin reached for another cookie. "Tell her to bug off. That's what I tell Millie when she turns into the fashion gestapo."

Alex chuckled. "I'm a fumbler, too, if you haven't noticed."

"No! You?"

He chuckled again.

She picked up the plate, offered him a cookie. "You're not eating. That's against the rules."

Alex reached out. But he knocked several cookies off the plate when Tinker barked suddenly at the window. "See there? I'm a fumbler. Just look at the mess I've made." He knelt on the floor.

Robin fell to her knees beside him. "Don't worry about it." Their fingers brushed as they hurriedly gathered cookies. She glanced up . . . and caught her breath. He was watching her, his face only inches away. Reaching for the belt to her robe, she pulled it tight.

"What about you?" Alex asked quietly. "What's your complaint?"

"I—" Robin's heart pounded to the beat of the love song crooning on the stereo. She drew a quick breath. "My mouth is too big."

His eyes lowered to her lips. "I'm not so certain about that." Slowly, he leaned toward her. Their glasses bumped.

"Oops," Robin whispered. She touched a finger to her frames and smiled. "It's the same problem you had as a boy."

"I'm not so easily humiliated these days."

Lifting a hand to the nape of her neck, he tilted his head to one side and tried again. Their mouths touched once . . . quickly, softly.

"I like your mouth," he muttered against her lips, his hand still pressed lightly to the back of her neck.

"I like your shaggy hair."

"You do, do you?"

"I've never cared much for polished men," she whispered.

Taking his time, Alex kissed her again. His fingers felt rough against her skin but his touch was gentle.

"So . . ." he said when they parted, the tip of his nose touching hers, "what else would you like to complain about?"

"I . . . I'm afraid."

He went still, leaned back, looked deep into her eyes. "Not of me, I hope."

Of you, of myself, of everything. Robin didn't know why she'd said it. She only knew she wanted to tell him. Tell him she feared leaving her house, feared an old family curse, feared falling for him.

"Maybe I am just a little afraid of you, but not in the way you might think." She sat back on her heels in the space between the sofa and the coffee table. "I'm afraid of that kiss and the fact that I liked it. I'm afraid to let it happen again."

Alex sat on the floor beside her, his knees up in front of him, his forearms propped on top of them. "What if I told you that kiss scared the hell out of me, too?"

She studied his face, saw that he looked dead serious.

"I've heard," Alex continued, "that the best way to defeat fear is to practice the scary deed again and again until it's second nature. Care to give it a go?"

After a moment of hesitation, Robin smiled and leaned toward him.

The kiss was tentative and tender, delicate as the tickle of a feather, dizzying.

"There now," Alex said softly when it ended. "That wasn't quite as frightening as before."

His grin was crooked and heart-stopping, his eyes so patient and kind she almost couldn't bear to look into them.

"I think we're going to require a lot more practice, though," he added.

Robin laughed. "You make me feel better, Alex."

He twisted the belt of her robe around his finger. "Call on me anytime."

She couldn't help thinking that Alex was good for what ailed her; the very best medicine. She could stand a healthy dose of him morning, noon and night. But Robin knew she wasn't being fair. If he knew what he'd be walking into by caring for her, he'd probably turn around and run. And that was what she found most terrifying—his probable reaction to the truth about her.

Easing away from him, Robin stood, then sat on the sofa. "I'm really glad you stopped by, but I should call it a day. I'm not very good company when I'm tired."

Alex crouched in front of her. "It's only six o'clock. I could take you to dinner."

"I already ate," she lied, knowing her excuses sounded lame.

He took her hand, moved it gently to the rhythm of the music. "Teach me to dance the two-step, Robin. Now that I'm a Texan, I should learn."

She shook her head. "I'm sorry, Alex. It's been a long day. Thanks for dropping by . . . for making me smile again."

"I'm not much good at pity parties, I guess." He released her hand. "I am a good listener, though. Another time?"

She smiled at him, nodded.

Alex touched her nose with his fingertip then stood and started for the back door. "I'll let myself out this way if you don't mind." He paused by the easel. "I guess I'll have to see your studio another time."

"Your sister's cookies. . . ."

"Keep them," he said, shifting his attention to the painting.

At least a full minute passed in silence as Alex stared at the canvas. When he finally looked up, he had an odd, unreadable expression on his face.

"Did you paint this?"

"Yes."

Adjusting his glasses and narrowing his eyes, he studied the canvas again. "It's quite good."

"Thanks."

The butterfly that had been hanging around her place lately, or another one like it, seemed to appear out of nowhere. It glided toward the painting, alighted on the dusty road right beside the saloon.

Alex scratched his head, chuckled quietly.

"What is it?"

"Nothing," he said. "It just reminds me of . . . something." His gaze shifted back to her. "Good night, Robin. I hope tomorrow will be a better day for you." He quickly let himself out.

Robin sat on the sofa and stared at the door. Twice today she'd tried to step beyond her comfort zone—first by attempting an outing with Millie, then by letting down her guard with Alex. Twice today she'd failed.

She slumped against the sofa cushions and reached again for the amulet that hung cool and heavy against her chest. She was tired of feeling vulnerable and helpless. She was disgusted with herself for letting the situation reach this point.

With a frustrated sigh, she stood and crossed to the phone on the kitchen wall. Lifting the receiver from its cradle, she punched in a number and waited through the rings. Knowledge was power. The curse had started all her problems. Maybe a little knowledge could end it.

"Uncle E," she said when he finally picked up. "Could you do me a favor? I need you to help me gather some research material. Go to the library tomorrow and find all the information you can about what was going on in the Texas Panhandle in 1888."

When he asked her to be more specific, she thought of the story of her great-great-grandmother, Hannah Sann. How the woman had supposedly died on a runaway stagecoach during an attempted holdup.

"Start with the outlaws," she said.

Hours later, Robin awoke abruptly with an uneasy feeling she couldn't explain. Uncertain what had roused her, she glanced at the clock and saw that the time was just after four A.M. She hadn't dreamed tonight, or if she had, the images had already slipped from her memory.

Searching for Tinker, she patted the bed. When she didn't find him, she murmured his name.

A noise downstairs caught her ears . . . Tinker's

low growl, the one that started deep in his throat, the one that always lifted the fine hairs along Robin's neck and started her adrenaline flowing.

Robin sat up and strained to hear something out of the ordinary, something other than the *plop, plop, plop* of the dripping bathroom faucet, the tick of the clock, the bedroom window creaking against the weight of the wind. But she didn't hear anything unusual, so she settled in again, hugging her pillow and willing her pulse to slow its erratic beat.

When Tinker's growl escalated into agitated barking, Robin's muscles tensed. In the pre-dawn stillness of the house she heard the doggy door squeak as Tinker passed through it. The sound seemed louder than usual, intrusive and eerie. Reason told her Alex's cat had probably riled Tinker, so she took a deep breath and relaxed, allowing the dog a minute to scare the mischievous feline back into its own yard.

A minute passed. Tinker kept up his tirade.

Crazy thoughts whispered through Robin's mind, thoughts she couldn't ignore. *What if it isn't the cat? What if someone's out there? What if destiny has finally arrived . . . my date with death?*

Her instinct was to pull the blanket over her head, to stay completely still. But she was determined not to let irrational fears paralyze her one minute longer. So, pushing the covers back, she climbed from bed and started downstairs. Alex's damn cat was toying with Tinker again, that's all. She'd put a stop to it and get back to sleep.

Pausing at the entry-hall closet where she kept her sports equipment, Robin located the slingshot Uncle E had made for her when she was only ten. Then, by feel and instinct, she made her way through the darkness of the house into the kitchen.

The bag of pecans Uncle E had brought sat on the counter where he'd left them, untouched and temporarily forgotten, along with the promise of making her favorite pie if she'd shell them. Just in case something more intimidating than Alex's cat awaited her, Robin reached inside and grabbed a handful.

It was either a moonless night or cloud cover blocked any light from the sky, she wasn't sure which. In the living room, she stood at the window and squinted into the darkness, trying to see something other than the inky silhouette of the big oak tree. Despite the warm night, goose bumps scattered across Robin's skin beneath her long T-shirt, and the tile floor felt cold against her bare feet.

When a light came on outside, she gasped and jumped. Unless Alex's cat possessed some extremely unusual talents, someone was out there . . . someone who walked on two legs, not four. A long, piercing beam illuminated Tinker. She couldn't see the intruder who held the flashlight, only her schnauzer, out of control on a snarling, barking frenzy at the base of the old oak tree.

Fear clutched Robin by the throat, set her heart to racing as she backed away from the window. She reminded herself that she was safely behind locked doors and tried to ignore all the other thoughts running through her mind. Particularly the idea that if such a thing as a curse existed, it wouldn't be stopped by a lock . . . or anything else.

For the first time in her life, she wished she owned a gun. Though Uncle E was a skilled marksman and hunter, Millie was a zealous advocate for the total banishment of guns. The issue had been one of their many battles during the years of Robin's upbringing. Millie refused to allow Ethan to teach Robin to shoot a gun. So he'd compromised by teaching her to shoot other things—a pea shooter first, then the slingshot she now held in her hand, later, a bow and arrow. All had remained favorite pastimes of Robin's, and she was a dead-on shot.

The beam left Tinker, slid upward from the ground into the branches of the tree.

With her gaze fixed on that bobbing ray of light, Robin backed toward the kitchen counter, laid the slingshot and nuts down, then picked up the phone and dialed 911. Her conversation with the operator on the other end was quiet and to the point. It ended when Robin gave the woman her address and hung up.

Trembling, Robin picked up the slingshot and pecans and returned to the window. The beam outside jerked and swayed like a drugged-out dancer at a rock-and-roll concert as the intruder moved about the base of the tree. It shined up into the wind-tossed branches, down to Tinker, then up again.

When Tinker's barking stopped, the sudden quiet was as startling as walking into a wall. But the silence was soon filled by a keening wail. The flashlight dropped to the ground where it slanted a wedge of brightness across the grass.

The next wail instantly transformed her fear into worry and anger. Robin didn't waste time thinking. Afraid the eerie sound might be coming from Tinker, she went to the door, freed the latch, eased it open and silently stepped outside.

As she crept toward the tree, the slingshot's wooden handle felt smooth and cool against her sweaty palm. Placing a pecan in the leather sling, she aimed toward the branches and pulled back the strap.

Chapter Nine

Alex sat on one of the lower branches of Robin's oak tree, which didn't seem particularly low considering he hadn't climbed a tree in twenty years. As he clung to the swaying branch above him with his one uninjured hand, he finally understood why Sheeba spent so much of her time quivering in treetops, refusing to come down. Amazing how a mongrel's wrath could motivate a person to do things he otherwise wouldn't. Cats were no different in that respect, he guessed.

The distraught barking below unnerved and frustrated Alex. It had taken a huge dose of self-control not to hit the dog when those needle-sharp canine teeth sank into the palm of his hand. He fancied himself an animal lover and, until Tinker, animals had always loved him in return. Alex couldn't conceive what he'd done to earn the dog's wrath. Certainly nothing deserving of a bite. When he'd bent to pet the schnauzer, he'd only intended to calm him so that Sheeba might be coaxed from the tree.

The barking continued. Alex glanced down. The schnauzer ran into the slice of brightness emitted from the flashlight that lay in the grass, then into the shadows. Back and forth, again and again.

The blustering wind blew Alex's hair into his eyes. As he pondered his next move, he heard a tiny *meow* just above his right ear. Twisting, he looked up. Two red, glowing eyes stared back at him. He knew better than to make any hasty moves toward Sheeba in her agitated state.

Grasping the branch above tighter with his left hand, he whispered the cat's name while slowly raising his maimed hand toward her. After a moment, she rubbed up against his fingers. He slid his hand under her belly, lifted her off the branch and brought her to him.

Alex decided he'd have to take his chances with Robin's dog or he'd be stuck in the oak tree all night wearing nothing but drawstring pajama bottoms. The possibility of Robin finding him there at sunrise, wind-blown and bleary-eyed among the branches in such a state of undress, was not a prospect he relished.

Sheeba purred in his lap as he broke off a good-sized twig to protect them from the canine.

He grasped it between his teeth, scooped the cat into the crook of his arm and started to climb down.

"Stop right there or I'll shoot!"

Startled by the sound of Robin's shaky voice, Alex lost his balance and his grip on the limb above him. Reflexively, he let go of Sheeba and, on his way down, caught hold of the branch he'd been sitting on. With his feet dangling eight feet above the ground, he held tight.

Sheeba held tight, too . . . to Alex's bare chest. The cat sank her claws into his flesh and hissed like a teakettle at full steam. Alex bit down tighter on the twig. Again, he lost his grip and plummeted toward the ground. As he fell, something hard and round smacked him on the forehead.

He landed in the grass. The next shot caught the right side of his glasses, cracking the lens but sparing his eye. With a wild, hellish screech, Sheeba withdrew her claws from his chest and took off. Tinker's barks followed.

Terrified, Alex rolled to his side, lifted his knees to his chest and sheltered his head with his arms. It crossed his mind that he hadn't heard the weapon explode. When he opened his mouth to yell, the twig fell out of it. "Don't shoot! I'm unarmed!"

He slid his good hand to his face, expecting to find pieces of it missing, expecting blood and splintered bits of bone. But his fingers touched nothing more than a bump the size of an egg. The bullet must have just grazed him, he assured himself.

Light spilled across him. Alex lifted his head, spread his fingers and peeked through them.

"Oh, my God!" Robin fell to her knees beside him in the grass. "Alex . . . I—I'm so sorry. I thought you were a prowler." She reached out to touch him, then pulled her hand back unsteadily. "You're bleeding."

Alex thought he must be in shock. The pain wasn't nearly as unbearable as he thought it should be. Just a dull, aching throb between his brows, though his hand and chest hurt like the bloody dickens. He rose to his knees and glanced at Robin. He could barely make out her features in the darkness with the flashlight shining in his eyes. What little he could see was distorted due to the fragmented lens of his glasses. "Is—" he swallowed and looked away, afraid to meet her gaze, afraid of the horror he'd detect there. "Is it bad?"

"Your chest?"

"My head," he answered. "Where the bullet grazed."

"Bullet?"

Warily, he looked at her. Thanks to the darkness and his cracked lens, it was difficult to tell for sure, but she didn't seem horrified at all. Instead, she seemed ashamed. Her left hand rose until the flashlight's beam shone on it, and Alex saw that she held something that resembled a slingshot.

"I hit you with unshelled pecans . . . compliments of Uncle E."

"Nuts. . . ." Alex didn't know which was stronger—his relief, his embarrassment or his anger. "Remind me to thank your uncle."

"He taught me to shoot."

"And did a bloody fine job of it." He tried to stand.

"Here. . . ." After draping the slingshot over her wrist, Robin clasped hold of his arm. "Let me help you." She stood up slowly, pulling him to his feet. "Anything broken?"

"Only my glasses," he huffed, deciding to nurture his anger. Anger, at least, offered a bit of gratification. He couldn't say the same for embarrassment. And as for relief, well, it had already passed.

She studied the frames sitting lopsided on his nose and winced. "Sorry about that. I'll pay for a pair of new ones. Better broken glasses than broken bones, though. Let's get you into the house and take a look at those scratches."

He showed her his palm. "And don't forget the dog bite."

She aimed the light on his wound, then glanced up at him. "Oh, no. Tinker?"

"How did you guess?"

The dog trotted up beside them, no longer barking and snarling but looking innocent and sweet as a newborn babe.

"Now, be fair," Robin said. With one hand, she held Alex's arm to steady him, with the other she pointed his flashlight ahead. They started toward her back door. "Tinker thought you were a prowler, too."

"Hold it right there!" a deep voice commanded from behind them. "Drop your weapons and put your hands in the air!"

Lifting both arms skyward, Alex froze.

Robin dropped the flashlight and slingshot and followed his lead.

Another light snapped on, shining over them from behind. "Not you, ma'am," said a different man's voice, a younger, higher, more hesitant one. "Just the gentleman. Is h-he the prowler you called about?"

Robin lowered her arms and slid Alex a side-long look of apology. "I called 911," she whispered, then made a face and turned. "False alarm, officers. It was only my neighbor. He was—" She spun back to Alex.

He kept his hands in the air.

"What *are* you doing in my yard in your pajamas, anyway?"

Facing her, he answered, "I'm rescuing my cat from being eaten up by your dog."

The flashlight shook nervously in the younger policeman's trembling hand. He turned it on

Robin so that Alex witnessed the narrowing of her eyes.

"Eaten?" she said between clenched teeth, placing her hands on her hips. "If your cat was so threatened by my dog, may I ask what she was doing in my yard in the first place? Surely you don't expect us to believe Tinker dragged her over here to munch on as a midnight snack?"

The young officer's light slid from Robin to Alex.

"Sir," the older cop said to Alex, "you can lower—"

"All I know," Alex continued, ignoring the man, "is that Sheeba disappeared from the house. I couldn't sleep, so I decided to look for her."

He'd be damned before he admitted to Robin that she was the cause of his insomnia. He wouldn't give her the satisfaction of knowing that in the ten hours, five minutes and fifty-five seconds between leaving her house and setting out to find Sheeba, he'd thought of little else but the way she kissed, her powdery scent, the downy soft touch of her breath against his face.

"I found Sheeba in your tree," he continued, "shaking like a leaf while your precious Tricker—"

"Tinker! His name is—"

"—slobbered and snarled, bared his teeth and eyed my cat as he might a juicy bone!"

The light shifted to Robin again. Her face appeared strangely disjointed through Alex's shattered lens. He closed his right eye and looked only through the good side.

Wind whipped hair about her face. She uttered a sound of disgust and crossed her arms beneath her breasts.

The light lowered slightly, zeroing in on her bosom. So did Alex's one open eye. He saw that she wasn't wearing a bra and realized he wasn't the only one who'd noticed.

"Jiminy, kid," the more seasoned policeman said gruffly. "What in the sam hill do ya think you're doin'?"

Quickly, the light came up to Robin's face again. "Sorry, O'Riley," the younger officer muttered, sounding sheepish.

Light or not, Alex couldn't quit staring. His gaze lowered further. She wasn't wearing pajama bottoms, either. Or shoes. Only a T-shirt that hit her mid-thigh. The T-shirt was streaked with slashes of paint and read, *Artists Do It with Flair.*

Clearing his throat, which had suddenly gone dry, Alex met her gaze. No glasses, either. She wasn't wearing her glasses and she looked . . . beautiful . . . and even more familiar without them. Like someone he knew in his dreams.

"Millie had it all wrong," she snapped. "The only thing you have in common with a bull is a hard head and the fact that you're full of it—bull, that is."

"I don't know what you're talking about."

The young policeman's light shifted to Alex.

"Sir?" O'Riley stepped forward.

Alex's chin came up. "Yes?"

"Your hands?"

Opening his eye, Alex followed the older officer's gaze overhead. His arms were still up, his fingers pointed skyward. He knew right then and there he should never have followed Doctor Dave's psycho-bloody-advice about facing his fear of relationships with the opposite sex, about using positive aggression and all of that rot. Look what it had done for him—placed him right in the spotlight, playing the part of the fool.

Both officers' expressions were openly amused when Alex glanced their way.

"Feel free to lower them whenever you're ready," O'Riley said.

Alex did, then returned his attention to Robin. "You need to do something about your dog."

"You need to do something about your cat."

"At least Sheeba doesn't bite."

"At least Tinker doesn't trespass."

"Obviously, you've forgotten the mess your animal made in my yard just yesterday. He didn't do it long distance."

"There are plenty of other dogs in this neighborhood. You can't prove that was Tinker's mess."

"Proof or not, I think we both know who did the dirty deed."

"Let's go, kid." O'Riley shook his head. "We can't help here."

Oblivious to the two cops, Robin uncrossed her arms and pointed at Alex. "Tinker howled before I came out. Can you explain that? He never howls."

"Well, I do. That was me you heard. Your precious pooch bites. I was trying to pry him off me."

"*Pry?* What exactly did you—" Robin stopped midsentence at the sound of O'Riley's voice.

"Lovers' quarrels," the older officer muttered as he and his partner started out of the yard. He slapped the young rookie on the back. "Get used to 'em, kid. You'll have plenty of these kind of calls if you stay on the force long enough."

Alex watched Robin watch the cops. She looked unnerved, completely taken aback by the brawny old officer's comment.

"I guess we do sound rather foolish," Alex said when they were alone again.

"I guess so." She faced him, her expression sheepish.

They both started laughing.

"I'm not the least bit sleepy," Robin said after a minute. "What do you say we continue this argument inside so we don't wake the neighbors?"

"We *are* the neighbors."

"Then why don't we make it a discussion rather than an argument?"

"A wise idea," Alex agreed. "We can try."

She picked up the slingshot and flashlight and headed for the house. "I'll make breakfast."

Jennifer Archer

"I'll run home and wash up."

"I'll leave my place unlocked. Let yourself in." She paused by the door. "I have some salve for those cat scratches if you need it."

"Thanks, I'll take you up on that. I'm afraid my medicines are still boxed up. Oh, and I'll need something for this, too," he added, lifting his hand, unable to resist the opportunity for another subtle reminder of her dog's bad behavior. "Tinker's bite, remember?"

Robin scowled at him over her shoulder. "Alleged bite," she said. "As if you'd let me forget."

Trying not to dwell on the fact that she was nervous, much less the reasons why, Robin brushed her teeth, slipped a clean pair of shorts on beneath the T-shirt she'd slept in, then pulled her hair into a quick ponytail.

After rummaging around in her medicine cabinet, she found the tube of salve she'd offered Alex. She slid it into her pocket, then grabbed a bottle of antiseptic, a few balls of cotton and an adhesive bandage. On her way past the bedside table, she picked up her glasses, slipped them on, then, with a quick glance at Tinker sleeping on the bed, started downstairs.

Irritated as she'd been at his accusations about her dog, she felt bad for Alex. He'd been through hell in the last half hour.

Robin laughed quietly. Caught in the beam of the officer's flashlight with his hands up, Alex

138

had looked completely miserable and, for some odd reason, totally irresistible. Leaves stuck out of his disheveled hair. His glasses were twisted and broken. He had a knot on his forehead and cat scratches across his chest.

The thought of Alex's bare chest was enough to make Robin pause on the stairway midway down. Silly as it seemed, she wasn't sure she could keep her cool while applying salve to Alex's scratches. She'd probably end up making a fool of herself again. But maybe everything would turn out okay if she thought of other things while playing nurse. Things less appealing than Alex's lean, hard body.

Robin blew a loose strand of hair out of her face, then resumed her descent down the stairs. Suddenly, she recalled how the curling dark hair on Alex's chest tapered into a thin line that trailed all the way down to his firm, flat stomach.

She paused again, drew a deep breath, blew it out through puffed cheeks. At this rate, she'd never make it to the bottom of the stairs. She leaned her hip against the railing and scolded herself for becoming so ridiculously rattled at the prospect of being alone with Alex when he was only half-dressed. She'd seen plenty of bare-chested males in her almost thirty years. For crying out loud! Alex was only a man. And she was a woman.

And that's what scared her.

She was lonely and vulnerable, and Alex was

patient, compassionate and interesting. Not to mention he had a surprisingly great body.

Robin took another step down. That was it! It was the surprise factor that had her so flustered. Alex was one surprise after another. Every time she thought she had the guy pegged, he threw her for a loop. For instance, the way he kissed. There was nothing at all clumsy about his skill in that particular art. And he couldn't possibly stay in the shape he was in by lecturing to a class all morning, hovering over a microscope all afternoon, then sitting with his nose in a book all night. Alex's body looked like it belonged to an athlete, or a lumberjack, or . . . a cowboy.

Robin forced herself to descend another step. She refused to lapse into that old fantasy again. And as for this new fantasy—Alex waiting for her in the kitchen wearing nothing but a smile— well . . .

To counteract the effect of that image, Robin thought of him fencing in his backyard, looking uncoordinated and comical. Maybe he'd just been out of practice, as he'd said. And maybe she'd been cooped up in this house far too long by herself. That was the only plausible reason why she, a sensible grown woman, was obsessing like a flighty teenaged girl about her neighbor.

He was bent over her dining table twisting the frame of his shattered glasses when she walked into the room. Lowering the glasses to the table, he looked up. "I was starting to worry about you."

"Couldn't find the salve," she lied.

To her disappointment, he wore more than a smile. He wore more than pajama bottoms, too. He'd changed into khaki shorts and a dark blue T-shirt and had slipped a pair of old dock shoes onto his feet. Robin couldn't imagine feeling any more unnerved if she had found him in her kitchen stark naked. She set the supplies on the table in front of him, then pulled a chair around so they faced each other, knee to knee.

Their gazes collided. An awkward moment of silence followed. His hair was damp. She smelled the clean scent of soap on his skin.

Moistening her lips, Robin reached for the antiseptic. "I'm sorry about your glasses."

"I have another pair stashed away somewhere."

She twisted the bottle cap. "We'll tend to the cat scratches first. It might be a trick to take off your shirt after your hand is bandaged."

"Of course, my shirt," Alex said. Crossing his arms at his waist, he pulled the garment over his head. He draped it across the chair and glanced down at the angry, red welts on his chest. "I can tend to these myself, but I'll need some assistance with the scratches on my back." He leaned forward, turning so that Robin could see.

Her gaze traveled down the side of his rib cage, just to the right of his spine where several jagged abrasions marred his skin—four or five short ones and a longer one that trailed beneath his waistband. "These look different from the others."

"Tree limbs," Alex said. "Must've caught me as I fell. Sheeba only made mincemeat of my front."

Hoping he couldn't tell how rattled his nearness made her, Robin lifted the cap off the antiseptic and soaked a cotton ball in the strong-smelling liquid. "Turn a little more," she said, then, wincing, paused just short of touching the wet cotton to his skin. "This is gonna sting like all get out."

Alex gripped the back of the chair. "I haven't a clue what 'all get out' is, nor how much it stings, but I'm prepared for the worst."

"You're a good one to tease," Robin scoffed with a grin. "Rubbers instead of erasers," she muttered. "What was the Brit smoking who thought up that one, anyway?"

He started to comment, but she pressed the cotton against him, stealing his words and causing his shoulder blade to jump as the antiseptic hit home.

Working quickly, Robin finished with the shorter scratches, then moved to the last one. She pulled back her hand, drew the corner of her lower lip between her teeth, wondering just exactly how far past his waistband that long, red slash extended. It would be more embarrassing if she made a big deal out of the situation, she decided. Her best bet was to act as if she felt perfectly comfortable sticking her hand down his pants, as if she did that sort of thing every day.

Inching the cotton toward his back, Robin touched the top of the scratch then skimmed lower. At the edge of his waistband, she hesitated.

Alex glanced back. "Is something wrong?"

She jumped. "This one scratch," she blurted, feeling her face heat. "How long is it?"

His brows drew together. "I'm not certain, I didn't pay much attention. Thirteen centimeters? Fourteen?"

Robin glanced again at the scratch. Slightly more than two inches visible. She did some quick calculating. If her math were correct, she'd have to venture dangerously close to private property to find the end of that scratch. And in the dark, nonetheless.

She swallowed. "You might want to slide your pants down."

"Pardon me?"

"Your pants . . . they're in the way."

Alex was silent for a few seconds. Finally, he chuckled. "Oh! You mean my trousers." He chuckled again.

Robin leaned back in her chair. "I'm glad you find this amusing."

"I'm sorry," Alex said. "It's just that pants, as far as we Brits are concerned, are underpants."

"Oh." Completely humiliated, Robin averted her eyes. "Well . . . those will have to go down, too, I guess."

"Don't worry about it." Alex sounded as if he

tried not to laugh. "I'll tend to that last one later myself."

"It's okay. I'll do it."

"No really—"

"I said it's okay." Careful not to look at his face, Robin doused the cotton ball with antiseptic again. For some reason, she felt compelled to prove to Alex, as well as to herself, that she wasn't as prudish as she suddenly felt.

Alex unbuttoned his khakis. The sound of his zipper made her heart take a dive. He shoved one side of his trousers, as well as the elastic band of his blue-and-white striped boxers, down to just below his hip where the scratch ended.

Without even a second of delay, Robin swabbed the area and sat back. "There," she said, as he turned around. "While those dry, we'll work on your chest."

He started to button up.

"Don't do that yet. I still have to put on the salve."

"I don't mind finishing," Alex said.

"They're easier for me to see."

She felt the weight of his gaze while dabbing his skin. It had been years since her stomach had fluttered so wildly. If this were one of her dreams, she'd probably look up, eye him straight and steady, and say something sassy. Seductive, even. But this was reality, and, unlike her alter-ego, the Robin in her dreams, she'd forgotten the art of flirtation a long time ago.

"We could put up a fence," Robin said, afraid if they didn't get down to business soon, she was going to do or say something asinine again. She reached for a fresh cotton ball. "Of course, I'd expect us to split the expense."

"I considered that earlier. But while it would keep your dog out of my yard, I'm afraid it wouldn't keep Sheeba out of yours if she had a mind to get in. Besides that, one of the reasons I bought a house in this neighborhood was the lack of fences. Seems rare for this part of the country. I find that strange. When I think of Texas, I think of that old song 'Don't Fence Me In.' "

Robin traded the cotton for the tube of salve. While the antiseptic dried on Alex's chest, she had him shift again so she could reach his back. "Okay then, your turn. I'm open to ideas."

"I suppose there are always leashes. Long ones that would allow Sheeba and Tinker to roam a bit." He shook his head. "I don't particularly like the thought of that."

"Me either. It's a horrible idea."

She felt more at ease touching him so intimately while talking about their dilemma. With Alex focused on a solution to their pet problem, Robin had the perfect opportunity to shamelessly focus on him. His skin felt warm and firm against her fingers, and, beneath it, the muscle was long and defined.

"What do you say we simply keep a closer watch on the two of them? Confine them inside unless we're outside, too?" Alex glanced toward the flap of the doggy door in her living room. "You'd have to make some adjustments but only for a while—until they feel more at ease with each other."

"And how is that going to happen?"

"We'll bring them together for a bit each day. For supervised visits."

Robin frowned. "Can cats and dogs be trained to like each other?"

He gave that some thought. "Who knows? It's worth a try. After a time, if it isn't working, Sheeba will simply be forced to become a house cat."

"Okay." Robin smeared a final dab of salve on the last scratch. "Supervised visits it is. Now . . ." she sat back. "Let's see the damage to your hand."

His palm rested on his knee. "It's only a nip," Alex said. He turned it up, held it out to her.

Robin cradled his hand in her own. "Tinker's up to date on all his shots." She looked quickly at his face, then down again. They sat for several seconds in silence as she skimmed damp cotton across his skin. "Could I ask you a personal question?"

"Ask away." Alex's mouth curled up in that one-sided smile she liked far too much. "No secrets here."

"How does a professor of science get calluses on his hands?"

"Projects," he answered.

Pausing, she looked across at him. His eyes held that curious light they so often did. She tilted her head. "Projects?"

"Gardening, woodworking. Tinkering about the house. I'm a do-it-yourselfer. And I play guitar some, too." He laughed. "Or, I should say, I try to play. And now my nephew and I are restoring an old automobile his dad left him. Trying to put some life back into the old girl."

"You?"

His smile crinkled the corners of his eyes. "We're learning as we go."

"And the woodworking?"

"Took it in school as a lad and haven't stopped since. I came to the States without a stick of furniture, but I did have my equipment and tools shipped over. Other than a few pieces I purchased right away, I've been making the rest of my furniture since I arrived. It's slow progress, but I enjoy it."

Robin studied his face for a moment. One surprise after another. Her new neighbor had more facets than a high-priced diamond. "And now you're taking up fencing, too?"

"Just playing around with it a bit."

That explained the calluses, Robin thought. But a man didn't get a lean, muscled body by simply playing around at hobbies. Still, curious as she was, she would bite off her tongue before broaching the subject of Alex's physique.

147

Robin smoothed some salve on the dog bite, decided it didn't need a bandage. "There." Sliding her hand from beneath his, she sat back in her chair. She felt strangely conflicted, relieved to be finished with her chore, but sorry, too.

"I have a confession to make." The look in Alex's eyes was as mischievous as his tone of voice. "You're the first lass I ever played doctor with. I was much too shy as a lad to do anything of the sort."

For just an instant, Robin felt like the coy lady in her dreams. She dipped her chin, looked up at Alex through her lashes. "Well . . . how did you like it?"

"It was well worth the anticipation. I'm just glad I waited for the right doctor."

Holding his gaze, she nibbled her lower lip. "How about breakfast?"

"Only if you'll promise to show me your jewelry studio afterward."

"Deal."

"And," he added, "if I can assist in preparing the meal. I make a fine omelet."

"You're on. I'll make the coffee. How do you take it?"

"I take my *tea* with cream and sugar.

With a sigh, Robin stood. "Tea." She shook her head. "A drink for wimps. We have a lot of work to do if we're going to turn you into a true Texan."

Chapter Ten

Robin's studio was tucked away in a first-floor room behind the staircase. Intrigued to finally see the place where she made her silver jewelry and hand-beaded purses, Alex took his time browsing. He asked question after question, loving the way her eyes brightened when she talked about her work.

The sun had come up by the time Alex finished his "tour." Together, they walked down the hall toward the living room, laughing and talking, the previous conflict over Sheeba and Tinker all but forgotten.

"Design something for me, Robin." Alex picked a leaf from his hair, one his quick shower and combing had missed. "I'll pay you, of course."

"What would you like?"

"Surprise me."

She pursed her lips and studied him. "Hmm. What kind of purse suits you best? One with a shoulder strap, or without?"

Alex laughed.

"You don't strike me as a man who'd wear jewelry, either."

She was right, he didn't wear jewelry. But for her he'd be willing to start. "If you made it, I'd wear it. Just keep it simple, I—"

"Millie!" Robin gasped, her hand flying up to her throat.

Millie McCutcheon stood beside the dining table, her arms loaded with grocery sacks, a suspicious look on her face as she stared at the remains of a breakfast table set for two. Her eyes lifted quickly, flicked over Robin, then Alex.

Alex glanced down at himself. He'd yet to put his shirt back on because of the salve. Before preparing their breakfast, he'd started to slip it on, but Robin had insisted the ointment should soak into his skin so it wouldn't stain his clothing.

He shifted his attention to Robin. Her feet were bare, and though she'd donned a pair of shorts, she hadn't changed out of her sleep shirt and still wasn't wearing a bra . . . a fact that had taunted him throughout the morning. He could bloody well guess what Millie must suspect. Only a second later, her suggestive smile confirmed his surmise.

Robin slowly stepped farther into the room. "What are you doing here?"

Millie set the sacks on the table beside the uncleared dishes. "I might ask the two of you the same question."

The delight in the older woman's tone was unmistakable. Alex dashed to the chair to grab his shirt. Hoping to spare Robin any further embarrassment, he tugged it over his head, but not before he caught Millie's perusal of the scratches on his chest.

"We've, uh, had a rather eventful morning," he stammered.

Millie's brows bobbed. "So I gather." She lowered her purse to the floor, then pulled back a chair and sat.

Alex winced, wishing he'd kept his mouth shut.

"Don't get any ideas, Millie," Robin warned, crossing her arms. "This isn't how it looks."

"You don't have to make any explanations to me, sweetie." Propping an elbow on the table, her chin against her knuckles, Millie grinned. "I wholeheartedly approve."

"The scratches on my chest are compliments of my cat," Alex said.

Millie shifted her smile to him. "Whatever you say."

"Seriously. Sheeba—"

"Forget it, Alex." Robin began clearing the table. "It's a losing battle. She'll believe what she wants to believe." Pausing in the middle of the kitchen, a plate in one hand, a coffee cup in the other, she asked, "What are you doing here at six o'clock in the morning, Millie?"

"I'm going in to the boutique early to do paperwork. I'd hoped to slip in here without waking you." She picked up one of the sacks. "I wanted to leave a few things to cheer you up. Thought you might need it after yesterday. But I see someone beat me to it." She winked at Alex. "No doubt your cheering-up methods were a damn sight more fun than mine."

Robin groaned. She placed the dishes in the sink, then walked to the table and peeked into a sack. "What did you bring?"

"Fresh, hot cinnamon rolls from the bakery, for one thing." She wiggled her brows. "I know the baker personally. For me, he opened up early. I brought some groceries and magazines, too. I bought them last night."

Robin peered inside another sack. "Why is everyone trying to fatten me up? Alex brings chocolate cookies—you bring cinnamon rolls."

"You brought chocolate, Alex?" Millie crooned. "Nice touch. Few men have the wisdom to think of such an approach." She motioned toward the chair across from her. "Have a seat. You look exhausted. Must've been some night."

Alex gathered his silverware, his own plate and cup. "I'll just help Robin tidy up." As he started into the kitchen, he sensed Millie watching him. His fork fell to the floor. When he stooped to pick it up, his knife clattered on top of it. Robin's stand-in mother possessed an uncanny ability to completely unnerve him.

"This afternoon," Millie said, returning her focus to Robin, "April's coming over to cut your hair and give you a manicure."

Robin set the sack of rolls aside. "April who?"

"My new hairdresser. I know you're used to Angie, but she moved to Dallas six months ago. I knew you'd balk at my flying you there for the day. After Angie left my self-image suffered for a while." She patted her hair. "Then I found April. You'll like her. She works miracles. And if you don't mind my saying so, sweetie, you're in dire need of a miracle right now. Your nails especially."

Alex watched Robin stare down at her fingers. The silver she worked with had tarnished her nails, as well as the skin around them, to a sooty gray. She had artist's hands—graceful, expressive, unadorned.

Robin glanced at Millie. "I can either make beautiful jewelry or I can have beautiful nails. I can't have both."

"Humor me just this once," Millie said.

Robin reached into a third sack. "What's all this?"

"Books. Ethan brought them by last night. Said something came up, and he wasn't sure he could make it over here or get to the library today to find the books you asked for. He had those at home and thought you might want them."

From the kitchen sink, Alex watched their exchange. While Robin flipped through the pages of a hardback volume, Millie reached for her purse on the floor beside her chair, then started rummaging through it.

Robin frowned. "Why didn't Uncle E just bring them to me last night? He knew I'd be home. It's not as if I'm going anywhere." She darted a glance at Alex, then quickly averted her eyes.

Millie kept rummaging. "He, um, needed to come by my place anyway."

"He did?" Robin sounded as baffled and surprised as she looked.

"Yes, he did," Millie answered defensively. She pulled out a nail file, lowered her purse to the floor, then proceeded to buff her nails with brisk, measured strokes. "We had some business to attend to."

Robin lowered the book to her lap. "Business? You and Uncle E?"

Millie kept her eyes on her nails. "Is that so shocking?"

Shrugging, Robin said, "I just can't imagine what kind of business you'd have with Uncle E."

"Why on earth do you want books about nineteenth-century Texas outlaws?" Millie asked, changing the subject.

"I'm interested in history. What's wrong with that?"

"I'd think a nice romance novel or a cozy mystery would be more relaxing. I'll make a visit to the library myself on the way home and find something interesting for you." Her gaze strayed to Alex. "Something sexy."

Intrigued by the subtle undercurrent of tension he sensed in the women's conversation, Alex turned off the water and stepped away from the sink. He dried his hands on a dish towel, stood quietly in the center of the kitchen with his arms crossed and listened.

"I don't want anything sexy or relaxing. I'm doing research, for crying out loud."

Millie stopped buffing long enough to tap her nails on the table. "Not that again. If you're up to what I think—"

"—I'm painting a western town," Robin interrupted, talking through clenched teeth. "I needed some research material. Can't we leave it at that?" She sent Millie an obvious warning with her narrow-eyed glare.

Clearing his throat, Alex walked around the counter. It seemed Millie was dancing at the edge of a subject Robin would rather he didn't hear. He didn't care to cause her any further discomfort. "Excuse me, ladies. I think I'll start home now. I'm tutoring later this morning. After that, I'm certain to need a nap."

He smiled at Robin. Her ponytail sagged. She looked sleepy and tousled and wonderful. "Thanks for everything, Robin. I apologize for the earlier incident."

She slipped off her glasses, smiled back at him. "You're forgiven."

"If you need help spraying your roses later, give me a call."

"I'll do that," Robin said. "Oh, and don't forget the supervised visit. The first one might be a doozy. You know how those two can be."

"Do I ever."

As if she watched a tennis match, Millie shifted her head repeatedly as they spoke. First to Robin, then to Alex, then back to Robin again.

He opened the door.

"Alex?" Robin said quickly, before he could step outside.

"Yes?" He paused, glanced over his shoulder.

"If you're ever in need of a doctor again, don't forget who's best."

Alex grinned. "No chance of that happening, I assure you."

After Millie left, Robin sat at the kitchen table and pored over the books Uncle E had sent. One, *The Outlaw Trail, Unsolved Mysteries of Wild West Texas,* was particularly intriguing. Hard-looking men stared back at her from the pages. Men with mean, black-button eyes and curling mustaches above grim-slashed mouths. Most wore gun belts. Few were elderly. Robin guessed their kind didn't live long, considering the profession they chose.

She kept flipping back to one photo; a full-length shot of an outlaw named Nasty Jack Tucker, a tiny bald man with cocky gleaming eyes. She felt his taunting gaze as if it were aimed at her personally, as if he offered her a dare.

He wore a long overcoat and a side-tipped derby hat. Beneath it, a jagged scar extended from his left temple to his jaw, and a black cheroot was clamped between his bared crooked teeth.

As Robin read the text under Nasty Jack's image, a chill ran up her spine. Holding the book in one hand, she left the table and went to call Uncle E.

"Listen to this," Robin said after a waitress at the Ten Pin tracked him down and put him on the phone. "I read it in one of those books you sent over. It seems that in the spring of 1888, an outlaw named Nasty Jack Tucker and his gang of five robbed a bank in Springer, New Mexico, of six thousand dollars then high-tailed it here to the Texas Panhandle. They hid out undiscovered for a time with the aid of some unnamed women of questionable reputation who lived on the outskirts of Tascosa."

"Doesn't surprise me," Ethan said. "From all the stories I've heard, Tascosa was a rowdy cow town, a hoppin' center of activity. All the ranches in the Panhandle relied upon it for supplies. It was the only trading point for two hundred miles in any direction."

"Yes, but most of the businesses there relocated across the Canadian River in 1887, the year be-

fore Nasty Jack showed up. By then, the Fort
Worth and Denver Railroad had bypassed the
town. Apparently it was still a good place for
scoundrels to hang out, though. That sort pretty
much made up the population. Jack and his en-
tourage would've blended right in."

"You've sparked my curiosity, sugar," Uncle E
said with impatience, "but cut to the chase. I've
got customers waitin'."

"Well, somehow or another, Nasty Jack misplaced the stolen money. There was some speculation that one of the women hiding him tricked
it out from under his nose. At any rate, Nasty Jack
ended up getting himself killed by a posse when
he and his gang went after one of the women who
was leaving town on the stage. A stage driver and
one of the passengers died, too."

"Who was the passenger?"

"It doesn't say but I bet I can guess."

Ethan sighed. "Don't get your hopes up, sugar.
A lot of people got killed on stagecoaches back
in those days. Your great-great-grandmother was
just one of many."

"But you told me she and her baby lived on
the outskirts of town with a crazy woman."

"That's right. The lady had the sight. Fancied
herself a healer. Could cast spells, too."

"See? The book says women of questionable
reputation helped the outlaws hide. When I first
read that, I assumed it meant they were prosti-

tutes. But it might not mean that at all. Maybe they were just eccentric."

"What happened to the money?"

"The book says it was never found."

There was a long hesitation on Uncle E's end of the line, then, "What do you want me to do?"

"Go to the library for real this time. Maybe the museum, too. See if you can find anything else on Nasty Jack Tucker. While you're doing that, I'll search the Internet and make some calls to see what I can come up with. I wonder if newspapers from that time period are preserved somewhere? Or if there's any way to track down the stagecoach company's records?"

"I'll go to the library tonight. When I come by, I've got another good-luck charm to bring you, and a recipe for a potion I'll make that's guaranteed to break even the strongest of spells."

"I don't want charms and potions, Uncle E, I want answers."

"I know, sugar, I know."

She thought of the business Millie claimed to have with him. "By the way, you have some explaining to do."

"What'd I do?"

"It's not what you did, it's what you're doing. Just what are you and Millie up to, anyway?"

"Up to? We're not up to anything. Why? What'd she say?"

"She didn't say anything. That's what worries me."

"Sugar, you're talkin' crazy. You sound worn out."

"I am worn out. I didn't sleep much last night."

"Wanna talk about it?"

"Later, maybe. Right now, I'm going to take a nice, long nap. . . ."

Robin awoke with the morning sun in her eyes. She lay in the cornfield on a velvet-soft bed of yellow rose petals. The gambler slept beside her, his hand in her hair, his Stetson on the ground at his side.

Somewhere in the distance a door slammed. A woman's laughter drifted like tinkling chimes on the gentle spring breeze, mingling with bird song before it slipped away into the sky.

Rolling to her knees, Robin rubbed sleep from her eyes. She shook the gambler by his shoulder. "Wake up!"

He blinked and stared up at her, his eyes stormy slashes of blue against the black of his mask. "You came back."

"Shhh!" she hissed. "Listen!"

Beyond the cornstalks at the field's farthest edge, two voices could be heard. Like the laughter of moments before, the first one, which was seductively feminine, rose and fell in smooth, clear waves of sensual delight. The other, a man's, sounded raspy and coarse, gritty as a West Texas windstorm.

The gambler sat up. Lifting his Stetson from

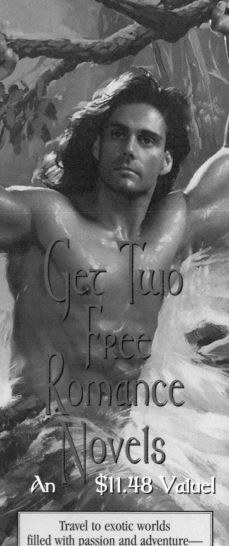

Thrill to the most sensual, adventure-filled Romances on the market today...

FROM  LOVE SPELL BOOKS

As a home subscriber to the Love Spell Romance Book Club, you'll enjoy the best in today's BRAND-NEW Time Travel, Futuristic, Legendary Lovers, Perfect Heroes and other genre romance fiction. For five years, Love Spell has brought you the award-winning, high-quality authors you know and love to read. Each Love Spell romance will sweep you away to a world of high adventure...and intimate romance. Discover for yourself all the passion and excitement millions of readers thrill to each and every month.

Save $5.00 Each Time You Buy!

Every other month, the Love Spell Romance Book Club brings you four brand-new titles from Love Spell Books. EACH PACKAGE WILL SAVE YOU AT LEAST $5.00 FROM THE BOOK-STORE PRICE! And you'll never miss a new title with our convenient home delivery service.

Here's how we do it: Each package will carry a FREE 10-DAY EXAMINATION privilege. At the end of that time, if you decide to keep your books, simply pay the low invoice price of $17.96, no shipping or handling charges added. HOME DELIVERY IS ALWAYS FREE. With today's top romance novels selling for $5.99 and higher, our price SAVES YOU AT LEAST $5.00 with each shipment.

AND YOUR FIRST TWO-BOOK SHIP-MENT IS TOTALLY FREE!

IT'S A BARGAIN YOU CAN'T BEAT! A SUPER $11.48 Value!

Love Spell ✦ A Division of Dorchester Publishing Co., Inc.

Get Two Books Totally
FREE —
An $11.48 Value!

▼ Tear Here and Mail Your FREE Book Card Today! ▼

PLEASE RUSH
MY TWO FREE
BOOKS TO ME
RIGHT AWAY!

Love Spell Romance Book Club
P.O. Box 6613
Edison, NJ 08818-6613

the ground, he shoved it onto his head. One hand slid to the Colt on his left hip, the other to the sword on his right.

The vigilant gesture increased Robin's pulse rate and stirred up her sense of excitement. "Let's go," she whispered. She started crawling, leaving her own hat behind.

On hands and knees, they crept through the field toward the voices, stopping when they reached the last row of towering stalks. Taking care to stay silent and hidden, they knelt side-by-side. Robin pushed apart ears of corn, and they both peered out.

In front of a small adobe hut stood an odd-looking couple engaged in a lustful embrace. The tall, willowy woman wore nothing but a white chemise and bloomers; even her feet were bare. Silver-streaked red hair tumbled around her pale shoulders in a wild, frizzy tangle, and her eyes were smudged with kohl.

Her bald male companion stood several inches shorter than she. He had one hand down the back of the woman's bloomers and held a bottle in the other. Leaning back, he tilted the bottle and poured a trickle of whiskey into the woman's abundant cleavage. The long, black cheroot he smoked fell from his teeth to the ground where he crushed it beneath the toe of his boot. With a feral growl, he buried his face in the tall woman's bosom and proceeded to lick the nectar from her breasts.

The tall woman moaned, a carnal sound that started deep in her throat. With her arm draped around the tiny man's neck, she threw back her head, giving him better access. "I declare, Jack Tucker," she crooned like a tarnished Southern belle. "You surely do live up to your nickname. You're a deliciously nasty little devil." She slipped the bottle from his hand and took a long swig.

Lifting his head, the bald man stepped back and glared up at her. "Shut your mouth, Lil," he snarled. "I told you not to speak my name. From now on, I'm J. T. Sweeny, even to you."

Robin felt the gambler tense beside her.

"Nasty Jack Tucker." He spit out the name in a whisper of disgust, as though it tasted foul on his tongue.

"You know him?"

"Our paths have crossed." With his gaze fixed on the couple in the yard, the gambler felt for the Colt .45 resting in the holster against his left leg. "Men best watch their backs and lock up their wallets, wives and daughters whenever Jack's around."

"And the woman? Who's she?"

"Folks claim she's a sorceress. Showed up here a few months back. Story is a passel of women ran her out of the Georgia town she lived in for casting love spells. They'd caught their fine young sons and faithful husbands in the arms of the red-haired witch. And some found worse." He

cleared his throat. "But that part of the story's not fit for a lady's delicate ears."

Robin propped her hands on her hips and cast him a reproachful glare. "Really, Gambler, I'm not the shrinking violet you think I am. After all, I cut my baby teeth on daytime soap operas and MTV."

She returned her attention to the enchantress. Ignoring Nasty Jack's scowl, the woman splashed more whiskey onto her breasts and suggested the outlaw resume his prior activity. When he didn't respond, she stroked a fingertip across his lower lip and laughed.

"Look at her chin," Robin whispered, fascinated by the woman's reckless lack of inhibition. "See the cleft in the center? 'Dimple on the chin, the devil within,' " she quoted. "It's the sign of a mischievous spirit."

Beside her, the gambler slapped his hand to cover his nose and mouth, then sneezed, muffling the sound with his palm. "Something in this field's gettin' to me," he said, sounding congested.

She turned to see him pull a red kerchief from his pocket and wipe his nose, which was equally as red. Then he withdrew an inhaler and took a quick hit. Just her luck. The so-called best detective this side of the North Atlantic suffered allergy attacks.

"We're all alone, you naughty little man," Lil cooed across the way. "Who's gonna hear me say

*your name?" She nodded toward a nearby ram-
shackle barn. "Those scoundrels you run with are
down for the count ... sleeping off last night's
drink. Besides, they know who you are."*

*"You're forgettin' the blue-eyed squaw," Jack
rumbled, with a quick glance over his shoulder at
the hut. "I don't trust her. She slinks around like
a cat. Always watchin' ... listenin'."*

*"Her?" Lil lifted Jack's hand, pressed it to her
breast. Smiling, she leaned forward and rubbed
up against him. "She and her baby girl have been
with me two weeks, and she's yet to utter a word.
She's no threat to you, darlin'. The squaw
woman's touched in the head over her man's
death. Deaf and dumb, too, far as I can tell."*

*Nasty Jack grabbed a handful of silver-
streaked hair, then tugged Lil's head back, forcing a strangled sound past her lips. "You better
hope you know what yer talkin' about, shrew."*

*"You're safe with me, Jack," she gasped. "No
one would dare touch you." She wiggled her fingers in his face, and hissed, "They're afraid I'll
hex them ... give them the evil eye."*

*"And what about me?" He tugged her hair
harder. "Should I be scared a you, too? What do
ya got in mind? Are ya plannin' to use those
magic powers of yours to trick me into tellin' ya
where I hid the money?"*

*"You surely do have a suspicious mind," Lil
said, her tone innocent. Her mouth curled in a
slow, erotic grin, "I don't want a single thing*

from you except more of what you gave me last night and this morning."

A rusty chuckle erupted from Jack's throat. "Dad-blast! You're a wicked Jezebel, Lil, that's what you are. I must be loco to get mixed up with the likes of you." He lowered his mouth to nuzzle her neck then, lifting his head, stared at her breasts where they strained against the thin, wet fabric of her chemise. "How's a man s'posed to think sensible with your ammunition aimed right at him like a pair a twin bullets?"

With another lecherous chuckle, Nasty Jack swept the witch off her feet, walked to the horse trough then, ignoring her screech, fell backward into the water with Lil on top of him.

Across the way in the cornfield, the gambler leaned back on his heels. He grasped Robin's arm and pulled her away from the stalks she held aside.

"Let's get out of here, ma'am. That's nothin' for a lady such as you to be seein'."

Something jabbed into her side as she slumped against him. Turning, she lifted a brow and said, "You seem more affected than me by their antics."

The corner of the gambler's mouth lifted. "That was the handle of my sword, ma'am." He drew her closer, settled his hands at her waist. "How does a fine, fancy lady like you know about such things as you're implying, anyhow?"

With her forefinger, she tipped up the brim of his Stetson. "I told you . . . I'm no shrinking violet."

"No, ma'am, you're more like a rose. Soft where it counts, but with a temper that can prick a man if he's not careful."

Their mouths inched closer. His hand skimmed up from her waist toward her bosom.

The gambler hesitated. "Maybe, for my own sake, I'd best give this some thought. First time I took liberties with you, I got slapped. Second time, you disappeared."

Robin slipped the fingers of one hand into the black curls at the nape of his neck. With her other hand, she traced the outline of a stallion etched into his silver belt buckle. "You know what they say, Gambler . . . third time's the charm." Grinning, she pressed his head toward hers until their lips touched.

A second later, a baby's cry startled them apart.

Robin turned and leaned forward to peek through the cornstalks again.

Sunlight glinted off the one grimy window in the front wall of the adobe hut. Just for an instant, Robin saw movement—the flicker of two wide eyes. A flash of long flaxen hair. Darkness.

"Did you see her?" she whispered, her gaze intent on the window.

Beside her, the gambler sneezed, but this time, he didn't muffle the sound.

Water splashed out of the horse trough. Nasty Jack Tucker jumped up, drew his gun and started toward the corn. . . .

Chapter Eleven

Alex tensed. His heart thudded like a drum. With a hair-raising shriek, he jumped up, grabbed the arm of the dark figure looming over him, then twisted it behind the attacker's back. Going to his knees, he forced the man to the ground, face-down.

"Uncle Alex! Let me up!"

The voice was frantic and young—not at all like Nasty Jack's. More like his nephew, Ty's.

"*Alex!* What on earth? Let go of him!"

Blinking, Alex squinted up into his sister's mortified face, covered his mouth . . . and sneezed. "Carin . . ."

He glanced down. Pinned beneath Alex's bent knee, Ty struggled to free himself. The lad's arm was wrenched at an awkward angle behind his

167

back, and it suddenly dawned on Alex that *he* was the one doing the wrenching.

Groggy and confused, he released his nephew's wrist, flexed his fingers and stood. "I'm sorry, Ty. I thought you—" Blowing out a long, calming breath, Alex removed his glasses and rubbed his bleary eyes. "You caught me dreaming."

Carin's laugh was perplexed. "Must've been a frightful dream. Thank heaven you weren't armed."

As he helped Ty to his feet, Alex decided against informing his sister he had been armed . . . in the dream, at least.

"Who taught you that move?" Ty brushed grass off the front of his shorts and T-shirt while affording Alex a wry grin. "Mom never told me you were a professional wrestler," he teased.

"Amateur," Alex said.

Ty's eyes widened. "No kidding?"

"As a university student."

"What haven't you tried?" the boy asked.

Carin crossed her arms, her eyes amused. "Not much of anything. Early in life, your uncle decided he would prove to the world there was nothing he couldn't do if he set his mind to it. And he had to be best. He was tenacious back then, your uncle. And from what I can tell, he's yet to grow up even a bit."

Alex regarded her smugly as he righted the lawn chair in which he'd been sleeping. In his haste to wrangle Ty to the ground, he'd kicked over the lounge. Since Sheeba had been secured by a leash to the chair, he freed her now, too, and lifted her to his chest.

"A stubborn lad in a man's body," Carin continued. "That's our Alex."

He was well aware of the subtle message hidden behind his sister's good-natured ribbing, but wasn't about to complain. At least she'd resorted to teasing rather than the dreaded, though well-meant, lectures she usually dispensed. He could no longer bear the long-winded orations about how he didn't need to prove anything to anyone, least of all himself. Despite what Carin might think, nothing remained of the lad he'd once been, desperate to impress their mum, to no avail. With Leigh, he'd temporarily slipped back into the old routine, but only for a bit.

Alex sneezed again. Yes, he decided, Carin's change of technique was welcome, indeed.

"Are you catching a cold?" Carin asked.

"No, just a bit sensitive to something in the air." Stroking Sheeba, he looked around the yard, then across the hedge toward Robin's house. "Probably another blasted butterfly. You never mentioned that this area was such a haven for the creatures. I've never seen anything like it."

"Butterflies?" Carin frowned. "I've never noticed."

"How could you possibly miss them?" He shook his head, shot another glance across the hedge. "Well, actually I've only seen one. But the

169

bugger's as persistent as you accuse me of being. I'm starting to think he wants me to adopt him. Perhaps it's just this neighborhood. Could be butterflies are as attracted to Robin's roses as I am."

Carin's eyes grew alert with sudden interest. "Robin?"

"My neighbor." Alex turned to Ty, who stood beside his mother looking restless and bored. "So . . . ready to get to work on the Mustang?"

"Yeah, I guess."

"I'm on my lunch break," Carin said. "I hope you don't mind if he stays until I've finished at work. I can pick him up at five-thirty."

"Perfect," Alex said. "That allows plenty of time for the two of us to thoroughly soil our hands." Ignoring his nephew's look of disdain, Alex handed him the cat and added, "Put Sheeba in the house for me, would you, Ty? I'll join you in the garage after I see your mum off."

As Ty walked away, Carin touched the bump on Alex's forehead. "What happened here?"

"I had a run-in with a pecan."

"A pecan?"

"Never mind. You wouldn't believe it."

Frowning, she tilted her head. "So, brother, tell me about your neighbor. She wouldn't be Robin Wise, would she?"

Alex's gaze ricocheted from his sister to Robin's rosebushes then back again. "You know Robin?"

"We've yet to meet, but I know of her. Tell

me, do you find her as attractive as you do her roses?"

"Why do you ask?"

Carin clasped her hands behind her back. "I'm not quite certain what tipped me off. Perhaps the sound of your voice when you spoke her name. Not to mention the fact that you've glanced over there at least five times in the last half minute."

"You exaggerate."

"Do I?" She strolled alongside him. "How is Robin?"

Alex frowned. His sister had lowered her voice to just above a whisper, as if she feared Robin might overhear their discussion. "She's fine." He recalled how depressed Robin had been the prior evening when he'd dropped by her house. Suddenly he wondered if his statement was totally true. "Why do you ask? Has Robin been ill?"

At the side of the house, Carin stopped walking. "So she hasn't told you?"

"Told me what?" Alex paused to face her.

She pressed her lips together and sighed. "Robin Wise is agoraphobic, Alex."

"Agora—"

"She hasn't left her house in a year, or close to that long."

"But I've seen her in her backyard," Alex blurted, not wanting to believe his sister's claim. "She tends her garden daily."

"Yes, I've heard rumors of that. Her house and her backyard are as far as she'll venture."

"Rumors!" Alex huffed. "I'm surprised you'd listen to such nonsense, Carin, much less believe it."

"Alex . . ." Carin stepped close and touched his arm. "Perhaps *rumor* was a poor choice of words. This is a small town. Everyone living here is acquainted with everyone else. The people I've heard speak of Robin's condition weren't ridiculing. They were genuinely concerned about her welfare."

Feeling strangely off-kilter, as if something or someone had tilted the world on its axis, Alex tightened his hands into fists and shook his head. "My God . . . a year alone in that house." Though he stood at the side of his own house and couldn't see Robin's yard or her roses, he turned to stare in that direction.

Robin's comment that she and Millie hadn't made it to the nursery yesterday afternoon came to mind. She'd sounded despondent when she told him that. He recalled, too, her admission that she was afraid after he kissed her. She had abruptly drawn inward to distance herself from him. Now, Alex had a clearer understanding of the reasons for her guarded behavior.

"An entire year shut away," he muttered, dazed by the very idea of it. He met Carin's eyes and swallowed. "Why?" he asked. "What could have happened to make such a smart, attractive, talented woman so utterly afraid?"

* * *

172

"See what you think." April offered Robin a large, oval mirror.

Regarding her reflection, Robin ran manicured fingers through her hair, which now swept the top of her shoulders. "I feel like a new woman. And these nails!" She lifted a hand and spread her fingers wide. "They're so white! Millie will be disappointed we didn't go with the Vampire Blood Red, though."

"Millie is something else." April gathered the supplies that lay scattered across Robin's dining table and began putting them into a case. "That woman knew just exactly how to bribe me over here on my day off. Chocolate and romance novels—my two passions. If you ask my husband, he'll insist they're weaknesses, but what does he know?"

Robin blew on her nails, though the clear polish was long past dry. "Well, I appreciate this. And I apologize for nodding off."

"Hey, if my dreams made me smile in my sleep like yours, I'd snooze every chance I got."

After securing the latches on the case, April slid it from the table to the floor. Her gaze flicked to the easel across the way in the living room. "I sneaked a peek at your painting when you were in the bathroom. It's good."

"Thank you."

"Mind if I look again?"

"Of course not." Robin stood and led the hairdresser across the room. They paused in front of the easel. "It's slow going with this one, I'm afraid."

"The town looks so real! And that cornfield off in the distance . . . it's cool how, at first glance, you don't notice it's there, but when you look again . . ." April nodded toward the stack of books on the floor beside the sofa. "Did you reproduce the picture from one of those?"

"No. As a matter of fact, I've actually been to that town. I've walked through that cornfield and stood right outside the door of that saloon. Been inside, too. But that's another painting."

"You're kidding, right?" After one last appraisal of Robin's work, April returned to the table and her supply case. "I didn't know places like that existed anymore, unless it's a tourist trap."

"They do in dreams. The saloon's called the Crazy Ace. I need to add a sign over the building."

"An old western town put that smile on your face when you nodded off in my chair?" April grinned and shook her head. "I don't think so. Next time I drop by, there'll be a good-looking cowboy leaning against that hitching post, am I right?"

"Nope . . . he's a gambler."

April laughed. "That's even better."

With a chuckle of her own, Robin escorted Millie's hairdresser to the front door.

Minutes later, she returned to study the painting. The gambler. Maybe he was the missing element. But, what if she couldn't capture his essence? Even worse, what if seeing him on the canvas, an imperfect caricature of the magnificent image she carried around in her mind, somehow ruined everything?

Robin slipped into the smock she always wore while painting and prepared to spend some time with a brush in her hand. Where this piece was concerned, she seemed to do best when she didn't think about it too much, when she let her mind wander, instead. The sunset had appeared in that way, the cornfield, too. In fact, after painting it, she'd been as surprised as April to discover the field there, off in the distance.

For the next half-hour, Robin lost herself in her work and the rambling musings of her mind. Much like the colors she applied to the canvas, her thoughts appeared, blended, then finally solidified into clear images.

A sudden yearning for the mother she couldn't remember swept over her. A longing to, just once, hear the sound of Emily Wise's voice, smell her scent, feel the touch of her hand. Robin wondered if her mother had experienced the same fears and doubts about the curse that she now felt? If Emily, too, had tried to subdue her foreboding with rationalizations?

Robin dabbed more color onto the brush. Once, when she was around eighteen years old, she'd asked Uncle E for specific details about her

mother's death. He'd told her that her father had
not allowed talk of the curse; that he hadn't believed in it any more than Millie. So, after Emily
married Nicholas Wise, she never spoke of the
strange fate that plagued the women on her
mother's side of the family.

Then late one night, soon after her twenty-ninth
birthday, Emily called crying and woke Ethan.
She admitted she was afraid of what providence
had in store for her sometime during the next
twelve months. But she resisted his spell-breaking
potions and good-luck talismans. Such things
would only cause trouble with Nicholas.

Robin nibbled her lower lip as she started on
the Crazy Ace's sign. Her mother must have felt
so conflicted—torn between respect for her husband's wishes and fear of a family hex that hadn't
faltered in three generations.

Uncle E said that when Emily died from a blow
to the head just before her thirtieth birthday, his
heart broke, but he wasn't surprised. He berated
himself for not insisting she take precautions, no
matter what Nicholas said.

And so, as Robin grew up in his care, Ethan
took no chances. He wasn't stupid. Robin was
sure he didn't completely believe in the superstitious precautions he practiced. Uncle E was much
like a man who didn't believe in God, but said a
prayer for mercy . . . just in case. Curses might or
might not exist. But, just in case they did, he
made certain Robin knew of the risk and saw to

it that she was aware of her family history. Over the years, he educated himself on every potential way, reasonable or otherwise, he might help her avert her seemingly predestined fate. If that meant making a fool of himself, so be it.

Stroking another slash of red onto the canvas, Robin smiled. Uncle E. She adored the big, burly man. He didn't care one iota if people talked and snickered behind his back about his superstitious obsessions. To save her, he would gladly risk looking asinine.

Tinker licked Robin's ankle, bringing her back to the here and now. Rubbing her foot against his soft gray fur, she paused in her painting to look down at his upturned face. "Hungry? I bet you need to go outside."

After Alex had left that morning, she'd block-aded the doggy door with a jumbo box of deter-gent. "Our new neighbors are cramping our style, aren't they, boy?"

Intending to take Tinker outside, Robin placed the paintbrush aside and slipped off her smock. Her gaze flicked back to the painting. She caught her breath.

A bed. Without even realizing it, she'd painted a bed right smack in the middle of the dusty West Texas road. And not just any bed, her bed. From the four brass posters and fat, plumped pillows, right down to the fluffy, red spread. Robin re-membered starting on the sign for the saloon and, sure enough, the letters *C* and *R* were lightly filled in across the top of the building. But she hadn't finished.

With a baffled shake of her head, Robin picked up Tinker and started for the door. A glance at her watch showed the time to be nearly five-thirty. She hadn't read the paper or listened to a newscast all day, but one look out the back window told her bad weather was headed her way. The sunny sky of only an hour before now appeared darkly overcast and foreboding.

Robin was glad she hadn't taken time to spray her roses. Rain would only wash away the effort.

Alex dodged the thrust of Ty's saber. They'd finished working on the Mustang for the day with minutes to spare before Carin was due to arrive. When Alex offered to instruct Ty in fencing, his nephew scoffed at the suggestion. Heaven forbid that someone might pass by and see the lad participating in such a foolish endeavor.

Alex thought he'd never met anyone so worried about the impressions of the rest of the world. Was it just an insecurity of Ty's generation? Or had teenaged males throughout history fretted over such matters with Alex simply an exception?

In his obsessive quest to learn all he could about everything he could, Alex felt quite certain he'd made a spectacle of himself numerous times throughout his youth. But unless he was under the scrutiny of his mum's critical eye, it never occurred to Alex to be self-conscious. At least not until Leigh dumped him for not "measuring up" to her expectations.

Even after enduring that dreary scene, he wouldn't change all that much about himself. Perhaps he was far from perfect, but that was life. He'd learned that lesson the hard way. Silly or not, he'd never consider giving up the activities that interested him in order to please a woman. He'd just as soon give up women, instead.

Alex had convinced Ty no one would likely stroll by the backyard.

"I'd still feel like a dork in that stupid mask," Ty insisted.

The comment made no sense at all to Alex. If Ty didn't want to be recognized, the mask was a perfect disguise.

Concluding that fifteen-year-old lads seldom made sense, Alex agreed to forgo the masks. Ty reluctantly joined in, and now, wonder of wonders, it seemed he had forgotten to be self-conscious and was actually having fun.

Ty jabbed the saber again and, this time, the blunt end made contact with Alex's chest. "Right in the heart!" he shrieked. "You're history. I win." Lifting the saber overhead, he bellowed a victory cry.

Making a strangled sound in his throat, Alex dropped to his knees. He moaned and choked while pawing at his nephew's leg.

Ty smirked down at him, then poked him again with the saber.

Alex fell backward onto the grass where he thrashed about like a beached fish. Sprawled flat on his back, he clasped his hands to his throat, gave a few final spasmodic jerks for theatrical effect, and went still.

"That's about the worst acting I've ever seen," Ty drawled.

From a short distance away came the sound of applause. "Bravo! More! More!"

Alex pushed up onto his elbows and turned toward the hedge. Robin stood on her side of the shrubbery, clapping.

"It's nice to know at least someone around here recognizes talent when they see it. Give your mortally wounded uncle a bit of help here, would you, Ty?" His nephew clasped Alex's hand and jerked him to his feet. Alex draped an arm across the boy's shoulders, and they walked to the hedge.

"Ty," Alex said, "I'd like you to meet my neighbor, Robin Wise. Robin, Ty Mitchell, my nephew."

Ty blushed profusely when Robin shook his hand. To Robin's credit, she spared him any further humiliation by not commenting on the mock duel she'd obviously witnessed.

Millie's hairdresser had apparently made her visit. Robin's hair was shorter than before and missing the wave her usual braid instilled. The cut flattered her face. Alex liked it.

The evening was warm and unusually muggy.

When a breeze blew in suddenly, Alex considered it welcome relief.

Strands of auburn hair fluttered across Robin's face. She tucked them behind her ears. "I see you resorted to a leash, after all," she said, motioning toward the door to his house where a restrained Sheeba paced back and forth, testing the limits of the cord.

"Only when I can't keep my eye on her. Since Ty and I were fencing, my attention was diverted."

"I hate to see animals tied up in their own backyards. You're giving me a guilty conscience."

"It's only been a few minutes. She'll survive, I assure you."

Ty started off toward the cat. "I'll take her in the house." He looked over his shoulder at Robin. "Nice to meet you."

"You, too, Ty." Robin waited until he was inside the house before shifting her attention back to Alex. "He's a good-looking boy."

"Yes, he is. I'm afraid he's having a difficult time of it with his dad gone."

"He's lucky to have you."

A low roll of thunder caused them both to glance up at the sky where fast-moving clouds seemed to darken before their eyes.

"I was about to suggest we let Sheeba and Tinker have their first supervised visit, but it looks as if we're in for some weather." Again, Robin shoved strands of hair from her face. "You're welcome to bring Sheeba over to the house later if you'd like."

"If the storm isn't too turbulent, I'll do that."

Alex's back door opened, and Carin stepped out. He watched her approach. "My sister's here to fetch Ty."

He'd barely finished introducing the women when the wind grew stronger and a light rain started to fall.

"I'm sorry to run off." Robin stooped to pick up Tinker. "But I guess I'd better take this guy inside."

"I heard on the radio that we're under a tornado watch," Carin said.

Alex knew tornadoes were a common occurrence in this part of the country, but they were a new phenomenon for him. An unsettling wariness crept over him. "My house has a cellar, does yours, Robin?"

"No, but if the weather service has only issued a watch instead of a warning, then nothing's been spotted. We're probably just in for a late-afternoon thunderstorm. Don't worry about me. I grew up around here. I'm used to this."

The tension around her mouth and eyes as she scanned the dark sky told Alex otherwise. He managed a strained smile. "Well, *I'm* not used to it. If things begin to look worse, please come over and ease my mind."

From the corner of his eye, he saw Carin watching him. Alex felt certain he knew what his sister thought. He'd been foolish to ask Robin to make use of his cellar. Her agoraphobia would prevent her from accepting.

Robin's face flushed. "We'll see." She adjusted her glasses. "I'll keep an eye on the weather reports."

Seconds later, Alex closed his back door on the storm.

"Alex . . ." Carin started.

"I know, I know. But surely she would find the prospect of riding out a tornado more frightening than stepping beyond her yard."

Carin's eyes scanned his. "You care for her, don't you?"

"Really, Carin, I've only known the woman a few days."

She smiled. "After only two hours with Ray, I knew he was my cup of tea."

Alex lifted his hand to her shoulder. "You and Ray had something extraordinary."

Carin steadied her gaze upon him. "It's okay to care for someone, you know? If you'd let yourself, perhaps you could have something extraordinary, too." She reached up and took his hand in hers. "You're an extremely lovable man, Alex. I hope you know that."

Determined to avoid a lecture, Alex smiled, then turned away to prop the fencing sabers in a corner. "How was work today, Carin? Lots of sick people?"

She wasn't easily sidetracked. "Any woman

with even a pinch of intelligence would see that you're quite a catch."

"Why don't I show you the Mustang? You'll be proud of what Ty has accomplished."

Her eyes narrowed. "That asinine ex-fiancée of yours—"

"Please," Alex interrupted. He mocked her look of offense. "If you don't mind, I'd rather not discuss Leigh and her inability to recognize all my sterling qualities."

Carin's expression changed to one of sheepishness. "I just worry about you, you know?"

"I know." He smiled. "I worry about you, too. But let's not go overboard. I'm doing all right."

Ty walked into the room and handed Sheeba to him. "Why don't you two stay over until this storm passes?" Alex suggested.

Carin gathered her purse from a nearby chair. "Thanks for the offer, but we have our own cellar, complete with Nintendo. Besides, I'm dying to shed these work clothes."

A special weather bulletin interrupted the music on the radio in Robin's studio. She set aside the earrings she had been working on, then lifted Tinker from the floor.

Hail hammered on the roof overhead. The schnauzer trembled in her arms. Outside the window, marble-size chunks of ice jumped like popcorn as they hit the ground.

"The National Weather Service reports a funnel

cloud on the ground approximately ten miles south of Canyon moving north, northwest," announced the disc jockey. "All residents of Canyon and the surrounding area should take cover immediately. I repeat . . . ten miles south of Canyon . . ."

Chapter Twelve

Holding Tinker in the crook of her arm, Robin hurried for the downstairs guest room. She would pull the mattress off the double bed and use it to cover up in the adjoining bathroom's tub.

When she reached the bedroom door, the phone rang. She returned to the kitchen to answer it.

"A tornado's headed your way," Uncle E snapped before she had the chance to say "hello."

"I know, Uncle E. Tinker and I are climbing into the downstairs bathtub just as soon as I can drag a mattress in there."

"I wish I wasn't so far away, sugar. I'd come over. Maybe I should start headin' that direction anyway—"

"Don't you dare! I don't want you out in this.

There's nothing you can do. I'll give you a call after the storm passes."

The pounding of the hail grew louder. Robin swallowed down a surge of anxiety. "I love you, Uncle E."

"I love you, too, sugar." He cleared his throat. "You and Tinker hold tight now, you hear?"

She'd no sooner replaced the receiver than the phone rang again. Robin considered ignoring it, but she suspected who was on the other end of the line. She snatched up the receiver again, her eye on the wind-tossed branches of the oak tree in the yard.

"Hello, Millie. I'm taking cover."

"Crack all the windows," Millie ordered.

Robin managed to smile. She knew it would do no good to point out that the practice of opening windows to equalize the pressure in the house was an old tornado myth that had long ago been disproved. Millie had grown up opening windows in tornadic weather, she believed it to be effective, and no wet-behind-the-ears meteorologist was going to convince her otherwise.

"I know the routine, Millie. I've got to go now, okay? Love you—"

"—Your downstairs guest bath is the best place for you to take shelter. It's an interior room, no windows. Drag a mattress in there and cover up in that big ol' whirlpool tub. At least you'll have plenty of room."

Robin didn't know whether to laugh or scream from frustration. "Good idea. Why didn't I think of that?"

"That's why I'm here, sweetie. Now, you call me the instant it's safe to go to the phone. I'm at the shop. And Robin . . . ?"

"Millie, I really need to get off the phone."

"If you're relating this tornado to that curse business, I want you to stop it right this instant. Your fatalistic attitude is dangerous, especially in an emergency."

A limb blew off the tree and slapped against the window. "Millie . . ."

"Don't invite a tragedy, sweetie. Think straight. Use that smart head of yours. Make sure you take every precaution."

Seconds later, Robin closed Tinker up in the bathroom. She ran to tug the mattress from the bed. As she yanked off sheets and blankets, the whistling sound outside grew louder, more shrill.

Tinker scratched frantically at the bathroom door. His barks became more agitated.

Robin tossed the last of the linens into a corner. She grabbed hold of the cloth handles on the side of the mattress and tugged, again and again, until she finally had it off the bed and standing on its side. As she started to drag it across the floor, the mattress wobbled and threw her off balance. It sagged against the wall.

"Well, shit." Robin shoved her hair from her eyes, caught her breath.

Something bumped against the window at her side. Shrieking, she jumped away from the wall.

She drew a deep breath to steady her queasy stomach, then struggled to stand the mattress upright. It swayed unsteadily, then fell in the opposite direction. Half of it lay on the bed, the other half on the floor. With a groan, Robin gave it a kick that ended up making her toe throb.

Each time Tinker barked, her nerves stretched tighter. She decided to let him out of the bathroom, but when she opened the door, he streaked past her and disappeared into the hallway.

"Tinker!" Robin ran after him. "Come back!"

A crash sounded overhead. Thinking Tinker must have gone up and knocked something over, Robin took the stairs two at a time.

The blinds banged against the open window. The curtains flapped and billowed. A plant stand, which normally sat beneath it, had blown over. On the floor lay a pile of clay pots, clumps of scattered dirt, crumpled greenery. Tinker was nowhere in sight.

Robin hurried back to the stairs and ran down. "Tinker!" She knew he probably couldn't hear her cries over the wind hissing through the ventilation system, the rattling doors and windows, the stutter of hail on the roof.

When she was halfway across the living room, the lights went out. The radio in Robin's studio stopped playing. She glanced toward the windows. The sky was an odd, pale shade of green.

It cast a surreal glow on the carpet of hail surrounding the oak tree. Rain fell in horizontal sheets.

Robin turned to continue her search for Tinker when something beside the back door caught her attention. The box of detergent she had barricaded in front of the doggy door was pushed aside. The thick plastic cover flapped back and forth, squeaking with each swing.

"Oh, no," she murmured. "Tinker!" Twisting the knob on the back door, she shoved it wide. The wind blew it back in her face and knocked her down. Her ankle caught between the door and its frame.

Without warning, everything stopped—the wind, the hail, the rain. An eerie stillness settled in the air, raising goose bumps on Robin's skin. She tried to catch her breath, tried to free her trapped foot. The town siren started, its unearthly wail a startling, baleful sound after the silence of moments before.

The door flew open. Robin felt a hand on her shoulder. She twisted around, looked up.

Alex knelt over her, his glasses streaked with rain, his face pinched with worry. Water dripped from his hair onto her shirt. From between the lapels of his denim jacket, Tinker, soaking wet and shivering, peeked out at her.

Robin sat up quickly and took the dog from his arms. "You stupid, stupid . . . !" Her throat constricted, preventing further words. As Tinker

190

licked her face, relief flooded through her. For the first time, she realized she'd been crying. If anything ever happened to her dog . . .

"Robin." Alex took off his wet glasses, dropped them into his jacket pocket, then caught her under one arm to help her to her feet. "We need to go to my cellar. Now."

"I'm staying here."

"You—"

The wind started up again, this time louder than before. The fiercely powerful sound of it reminded Robin of the summer before sixth grade when Uncle E and Millie had taken her to Niagara Falls. The noise of the water had been overwhelming. This was no different. Pressure built in her ears. Her heart pounded like the hail had moments before.

Alex took her by the shoulders, shook her gently until she looked at his face instead of out the door. "I don't care if I have to carry you, you're going to my cellar."

In the few days Robin had known him, days often filled with tense disagreement, his voice had never sounded so stern. "I can't. I know you don't understand, but I can't leave."

His eyes softened. "I'll be right beside you. Every step, Robin. I won't let anything hurt you."

I won't let anything hurt you. Stunned, Robin stared into his face. She'd heard the same promise before . . . in a field of dying yellow roses.

"At least try," Alex pleaded. "Please."

Confused and terrified, Robin blinked away the hazy memory of an old dream. Something about the way Alex looked at her, something in his voice and the touch of his fingers told her he knew. *Alex knew.* He understood that the tornado wasn't what paralyzed her.

Still, Alex was right. Staying in this house might be signing her own death warrant. She didn't want to give in to her fear and die because of it.

Robin licked her lips, then whispered, "Let's go."

"Do you think you can run?"

"Yes. My foot's not hurt."

He took Tinker from her arms. For once, the dog didn't protest. "Ready?"

She nodded, and they started out the door.

The hail had stopped, but torrents of rain drenched Robin head to toe. True to his word, Alex stayed at her side. She made it as far as the hedge—then stopped.

"What's wrong?" Alex yelled.

Robin barely heard his words over the rush of wind and rain. "I can't!" Her body trembled uncontrollably. "Oh, God, Alex, what's wrong with me?"

He reached out to her. "I'll help you."

Before she could respond, Alex's head turned slightly. His eyes widened. His arm fell to his side.

Robin pulled off her rain-fogged glasses,

glanced over her shoulder in the direction he stared.

It was beautiful and frightening at the same time, a nightmare come to life, a moving, twisting shaft of boiling black smoke about a mile from her house. Robin's breath caught. Her glasses slipped from her fingers and fell to the ground.

"We're right in its path!" Alex yelled. "Are you really willing to take your chances with that?"

Robin couldn't answer. She was mesmerized, caught up in the twister's almighty spell.

Alex's fingers dug into her shoulder. "We've still time to make it to my cellar."

Millie's words came back to her . . . reasoning . . . pleading . . . commanding. *Don't invite a tragedy . . . Think straight . . . use that smart head of yours.*

Robin faced the hedge. Beyond it stretched Alex's yard, his picnic table, his house. Familiar territory that somehow felt off-limits. She leaned forward, told her feet to move. The dark images blurred and swam. Her air supply shut off. She suddenly felt so dizzy, her head seemed to leave her shoulders.

Robin covered her face with her hands and turned away. She took great gasps of air, choking on her tears and the shattering sobs that racked her chest. "Take Tinker and go," she screamed. "Please, Alex! Hurry! I'll get in the bathtub. I'll be okay."

Seconds ticked by in slow motion while she

stood there, crying and shivering as cold rain sliced down her skin.

Then Alex grabbed her about the waist, half-carried her, half-dragged her . . . toward her own house.

"We're out of time!" he yelled. "I won't leave you alone."

When they stepped inside the door, Robin's knees buckled. Tightening his hold around her waist, Alex lowered Tinker to the floor. He slid one arm beneath her legs and carried her the remaining distance to the bathroom. He was thankful he'd toured her house earlier. Robin was so upset, so miserable and emotionally drained, he didn't think she could have guided him if she'd tried.

It wouldn't be comfortable, but he, Robin and the dog could easily squeeze inside the deep whirlpool tub. When he sat her in it, Robin wrapped her arms around her knees and hugged them tightly, shivering.

With a quick glance back at her dark, wet head, Alex ran into the guest room. He grabbed hold of the mattress that already hung halfway off the bed. While he tugged, he listened for the sound of a train—a sound he'd heard tornadoes often mimicked.

The bedroom window shattered and a tree branch jutted through it, followed by a cold blast of air. Alex's adrenaline pumped overtime as he forced the mattress through the bathroom doorway and leaned it against the wall. Then he lifted Tinker from the floor and climbed in next to Robin.

He touched her arm. "Lie down. I'm going to pull the mattress on top of us."

She didn't respond at all, just sat there shaking, her face pressed to her knees. Alex heard her teeth chattering and wondered if she'd gone into shock. He wrapped an arm around her waist and jerked her down beside him. Then, with a strong tug, he pulled the mattress over the tub, cocooning them inside.

He hardly noticed his discomfort—the cramped quarters, his clinging wet clothes, the water tap poking into his shoulder. He was too preoccupied with worrying about all of them—Robin, himself, even precious Tinker who trembled at his feet.

It was pitch-dark and stuffy beneath the mattress, but at least it muffled some of the noise of the wind. Alex only wished it would block out the terrifying sounds entirely.

Robin didn't speak, but the muscles in her body quivered and jumped, telling Alex all too clearly of her fear. She was strung so tight that, if they survived this, he wasn't sure she'd ever unwind. But the worst of it was that he didn't know what to do or say to console her. So, he just held her tightly about the waist and whispered inane words of comfort, reassurances he wasn't quite sure were true.

Pressure built in his ears until he thought they

might explode. And then he heard it—a roar so loud and terrible, so powerful, he knew it could only belong to that angry black monster they'd spied in the distance. It hovered over the house, sounding like a fleet of helicopters.

He hadn't taken the time to close the bathroom door. It slammed and banged, again and again. Cabinets clattered. Toiletries clinked, then crashed as they hit the floor.

Robin gasped and fumbled for his hand. When her dog whimpered, she stirred and said, "Tinker?"

"He's right at my feet." Alex squeezed her fingers and tried not to think of stories he'd heard about cyclones tearing off roofs, ripping bathtubs from foundations, sucking people and appliances right up and carrying them for miles before finally letting go.

He drew a deep breath. "We're going to be okay," he murmured in her ear, praying he spoke the truth. "The worst's almost over." It wasn't enough, but it was all he could think to say.

An enormous crash sounded in the next room, as if something had flown into the house through the broken window. Tinker yelped. Robin made a startled sound, but didn't speak. She clenched his fingers so tight the tips went numb.

Then, as suddenly as the noise had arrived, it shifted away from the house, gradually becoming dimmer and dimmer until Alex could no longer hear it.

"It seems to have moved on," he finally said when his heartbeat had slowed to a more normal rate. "I believe I'll chance a look."

"Wait!" Her fingers dug into his palm. "It might be too soon. Just another minute . . . please?"

It was the first sentence she'd uttered since he'd carried her into the house. "Okay," Alex said, sensing her fear of being left alone.

"I'm so sorry. . . ." Her voice choked with emotion. "Thank you for staying."

"It's all right, Robin. I wouldn't want to be anywhere else other than right here with you."

"Liar," she replied with a tear-strangled laugh.

Alex stroked her hair and quietly held her until her muscles relaxed. It felt so good to have her safe in his arms; he was surprised at how good it felt. When the tornado warning was issued on the television, Robin was Alex's first worry—a fact that astonished him considering the short amount of time he'd known her. Even before Carin and Ty, he'd thought of her, alone and afraid, held prisoner by a phobia he didn't quite comprehend.

He'd taken a few minutes to call Carin while waiting for Robin to show up, hoping common sense would prevail over irrationality. Hoping she'd find the courage to protect herself by taking the few steps between her house and his. When the hail started coming down really hard, he tried to ring her up, but received a busy signal. That was when he'd decided to take matters into his own hands.

"It's been quiet for a time now," Alex said, remembering how frightened he'd been to find Tinker outside, to see Robin on the floor, crying and dazed. "Ready to give it a go?"

She momentarily tensed up again, then quietly muttered, "Okay."

Alex lifted the edge of the mattress. Pushing up with his head, he positioned both hands on the floor and moved forward until his upper body was out.

"Be careful. Some of your things slid from the vanity. There's broken glass on the floor." He climbed from the tub. "At least the walls are still standing."

Robin followed his lead. As if dreading what she'd find if she joined him, she held Tinker and stood just inside the bathroom door while Alex appraised the guest bedroom, the hallway and the living room and kitchen beyond.

"You have a tree limb through the bedroom window and debris on the floor that blew in through the hole it made," he called back to her. A few seconds later he added, "Some picture frames have fallen from the walls and your furniture seems to have jumped about but, other than that, everything looks fine."

"What about my painting?"

Alex turned toward the place where the easel

normally stood. "It's unharmed and exactly where you left it."

He took a moment to study the odd addition she'd made to the scene since he'd last taken a look. A brass bed sat in the center of the dusty road, adjacent to the saloon. And over the swinging doors of that building she'd stroked the letters *C* and *R*.

An uneasiness settled over him. Shaking it off, he returned to the bathroom. "Funny, isn't it?" he asked. "The furniture moved about, but the easel stayed in place."

For some reason, he didn't feel comfortable asking her about her work, about the word left unfinished above the saloon. He told himself his hesitance was due to the fact that, at the moment, more urgent matters required their attention. But he suspected something more caused his reluctance.

Together, they took inventory of the upstairs. Here, too, several of Robin's paintings hung crooked on the walls or had fallen off altogether. Because the bedroom window had been left open, wind had not only toppled over her plants, but had blown her phone and radio off the nightstand and thrown a jewelry box and bottles of perfumes and lotions off her dresser.

"You'd better go see if your own house is standing," Robin told him. "Tornadoes have been known to skip over one residence and flatten the one next door."

She'd pulled herself together with remarkable speed, though Alex noticed she avoided looking at him, as if she felt ashamed. Confident she was safe now, he promised to return and report in, then left her straightening her bedroom.

The moment he stepped into her backyard, his heart sank. Though his house still stood, Robin's roses had not fared as well. The few bushes that hadn't been beaten down were uprooted and strewn about the hail-riddled lawn.

The branch of her oak tree, on which he'd taken refuge from Tinker only the night before, had snapped in two and lay on the ground at his feet. Many of the remaining limbs were stripped of leaves, leaving them as bare as if it were winter rather than spring. In addition to scattered foliage and chunks of ice, the yard was littered with roof shingles and other miscellaneous debris.

After a glance toward Robin's bedroom window, Alex ran to his house for a quick inspection. He wanted to return to Robin before she discovered the damage. She loved those roses. That much was evident by the amount of time she spent nurturing and pampering them, by her concern about the black spot they'd recently contracted.

He wondered how he'd fill his days if he never left the house? Working at home would keep him busy enough. But he couldn't imagine the loneliness of rarely making face-to-face contact with another human being, even if it were only in passing. Alex could easily understand how Robin might have become emotionally attached to her roses.

His property was in no worse shape than hers. He guessed the funnel hadn't touched down, at least not on their block. After releasing Sheeba from the cellar, he tried to ring Carin and Ty. The lines remained down, though, so he headed back to Robin's, certain his family was safe inside their own cellar.

He found Robin sitting in a puddle of rain on her back step, surveying the remains of her garden with forlorn eyes. A bedraggled rose dangled from one of her hands, her broken glasses from the other.

Alex sat beside her. "I'm sorry."

She wouldn't meet his gaze. "It could've been worse. It could've been the house, or our lives."

"They were beautiful roses, Robin. You have a natural talent for creating lovely things—gardens, jewelry, your paintings."

"I can always start over. It's not as if I don't have the time." Her voice cracked on the last word. She sniffed. "Where was Sheeba during all the excitement?"

"Safe and sound in my cellar where I'd left her."

"It's a pretty sad state of affairs when a cat has more sense than I do."

"I'm not so certain about that. Sheeba and Trinket confined together in a basement might have caused more damage than any tornado."

"Tinker," Robin said.

"Excuse me?"

"You called him . . ." She giggled, then sniffed again. "Never mind."

"He stinks, by the way."

"Tinker?"

Alex nodded, relieved to hear her laughter. "When we were under the mattress." He wrinkled his nose. "Nothing's more fragrant than a wet dog."

She laughed at that. Then, without warning, she turned, looked up at him and started to cry.

Alex opened his arms. Robin dropped the rose and her glasses and leaned into him. Hugging her close, he sighed.

Her body shuddered with silent sobs. Finally, she eased back, wiped her cheeks with the back of her hand. "I'm a real piece of work, aren't I? Bet you had no idea what a nutcase you were getting for a neighbor. Or did the realtor tell you? Is that how you knew about me?"

Without her spelling it out, Alex understood she referred to her condition. He wondered if he'd said something to her during the confusion of the storm that indicated he knew.

Deciding to be honest, Alex shook his head. "Carin told me just this afternoon."

"I guess she thinks I'm crazy. I wouldn't blame either one of you for thinking it. I'm sure I've kept tongues wagging this past year."

Alex frowned. "I don't think anything of the sort and neither does Carin. And in the six months I've lived here, not a single person has mentioned your problem to me."

"Problem?" Robin's chin came up. Her gaze flicked briefly to his, but it was long enough for him to catch sight of her pain. "More like an obsession, don't you think? You don't have to be polite, Alex. I'm bordering on psychotic. I know it."

"Well, I don't know it."

"I behaved like a helpless child after I saw that funnel. If you hadn't been here . . ."

"You behaved like a strong woman with too much to face."

She huffed and shook her head.

"Even strong people have weak moments, Robin. Times when they need someone to lean on."

She stared at him directly then, her expression defiant and humiliated all at once. "Why are you being so nice to me?"

"Why are you being so hard on yourself?"

When she turned away and started to rise, he grabbed her wrist. Not allowing her time to protest or to speak another word, he crushed his mouth to hers.

She was unresponsive, her lips unyielding, her body tight and strained. Sliding his palms up the sides of her face, his fingers into her hair, Alex just kept kissing her, brushing his mouth against hers in small, soft strokes. He didn't quite understand what drove him on or what emotion he felt. He only knew that Robin was suffering and that her misery hurt him, too.

Chapter Thirteen

All of Robin's defensiveness and humiliation trickled away until nothing remained but need. A need to feel Alex's arms secure around her . . . to wrap herself in his heat . . . to let that heat seep into her pores and fill the terrible hollowness inside her. She didn't want to need him, but she did. Right now, she needed him more than anything.

Alex's grip on her arm relaxed as her lips parted and she slowly responded to the touch of his mouth against her own. And then, before she realized what was happening, the kisses that had started out sweet and full of comfort suddenly became hot and hungry and thrilling. Robin didn't know who had instigated the shift. She only knew that, even if she'd wanted to stop it from happening, she couldn't have . . . and that stopping it was the furthest thing from her mind.

Without losing contact, Alex pulled her to her feet, backed her up against the house. He leaned into her, his warm palms pressing gently against the sides of her face, his fingers splayed through her wet hair.

Robin slid her hands between the damp lapels of his jacket, curled her fingers into the spaces between the buttons on his shirt. She wanted to touch his skin, but when she did, when her fingertips brushed across his chest, it wasn't enough. She needed to feel him against her, needed to feel his warm, firm flesh next to her bare breasts, his hard angles pressing into her soft curves, no barrier of clothes, no excuses.

When his kiss moved from her mouth to her neck, Robin tilted back her head, closed her eyes and lost herself in pleasure.

"You taste so good," he murmured against her throat. "You smell like rain."

Somewhere in the distance, a police car or fire truck siren started, piercing the bubble of intimacy that had closed out the rest of the world. Robin opened her eyes. "We're standing in a puddle of water." Her laugh was breathless. She hardly recognized it as her own.

Alex didn't look up. "I know."

"Someone could show up at any second to check on me."

His hands moved to her waist, skimmed up

along the sides of her breasts, momentarily stealing the breath from her lungs.

"My yard is trashed. I have a tree limb through my . . ."

His mouth covered hers, cutting off her words. His hands kept moving.

For a long time after he pulled back, Robin couldn't speak. She could only stand with her face close to his, feeling his breath on her lips and wondering how something this crazy and wonderful could possibly be happening between them. "Have you called your sister?" she finally whispered.

Alex lifted a wet strand of hair away from her cheek, then flattened both hands against the brick wall of the house at either side of her head. "The phones are down." His gaze swept over her face as if he couldn't stop looking at her, as if he were memorizing every one of her features.

If she let herself, Robin knew she could easily return to that bubble and forget about everything else—the storm damage, her soaking wet clothes, the rest of the world. If that damn siren would only quit squealing, she would do just that.

She stared into his eyes. They looked more intense than she'd ever seen them. They focused on her with a long, measuring stare of unconcealed desire. "You should check on your family," she insisted.

"Carin has a cellar."

"They might need you. What if they lost their house?"

He scowled a little. One corner of his mouth curled up. "Why do you have to be so sensible?"

She smiled. "Do you have a cell phone?"

He shook his head. "I've resisted the trend. I like to think I can at least escape the phone while in the car. How about you?"

"I gave mine up when I quit going out."

After a moment of contemplative silence, he asked, "Will you be okay alone?"

"I expect Uncle E and Millie will show up any time now."

He lowered his arms, but his eyes held hers steady. "I'll be back."

"I'll be here."

For several long seconds, he stared at her in a way that made her tingle all over, made her pulse jump and her nerves scatter in ten different directions. Then, he turned and started toward the hedge.

As Robin watched him go, she worked on getting her breathing back to normal. She felt off-center. Her body ached with lust.

A minute later, she stood inside her own house, her back against the door. Tinker trotted into the living room and sat at her feet. Robin glanced down at him. "What am I going to do about Alex?"

When Tinker tilted his head and whimpered, Robin closed her eyes. "That kiss . . . it was probably nothing more than an after-effect of surviving the storm together."

Even as she spoke the words, she knew they weren't true. She had never felt anything as mindboggling as that kiss. Judging from Alex's reaction, she suspected he hadn't either.

"Starting something with him would be a big mistake." She opened one eye. Tinker was scratching his ear, apparently unfazed by her dilemma. It didn't matter. No one needed to tell her it was too late. This evening, she and Alex had crossed the line between friendship and something more. When he'd said he'd be back, she knew there was a lot more on his mind than helping her straighten the house.

Robin sighed. "I'm an emotional wreck. How can I get involved with anyone when I'm in this kind of shape?"

She opened her other eye and searched the floor for the books Uncle E had sent over. What would Alex think if he learned the cause of her panic disorder?

She recalled how he'd looked at her just minutes ago. With one smoldering glance, he'd made her feel beautiful and desirable in a way nothing or no one ever had before. If he found out the truth, his opinion of her would undoubtedly change. He'd never look at her in that same way again. How could she expect that he might? Alex was an intelligent man. And she was a woman researching the origins of a curse, not out of simple curiosity or interest, but because she feared it. He would find that pitiful.

Robin tugged her wet shirt over her head. Alex's pity would be more than she could bear. She would break into a million tiny, humiliated pieces in the face of it. And if she couldn't bring herself to be honest with him about herself, then she had no business taking their relationship to another level. No matter how enticing that sounded, following through on her attraction to Alex wouldn't be fair to either one of them.

Pushing away from the door, Robin started for the stairs, anxious to get out of her wet clothing. She looked over her shoulder at Tinker, who followed at her heels. "By the way, buster, you scared the crap out of me when you ran outside during the storm. You and I are going to have a little talk."

At the stern sound of her voice, Tinker came to a halt at the foot of the stairs. He lay down, placed his head on his paws and eyed her cautiously.

She stopped on the second step to point a finger at him. "Don't think for one minute you can sway me with those big, dark, woebegone eyes, either."

It was near nine o'clock before Alex arrived home. Carin's house had sustained several broken windows and lost more than half its shingles. After helping her and Ty sweep up glass and board over windows, he'd checked on neighbors and a few of his students. Then, he drove by the university and found it all intact.

All the while he was helping Carin and visiting acquaintances and friends, his mind had continually strayed to Robin. In a matter of minutes, things had changed between them, and all because of a kiss. The other kisses they'd shared had been nice, but not threatening. If he and Robin never became anything more than friends, they could easily put those first kisses in the past without any awkwardness between them.

But their last kiss was quite another matter. In the past, Alex had landed in bed with a woman or two after kisses not half as intriguing as that one. Had circumstances been otherwise, had there not been family to look in on and sirens blaring in the distance, he wondered if he'd be in Robin's bed right now instead of under a cold, eye-opening shower.

The thought conjured erotic images that urged him out from beneath the spray a bit faster, had him dressing quickly so he could see her again.

But once outside, he eyed her house with wary speculation. Robin didn't seem the sort of woman to hop into bed with a man she'd known only a few days, no matter how hot the kiss. Besides, this wasn't something he could just walk into without some thought. They were neighbors, after all. That made their situation sticky, indeed. Judging from his past experiences, the relationship would likely end one day, whether he wanted it to or not. And when it did, living next door to each other might prove uncomfortable.

Deciding there was no time like the present to deal with the issue, Alex proceeded down the sidewalk. He would tread gingerly around the subject, remain open-minded and accept whatever she decided. Robin obviously had enough problems without adding an unwanted affair to the list.

As he strolled up her front walk, he met Ethan and Millie on their way out. Engaged in a heated argument, the couple almost ran over him before they glanced up.

"Oh . . . Alex." Millie stepped back. "I didn't see you." For once, not even a hint of mischief flickered in her eyes, only worry and irritation.

Alex didn't waste time with pleasantries. He cut right to the subject that weighed on his mind. "How's Robin?"

Ethan gave him a congenial slap on the back. "Fine, thanks to you, son."

"I didn't do anything special."

"Bull," Ethan blustered. "You were here for her when we couldn't be."

Millie crossed her arms. "I don't care if Robin kicked and screamed to high heaven, you should've thrown her over your shoulder and hauled her skinny little butt down to your basement. When I think of the risk you both took—"

"For God's sake, Mil!" Ethan shoved a hand across his balding scalp. "The man deserves a pat on the back, not a dose of your bitchin'."

She exhaled a long, loud sigh. "I'm sorry, Alex. I do appreciate what you did for Robin. It's just that I get so frustrated with her." She shot a sharp glance Ethan's way. "Among other people."

"I understand," Alex said. After witnessing Robin's reluctance at the hedge while the tornado bore down on them, he could easily sympathize with Millie's frustration.

"She told us you know about her agoraphobia," Millie said, glancing back at the porchlight.

"Yes." Alex nodded. "I was wondering . . . has she sought help? You know, from a physician or a psychiatrist?"

Millie shook her head. "I've tried. But, as you found out for yourself, we'd have to knock her unconscious to get her out of that house. And whenever I suggest bringing a doctor by for a visit, she insists it won't do any good." She gave Ethan another dark look. "Robin's been brainwashed into believing there's no medical or scientific cure for what ails her."

Ethan cleared his throat and averted his eyes. Reaching into his pocket, he pulled out a toothpick and stuck it between his front teeth.

Millie slipped her purse strap over her shoulder. "It's been a long day. I'm going home. Thank you again, Alex." She stepped around him and started toward the driveway.

"See you in a little while?" Ethan called after her.

Millie didn't slow her pace or turn around. "I don't think so."

With that, she climbed into her BMW, started it and backed out, leaving only Ethan's dilapidated old pickup in the drive.

The toothpick in Ethan's mouth bobbed up and down as he watched her go. "Don't mind Millie," he said. "She likes to act all high and mighty with her fashion-plate duds and haughty attitude. But, underneath all the show, she's still a small-town farmer's daughter. Fort Cobb in Cole Hahns . . . that's Mil."

"Fort Cobb?"

"The little town in Oklahoma where she grew up. My daddy was from Fort Cobb, too. That's how Emily and I met Mil when we were kids. We'd go there in the summer to visit our grandparents."

He stared after the Beamer's receding red taillights. "Millie's from good stock, salt-of-the-earth folks. Don't know why she feels compelled to put on airs."

Alex tried not to smile. Ethan didn't fool him for a second. Alex had seen his expression as he watched Millie walk to her car. The old boy fancied the way she fit into those "fashion-plate duds" she wore. No doubt, he thrived on her sassiness, too.

"If you don't mind my asking," Alex said, "what happened to trigger Robin's agoraphobia?"

Pulling a key ring from the front pocket of his

jeans, Ethan slipped it over his finger. "She didn't tell you?"

"It didn't come up."

Ethan looked down at the cement walk, shoved a shingle aside with the toe of his boot. "I'll have to call somebody to come clean up this mess," he muttered.

"I know of some teenaged lads who could use a bit of extra spending money."

"They're hired. Send 'em over tomorrow."

His toothpick wiggled as he stooped to pick up a twig. "Ever hear of a lucky break, Alex?"

"Of course."

"Back in primitive times, when tribesmen wanted to protect their loved ones from the mischief of unseen evil-doers, they'd break a stick in half. They believed the loud snap would scare off the wicked no-good hooligans." He looked over his shoulder at Robin's house, then bent the twig. The wet wood refused to split.

"A lucky break." Ethan frowned as he tossed the twig away. "Robin could surely use one of those."

"Looks as if you're back in order," Alex said as Robin led him into her living room.

"Uncle E and Millie were a big help. They boarded up the broken window in the guest room. I'll have to call my insurance agent tomorrow about that and the roof."

"I spoke to your uncle outside. He's hired Ty

215

and one of his chums to clean up your yard. I'll see that they stop by tomorrow."

"Oh, good. Tell Ty to let me know when they're finished, and I'll pay them."

Feeling skittish and self-conscious, she paused at the sofa to face him. "Could I get you something to drink?" She hoped he wouldn't decline. She desperately needed something to do with her hands, something to occupy her attention so she wouldn't have to look at him. It would be too easy to walk into his arms and forget about all of the reasons she'd come up with over the last several hours why they should stay at a nice, friendly distance and quit spending so much time together.

"A small glass of wine would be nice," Alex said.

Robin went into the kitchen. "With all that happened tonight, I missed dinner. I have frozen egg rolls in the oven. I'm happy to share."

"That sounds good. I didn't eat, either. After cleaning up over at Carin's, I drove around and looked in on friends."

She took two glasses from the cabinet and pulled the cork from a bottle of merlot. "How does the town look?"

"It appears the funnel only touched ground twice. It plowed through a field, then came down again at the trailer park just outside the city limits."

Returning to the living room, Robin handed

Alex his wine, then sat beside him on the sofa. "How bad was the park hit?"

"Two trailers were overturned and partially flattened. A few of the residents had minor injuries—scratches and cuts, that sort of thing. Everyone made it to the park's cellar before the worst of it."

"Thank goodness no one was killed."

He nodded. "You can't imagine the amount of debris littering the roads. Roof shingles and trash everywhere. Uprooted trees, billboards toppled over."

They sat in silence for a moment. Robin glanced at the glowing lamp on the table beside her. "The electricity's back on. . . ." Heat spread up her neck. "I guess you can see that for yourself."

"Yes. But the phones are still down. At least, mine is. Since you can't ring, I should've thought to ask if there was anyone you wanted me to look in on for you."

"No . . . there's no one."

She was as startled by her declaration as he looked. For more than five years, she had lived in this town. She had moved here straight out of grad school rather than returning to Amarillo, where she'd grown up and where Millie and Ethan still lived. Yet during all that time, she hadn't become close to anyone. She had plenty of acquaintances. People with whom she used to chat when they met at the grocery store or on the street before her panic attacks confined her. But that was the extent of it.

Robin stared into her wine. It suddenly hit her why she'd moved here, where she'd known no one, instead of to Amarillo, where she'd once had friends: to avoid getting close to anyone. Because of the curse. Without even realizing it, she had convinced herself that she wouldn't be around long enough to make deep attachments.

Next to her, Alex toyed with the stem of his glass. When she couldn't stand it any longer, she glanced up and met his eyes.

He smiled. "How are you?"

"I'm okay."

"We should talk—"

"I know. I'd like to apologize for falling apart earlier. . . . I don't know why I can't get my act together. Sometimes I do the craziest things. It's really pathetic. I—"

"—Have I told you about my ex-fiancée, Leigh?"

She took a deep breath, baffled yet relieved by his interruption. "You were engaged?"

"Yes. We broke up shortly before I moved to the States."

"I'm sorry."

"I'm not." He set his wineglass on the coffee table. "Leigh's a nice enough woman. A newspaper reporter. Covers all the significant social events. She loves her work, and the paper couldn't have hired anyone more perfect for the

218

job. Leigh is the most together woman you'll ever meet. Anyone who knows her would tell you she's a class act."

Eyeing him with interest over the rim of the glass, Robin sipped her wine. "So why did you break up?"

Alex shrugged. "A lot of reasons. For one thing, we were a terrible match. For another, I couldn't care less about what people wear, least of all myself."

"And Leigh did?"

He chuckled. "She often referred to people by their style of dress instead of by name. We'd be at one of her functions, and she'd say to me . . ." He placed a hand on one hip, held an imaginary cigarette with the other. "You know who I'm talking about, darling. Miss Chunky Heeled '70s Geek-Goddess over there in the corner. See? Standing next to the Carolina Herrera Embroidered A-Line and those to-die-for gold stilettos?"

Robin laughed. "How on earth did the two of you ever hook up?"

"Leigh liked a challenge, and I was a huge one. I'm a secondhand shop reject, you know." He glanced down at his wrinkled clothes before taking a drink. "She has a ten-year-old son, Aaron. A couple of years ago, he took a summer workshop I taught for children interested in science. That's how I met Leigh."

Robin spied a trace of affection in his expression before he blinked and glanced away. He reached for his wineglass.

"Why are you telling me all this, Alex?"

He swirled the crimson wine round and round in his glass. "Maybe I'm trying to point out that you're not the only person who does crazy, pathetic things. Leigh, for instance. She was crazy to convince herself that a woman with her expectations could love a man like me. She was even crazier to think she could change me. And then, there's me." He smiled. "The pathetic one. Long after I knew we were doomed to fail as a couple, I stayed with her. The thought of admitting I'd made a mistake . . . that I'd failed." He shook his head. "I can't bear failure. So I simply proceeded to make the poor woman miserable until she dumped me."

Robin watched the play of emotion on his face. He might be over Leigh, but he wasn't over the incident, that much was clear. Still, she was confused. It seemed his pride would have incurred less damage if *he'd* ended the relationship instead of the other way around. As she watched him, the reason he'd chosen to do otherwise suddenly came to her. "It was Leigh's son, wasn't it? You couldn't stand for him to think you'd failed him."

He was quiet for a second, then asked, "Am I that transparent?"

"I saw how you looked at your nephew this afternoon. You looked the same when you spoke Aaron's name a minute ago."

"I told you I was pathetic." His tone was self-derisive. "I stayed with Leigh far longer than I should have because I'd become attached to her son. I didn't want to hurt him. What's more, I didn't want to hurt myself."

"That's hardly pathetic. It's admirable that you cared so much for him."

"What I did wasn't admirable." Alex ran a hand through his unruly hair. "I took the selfish way out and let the blame fall on his mother's shoulders instead of my own. I made Leigh look like the bad guy so Aaron wouldn't think less of me. It was a terrible thing for me to do to the lad—setting him at odds with his mum like that."

Robin studied him, impressed by his honesty. "Now that you mention it, it wasn't only a rotten thing for you to do to Aaron, it was a rotten thing for you to do to your ex-fiancée, too," she said.

He blinked at that, as if her comment took him by surprise. Robin guessed he'd expected her to defend his actions, not point out further offenses.

"You're right." He cleared his throat and smiled. "It was rather rotten of me."

She shrugged. "You're human. Everyone has their less-than-commendable moments."

"Your turn," Alex said, throwing her off-guard this time. "I've exposed a few of my many frailties. Now, tell me yours."

Heat rushed to her cheeks. She clasped her hands together in her lap, thinking she should have known there was a catch to his baring of the soul. "You've seen my shortcomings firsthand. I'm afraid of the world beyond my own backyard."

"But why? Something must've precipitated the fear."

She drew a shaky breath and looked down at her fingers. "There are some things you'd rather not know about me, Alex. I—"

The oven timer went off. Robin jumped up, thankful for the interruption, for an excuse to avoid his question. "The egg rolls are ready."

In the kitchen, she turned off the timer, grabbed a hot pad and slid the cookie sheet of sizzling egg rolls out of the oven. She set them on the counter, then, standing on tiptoe, reached to the top shelf of the cabinet for a serving platter. When she turned around, she almost dropped it.

Alex had slipped into the kitchen. He stood behind her, leaning against the wall, his arms crossed. When his gaze lifted, she realized she'd caught him looking at her backside.

Robin narrowed her eyes. "I thought you couldn't care less what people wear?"

His mouth curled up at one corner. "Until now, I couldn't. But if you wore those shorts every single day, I'd be a very happy fellow." He stepped toward her. "Teach me to dance the two-step, Robin."

"There's no music playing."

"We don't need music. I'll hum."

She tilted her head and smirked at him, hoping

he couldn't see the nervousness beneath her teasing. "I think you're just looking for an excuse to get your hands on me."

"Do I need an excuse?" Taking the platter from her, he set it on the counter, then slid his hands up her arms. "You lead, I'll follow."

"You're crazy, you know that?"

Circling his arm around her waist, Alex drew her against him. Robin felt his breath, feathery soft against her ear, as he alternately hummed and sang the words to "Crazy." Though he carried a tune well enough, he was no threat to Patsy Cline. As for his dancing, after a slight stumble or two, he moved in step with her as if they'd danced together all their lives. Robin wondered how she could have ever thought him clumsy.

Soon, his humming stopped. They stood in place, holding each other, their bodies swaying to an unheard beat.

"I came over here intending to logically weigh all the pros and cons of our getting involved," Alex murmured. "Right now, I can't think of a single con."

Robin's head lay against his shoulder. The sound of his heartbeat was a comfort, so steady, so strong. His palm pressed at the base of her spine, his fingers kneading. The solid length of his body felt right against her own—a perfect fit. For the first time since she was a child, protected by Ethan and Millie, Robin felt safe. How could she feel this way with him after so few days?

Lately, every time they were alone in the same room, they wound up touching or kissing each other.

"I'm not sure I'm ready for this." She stepped back. "If you knew certain things about me—"

"Is there someone else?"

For one absurd second, the gambler flashed to mind. Robin's gaze flicked toward the easel where the painting sat. The thought was so ridiculous, so outrageous, she almost laughed out loud. It was just that, with the gambler, she would never hesitate, never question the rationality of his needs or her own. If she wanted something, she would take it. If she didn't want it, she would simply walk away. In her dreams, it was that simple.

But this was no dream.

"No," Robin said, her attention returning to Alex. "There's no one else."

"That's all I need to know."

Her heart jumped. "But maybe we should discuss pros and cons. I'll start with the cons—"

"Don't." His fingers tightened around her arms. He pulled her closer. When her head tilted back, he lowered his mouth toward hers and mumbled, "Don't say anything."

A second later, the phone rang. They both jerked away from each other, as if they'd been caught doing something they shouldn't be doing.

"Guess the phones are back up."

"Damn." Alex laughed. "Sirens, oven timers,

telephones. If I didn't know better, I'd think someone was out to sabotage me."

"Maybe it's a sign."

"I don't believe in those." The phone kept ringing. "Let me guess . . . Ethan?"

"Or Millie."

"Have they had enough time to drive home?"

"Just barely." Robin leaned across the kitchen counter and reached for the receiver.

She'd guessed correctly.

"Is Alex still there?" Millie asked.

"Yes, Millie, he's here." Robin grinned when her eyes met Alex's.

Grinning, too, he held her gaze while reaching across to tuck a strand of hair behind her ear. The gesture was so purely intimate it set off tiny tremors of need throughout Robin's body.

"Apologize to him again for me, would you?" Millie asked. "He'll know what I'm talking about. And Robin?"

"Yes?"

"Don't run the man off. He's good for you."

"Maybe so." She held her eyes steady on Alex's, her words spoken to Millie, her message intended for him. "But I'm not so sure I'm good for him. Things are moving a little fast for me."

Alex quit smiling, but he didn't look away.

"Things . . . ?" Millie's surprise echoed across the line. "I didn't know . . . oh, that's wonderful! So something was going on when I found him at your house with no shirt on."

225

"A little distance between us might be wise right now . . . some time to think . . ."

His eyes softened with understanding.

"Don't think," Millie ordered sharply. "Take my advice and obey your hormones. He's a . . ."

Struck deaf and dumb by the blue intensity of Alex's gaze, Robin could barely discern Millie's words, much less respond to them.

Touching her beneath her chin with his fingertip, Alex gave her a quick, quiet kiss, then turned and walked from the room.

Chapter Fourteen

Ethan had almost forgotten how much he enjoyed the pleasure of lying naked in Millie's king-size bed. Almost, but not quite.

Six months. Until the barbecue dinner at Robin's a few nights ago, Millie had dodged him for six long, frustrating months. It was a dry spell he didn't want to repeat, and wouldn't, if he had his way. The only other times they'd lasted six months or more had been during each of Millie's marriages. Millie was no cheat. Except for the 'til-death-do-us-part bit, she took her vows seriously.

It wasn't that Ethan had been worried. He knew they'd wind up in bed again sooner or later. They always did.

On most matters, he and Millie might mix like

227

oil and water. But when it came to sex, they were biscuits and butter. When one got hot, the other melted. For forty-three years, it had worked that way—ever since, at the tender age of seventeen, Millie had punched him in the gut for calling her a phony, and they'd ended up stark naked in the hayloft of her daddy's barn.

"Ouch!" Flat on his back, his head propped up on a pile of pillows, Ethan scowled at her. Dressed in his favorite negligee, Millie sat at the edge of her bed leaning over him, a pair of tweezers in her hand. "Go easy on me, woman. This wasn't exactly in my plans for the evening."

She gripped another eyebrow hair and jerked. "Your brows are bushier than Tinker's. If they get any longer, you won't be able to see. When's the last time you had a good plucking?"

"You ought to know." Ethan winced as she yanked out another. "You did the honors."

"That was almost a year ago!"

"See, honey bun, I need you. I just go to pot whenever you're not around."

She paused to point the tweezers in his face. "I'll honey your bun—"

"Please . . ." Ethan groaned, but a smile twitched the corner of his mouth. "Could we wait at least another half hour? I'm an old man, Mil. My juices gotta regenerate before I can give it another go."

Leaning back, she crossed her arms. "Very funny. Why do you have to be so damn good in the sack? If it weren't for that, I wouldn't give you the time of day. You know that, don't you?"

Ethan chuckled. Lifting both hands to her shoulders, he started to rub. "When are you just gonna give up and marry me?"

She stared down at him, her eyes narrowed and full of the fiery mischief he loved.

"If we got married, Ethan Yarborough, it would ruin everything, and you know it. We'd kill each other. The only place we get along is in the bedroom."

With one hand, he grabbed her neck and pulled her toward him. Then he lifted his head and nibbled her earlobe. "Well, I guess we'd just have to spend all our time in bed."

When he lay back down, Millie took hold of his chin with one hand. "Hold still, you old coot. I'm not finished with you yet." Like a woman on a mission, she resumed her work with the tweezers.

"I can think of worse ways to spend my time than fightin' with you, Mil. Besides, we've got more in common than you like to admit."

"Only Robin. And we can't even seem to agree about her."

When he saw the strain in Millie's eyes, Ethan took hold of her wrist and lowered it to his chest. "You're as worried about Robin as I am, aren't you?"

"Yes, but not for the same reasons. I think she's getting worse. My God, Ethan, she couldn't even leave that house to escape a tornado!"

"I've been thinking maybe it's time to give her Emily's ring. It might be just what she needs to cheer her up."

Millie's forehead wrinkled. She set the tweezers on the bedside table. "You know good and well Emily intended for Robin to have that ring on her wedding day or her thirtieth birthday, whichever came first. The least we can do for your sister is respect her wishes."

"It's close enough to Robin's birthday. We could throw a little party this weekend and give the ring to her then. Maybe even invite Alex over. They seem to hit it off pretty good."

"Better than you know."

"What do you mean by that?"

Her left brow arched provocatively.

Ethan stroked his beard stubble while contemplating her silent insinuation. "You don't say. . . ." The news was unexpected, but he didn't object to the idea of it. "That Alex seems like a nice enough kid."

"He's hardly a kid, Ethan. The man has a PhD."

He sniffed. "Well, hell. Good for them. Let's make it a real celebration then. I know some of the folks at the Ten Pin would get a kick out of seeing Robin. They ask about her all the time. What about that gal who works at the boutique? We could ask her, too."

Folding her arms beneath her breasts, Millie

scrutinized him with hostile demand. "Why not wait until the following weekend? Robin's real birthday?"

He cleared his throat, stared up at the ceiling. "When Emily said she'd give the ring to Robin on her thirtieth birthday, she was only aiming to convince Nicholas she wasn't puttin' any more stock in the curse."

"I knew it." Millie's voice seethed. She shook her head. "But you still put stock in it, don't you? After all these years, I don't know why I can't accept that you really believe in that ridiculous nonsense. It's not as if you're an illiterate fool." She paused for a beat. "Well, maybe a fool, but definitely not an illiterate one."

"My common sense knows better. But you have to admit . . . four generations of women in my family dying due to freak accidents right before turnin' thirty seems more than coincidental."

"Look at me, Ethan."

He met her eyes. To his surprise, she no longer looked angry, she only looked concerned.

"If you give Robin a party a week before her birthday, it will be the same as telling her you don't believe she'll be around for the real one. That's the last thing she needs right now. She needs to get her mind off all that crap so she can start to get well again."

"She'll get well when her birthday's over and she's still breathing."

"Maybe, maybe not. The psychologist I spoke with said there are no guarantees."

Ethan hated to admit Millie might be right about anything. But, worse than that, he hated thinking he might be contributing to Robin's illness.

"Okay, okay." He patted Millie's hand. "We'll plan the party for the weekend after next."

"Why, Ethan Yarborough, you listened to me." Millie's smile was smug. She picked up a pillow and struck him gently over the head with it. "And it only took forty-three years."

Alex faced lane twelve, a black bowling ball between his palms, his focus on the center pin. During his morning run, he'd decided that after he met with the student he tutored every Thursday, he'd accept Ethan Yarborough's offer of lunch at the Ten Pin. The truth was, he had ulterior motives. He hoped to coax some information about Robin's condition out of the man.

He'd refrained from seeing her for several days. The day after the tornado, Ty and a young friend had gone over to clean up her yard, but Alex stayed away. He had busied himself by clearing his own yard and tending to minor repairs his house required. If Robin needed time to think about their relationship, he'd give it to her. In truth, he was relieved she'd had the good sense to suggest it. Normally, he, too, approached any decision with caution and consideration. But, the intelligent prudence upon which he prided himself took off on holiday every time he looked into Robin's sexy brown eyes.

Shifting his stance, Alex glanced to his left. Beside him, at the next lane, a skinny elderly gentleman wearing a brown, one-piece polyester jumpsuit started toward the line, knees bent, ball poised at one bony hip. The ball made a satisfying thump when it hit the polished wood floor. Curving, it hugged the gutter's edge and picked up speed on its thundering race toward the pins. A second before impact, the ball hooked left and crashed into the center pin, flattening it and the nine others behind it.

Spinning around, the old man bowed, then with a bit of a skip, sauntered back toward his whistling, jeering cronies.

"Good job!" Alex said as the bowler neared.

The old man grinned. "Not half bad if I do say so myself."

"Gotta keep your mind on the game, son, not your neighbor," Ethan bellowed from behind.

Alex snapped to attention. For a moment, he wondered if Robin's uncle was a mind reader. Then he realized that the "neighbor" Ethan referred to was the old codger in the next lane, not Robin.

"Line up your thumb with that center pin," Ethan instructed.

Thirty minutes later, Alex had a score of one hundred and one and a sore big toe. On his first time up, he'd dropped the ball on top of his red-and-green bowling shoe.

Ethan slapped him on the shoulder as they headed back to the cafe where they'd shared lunch an hour earlier. "A little trouble on the get-off, but not bad for a beginner. I was worried after you dropped the ball, then guttered your first two throws. You started out lousy, but you caught on fast."

"I thrive on a challenge."

Ethan's straightforwardness made Alex think of Robin and the way she'd accused him of being rotten to Leigh. Her frankness wasn't as frequent as her uncle's or as brassy and ingrained as Millie's. It slipped up on a person unexpectedly, a startling yet engaging surprise.

While Alex slid into a booth, Ethan went to get them something to drink. He returned with two bottles of beer.

"I was thinking more along the lines of water," Alex said. "It's a bit early in the day for me."

Ethan sat across from him. "One won't hurt. It'll put some hair on your chest."

"I wasn't aware I was lacking in that department."

Ethan chuckled. "Just an expression, son." He took a drink, the look in his eyes turning thoughtful. "Can I ask you about something?"

"Of course."

"You might've noticed that I have what some people call a superstitious streak."

Nodding, Alex sipped the beer, then pushed it aside.

"You being a man of science, I was wondering what your thoughts are about such matters? Seems as though men like yourself always come up with a reason for everything. Even things that seem unexplainable."

"What exactly are you referring to? Ghosts and goblins? Spells and potions and—"

"—Curses and coincidences and such," Ethan finished for him.

"Unless I have solid proof of something, I tend to be a bit skeptical of its existence. If you look hard enough, there's usually a logical explanation for everything."

"I figured you'd say that." Nailing Alex with a contemplative stare, Ethan took another swig of beer. "Maybe you could mention your views on the subject to Robin sometime. You know, tell her how you go about figuring out those logical explanations."

"Why would she want to discuss something of that sort?"

Ethan avoided Alex's gaze. "You'd have to ask her that question."

After a moment, the older man looked back at him. Silently, they studied each other across the tabletop. Ethan nursed his beer. Alex tapped the neck of his bottle. He didn't have a clue what thoughts ran through Ethan's head. As for himself, he was recalling a recent conversation about

235

the origins of the "lucky break" and wondering how that figured in to all of this.

"If you don't mind my saying so, sir," Alex said, "you tend to speak in riddles."

"So I've been told." Ethan grinned. "I'm glad you came out today and let me buy you lunch."

"I enjoyed the chicken-fried steak. The bowling, too. It was my first time for both."

"I suspect I didn't let you get a word in edgewise. Did you have something on your mind you wanted to talk about?"

"As a matter of fact, I do. The other night when I met you and Ms. McCutcheon outside Robin's, you didn't answer my question about what triggered her condition."

For what seemed like ten minutes, Ethan didn't say anything. He watched the waitresses go about their work, pulled the paper napkin from around the knife and fork in front of him, then toyed with the utensils.

Alex listened to the clink and rattle of dishes and silverware, the sizzle of meat on the grill. A dozen conversations mingled with rowdy laughter and, over it all, country music blared. In the next room, bowling balls rumbled, and pins clattered.

Ethan lifted the knife and fork in front of his face and stared at them. "Did your mama ever warn you not to cross sharp objects?"

"Why . . . yes," Alex answered. "I seem to recall that she did."

"Truth is, she probably didn't know why you

should avoid doing so any more than you did."
He placed the utensils on the table side by side,
careful not to let them touch. "It all stems back
to a time in history when crucifixion was the cap-
ital punishment of choice. When objects were
crossed, it reminded folks of the horrible price
they'd pay if they slipped up."

Alex realized he would get no useful information out of Ethan Yarborough. Still, instead of
scorning the man's stories, he found them entertaining. By revealing their origins, Ethan chal-
lenged the authenticity of the very superstitions
by which he obviously lived. The old boy was an
eccentric enigma, and Alex loved a good puzzle.

"Millie tells me you and Robin are kinda fond
of each other," Ethan said, switching the topic of
conversation in midstream.

Alex had an uneasy feeling this strapping
Texas good ol' boy was about to ask his intentions toward Robin. The vinyl beneath his legs
squeaked as he shifted positions. "Your niece is a
wonderful woman. I have nothing but respect—"

Ethan slapped the table and belted out a laugh.
"Calm down, son. I'm not fixin' to point a shot-
gun at you and force you to marry her. I just think
that if what Millie says is true, you should be
asking Robin these questions, not me."

"Fair enough," Alex said, feeling relieved.

"Since you're going to be talking to her, would
you deliver some books and articles I picked up
this morning at the library?"

"Of course. I wish I'd known Robin needed books. I could've saved you a trip. I'm stopping by the library myself on the way home." He'd finished *Amigo's Justice*. With any luck, the first book of the trilogy had been returned by now and he could check it out.

Ethan seemed preoccupied by his own thoughts. He drummed his fingers on the table and stared into space. "I have something else I'd like you to give Robin," he said slowly. "It won't take a minute for me to get it out of the safe in my office."

It seemed to Robin she'd spent the past two days on the telephone. After speaking to her insurance agent, a couple of roofers and a glass company about repairing her window, she'd turned her attention to Nasty Jack Tucker and the curse.

She'd done a lot of thinking after Alex's last visit. Fact or fiction, she was going to have to get to the bottom of the curse, at least in her own mind, before she could ever have a relationship with Alex—or with any man, for that matter.

After hearing stories Uncle E and Millie had told her about her parents, she realized that her mother's superstitious fears had been an issue between them. And Robin had often wondered if Millie and Uncle E might have become a couple if not for Ethan's obsessive preoccupation with magic and folklore.

To get started on her quest for more informa-

tion about what was going on in the Texas Panhandle in 1888, Robin called the newspaper
library in Amarillo. She was told they didn't have
bound volumes of newspapers before nineteen
hundred. Older copies were kept on microfilm,
but the issues were sporadic and carried little detail. She might find a paragraph or two, but no
long stories.

According to the clerk, the information was not
indexed by subject. Robin's best hope of finding
what she needed would be to read the microfilm
page by page. And that might take hours. The
woman suggested she try the public library. It
also kept old newspaper issues on microfilm, and
it was open after regular working hours.

Robin had left a message at the Ten Pin asking
Uncle E to go by the library and do the research
for her. They'd have to keep quiet about it. Millie
would be upset if she found out they were spending time investigating a so-called curse.

Between phone calls, Robin had worked on the
painting. She never knew what to expect when
she touched her brush to the canvas. Her thoughts
would wander and, when she came back to reality, a surprise always awaited her. Yesterday,
she'd stared at the four-poster bed in the center
of the dusty road and, before she realized it, she
had painted a single yellow rose on top of one
pillow. Today, she'd finished the Crazy Ace sign
and added a saber alongside the rose.

Though she realized the image unfolding before her eyes symbolized her dreams, anyone else would simply see it as a very odd painting. Robin wondered what Millie would read into it and looked forward to her reaction. But she sensed the painting wasn't complete. Something was missing. She didn't want Millie to pass judgment until she figured out what that "something" was. Later, she decided, she'd move the canvas and easel into her studio, away from prying eyes and well-meant opinions. The natural light the living room window provided would be missed, but that was a trade-off she would take.

When the doorbell rang, Robin set aside her brush and slipped off her smock.

Alex's nephew stood on her front porch clutching a grocery sack to his chest.

"Why, hello Ty." She opened the door wide and stepped back. "What are you up to? Would you like to come in?"

His face flushed almost the same shade of red as his hair. He shook his head. "That's okay. Uncle Alex asked me to bring you this sack of library books that your uncle sent home with him."

"Alex saw Uncle E?"

"I think they had lunch together."

Robin took the sack from him. "I see." Suspicion ran unchecked through her mind. She could think of only one reason Alex and her uncle would have lunch together: to discuss her. If she'd learned anything at all about Alex, it was the fact that he had an inquisitive mind. As for

Uncle E, he had a tongue that seldom ceased wagging. Yet she thought she could trust him to mind his own business and keep his mouth shut about hers.

"Are you sure you won't come in?" she asked Ty. "I can fix you a glass of lemonade or a soft drink."

He shook his head. "Thanks, but I'd better get back to work on the Mustang."

"How's it going?"

"Slow."

"You'll get there. Something tells me when your uncle sets his mind to a project, he never gives up." She smiled. "Thanks again for doing such a nice job on my yard."

"Too bad about your roses." He stuck his hands in his pockets. "Well . . . see ya later." Ty turned to leave, then looked back at her over his shoulder. "I almost forgot. Uncle Alex said to tell you there's a note in the sack that you need to read."

"Oh, really?" More than a little curious, she frowned, then lifted a hand to wave. "Thanks, Ty. Take care."

Sitting on the couch in her living room a minute later, she tore into the envelope with her name written across it in Uncle E's handwriting.

Robin, the note said, *here's all I could find at the library. I'll hit the museum tomorrow. I sent along something else, too. A birthday gift from your mama. Unless you plan on eloping before the big 3-0 next week, you might hold off on open-*

ing it until then. Emily wanted you to have it on your wedding day or your thirtieth birthday, whichever came first. I'll call as soon as I get a breather. Love ya, E

Robin's hand trembled as she lowered it into the sack. She dug past several books, so dazed she didn't see their covers or titles. Finally, her fingers closed around a small box. She lifted it out of the sack. Made of smooth, buffed rosewood, the square container with rounded corners fit perfectly in the palm of her hand.

Why had Uncle E sent it if, as his note indicated, he didn't want her to open it until her birthday? With any luck, he'd see her next week at the party Millie had called about yesterday.

Millie had made a big production of planning a special catered dinner to be held on the night Robin turned thirty. In addition to Uncle E and Millie, Alex, Karla from the boutique and a few Ten Pin employees would attend. The party was, no doubt, Millie's way of proving she absolutely believed Robin would be alive and able to join in on the celebration.

Robin had teased that, if she didn't survive the curse, Millie could just make the event a wake instead of a birthday party. Millie made it clear she found no humor in the macabre joke.

Robin guessed Uncle E's gesture of sending her mother's gift early was intended to give her hope and determination, to let her know her mother had held faith she would be an exception to the rule of their heritage, that she would break the chain of history if Emily didn't do it first.

Or maybe Ethan had simply been afraid to wait until her birthday—afraid she'd never see what lay inside her mother's box if he did.

Either way, Robin couldn't help believing he wanted her to open it now, despite the message he'd sent.

No hinges secured the lid to the lower half of the box, so it lifted off completely. Robin's breath caught when she looked inside.

Nestled against blood-red velvet, the exquisite gold-filigreed ring held three tiny, deep-blue gemstones. They sparkled like a moonlit ocean when they caught the light. As Robin stared down at the beautiful piece of antique jewelry, something fluttered from inside the lid and fell to her lap. Tearing her gaze from the ring, she glanced down.

Written across a cream-colored card in bold cursive strokes were the words: *Given with love and pride to my precious daughter, Robin Wise, from her mother, Emily Yarborough Wise, on this very special occasion.*

Chapter Fifteen

Alex glanced away from Carin when Ty came through the front door. "I'm sorry, Ty," Alex said, "but I left one of my own books in that sack you took to Robin. Could you run back over and get it for me?"

Ty's shoulders sagged. He gave a disgruntled sigh. "Geez, do I have to?"

In the chair across from Alex, Carin shifted her position. "Of course you don't have to. Nevertheless, you'll do so out of the goodness of your heart." Her eyes narrowed. "Or else."

Looking peeved, Ty turned and retraced his steps to the door. "Whatever."

"The book is entitled *Amigo's Gold*," Alex called after him.

The door slammed.

Carin stared at the closed door. "Ever since Ray's death . . ." She blew out a noisy sigh. "He's not getting any better."

"Are you sure? At times, when we're working together, he seems to let down his guard. He's talked to me a bit about this and that."

His sister's eyes brightened. "Really?" Propping her forearms across her knees, she leaned forward.

Alex could see that she was grasping for any shred of hope that her son might be his old self again one day. He nodded. "We've even shared a laugh or two."

"With me, he's always so distant . . . so angry."

"Some of that is simply normal teenage behavior."

She leaned back. "I suppose you're right. I worry about him, though. I wish he didn't have to be alone while I'm at work. Sometimes when I call, he doesn't answer the phone. Yet, when I ask, he doesn't have an explanation about where he's been. I'm certain he's bored. You know what they say about idle hands."

"Why didn't you tell me sooner? He can spend more time with me until my classes start up again."

"I'm off next week," Carin said. "I'm thinking of taking Ty and going on a holiday. We could drive to our cabin in Colorado. We haven't been up there since—" Averting her eyes, she paused.

"The mountain air would probably do us both good. Why don't you join us?"

Alex hated to disappoint her. He had moved to the States more for her and Ty than for himself. Still, he had responsibilities he couldn't shirk. "I would, Carin, but my summer classes begin the week after, and I haven't prepared." He sneezed. "Besides that, I think I might be catching a cold." Probably from running between his house and Robin's in all that rain, he mused.

She put up a hand. "I understand. Ty's leaving won't ruin your plans for restoring Ray's car, will it?"

"Don't worry about it. We can take our time with the Mustang."

After a thoughtful pause, she said, "Well . . . it's settled then. We're off to the Spanish Peaks. Perhaps Ty simply needs a dose of my undivided attention."

Carin seemed pleased with her decision and immediately more at ease.

"Now," she said, smiling. "Tell me how things are coming along with you and Robin Wise."

He pulled off his glasses and polished the lenses with his shirt hem. "I don't know what you mean."

She laughed. "Really, Alex, I'm not daft. You had lunch with the woman's uncle, and now you're obviously avoiding her by sending Ty to run your errands. What's wrong?"

Averting his gaze, Alex slipped his glasses

onto his nose. "She needed some time and space," he mumbled.

"Hmmm. Getting too close too quickly, are you?"

With a slow smile, he glanced back at her. "That's Robin's opinion. As for me, when I'm with her I can't get close enough quickly enough."

"Your uncle is dead meat."

Robin clutched the telephone receiver with one hand while holding her mother's box in the other. "Just answer my question, Millie. What's the story behind this ring?"

"I told him not to give it to you until next week, that's the story."

Robin sneezed.

"Are you catching a cold?"

"Maybe." She sniffed. "Guess that's what I get for standing outside in the pouring rain. But don't think you can sidetrack me by changing the subject. If you won't tell me about this ring, I'll just wait until Uncle E has time to talk."

She'd tried calling him first, but he'd been tied up again with some problem at the Ten Pin and couldn't come to the phone.

"All right." Millie sounded hesitant, yet resigned. "Your mother . . . she wanted so much to give it to you herself. She hoped she'd be the first."

"The first?"

"Counting you, the ring has been passed down from mother to daughter for four generations. But, so far, no mother has lived to see her daughter reach the age to wear it."

Tilting her head and lifting her shoulder to hold the receiver to her ear with no hands, Robin took the ring from the box and slipped it onto her right third finger. It fit loosely, but there was no danger that it might slip off. "How did you know—"

"Right after you were born," Millie interrupted, "Emily told Ethan and me that if anything ever happened to her, we were to take the ring off her finger and put it in the rosewood box she kept in her hope chest. When the time came for us to do as she had asked, we found the card inside already addressed to you."

Her mother had prepared for the worst. Tears stung Robin's eyes as she pictured Emily writing the message. She could only imagine the heartache a mother would feel, believing she might never see her baby grow up.

When a knock sounded at the front door, Robin turned. "Millie," she said, "tell me one more thing, then I have to go. You said the ring had been passed down through four generations. How did my great-great-grandmother come to own it?"

"Emily didn't know," Millie answered. "She wondered the same thing herself."

Robin wasn't surprised to find Ty on her doorstep yet again. After the string of recent events— the tornado, her painting, the ring—nothing else could surprise her. This time, Alex's nephew accepted her offer and came inside, though he didn't seem comfortable doing so.

"Uncle Alex left a book of his in that sack. *Amigo's Gold* or something like that."

Robin led Ty into the living room where she'd left the sack. She lifted it onto the coffee table. "Let's see," she said, digging around inside of it until she found a paperback novel. "This must be it." She pulled the book out. "Oh, my God. . . ."

Her knees went weak as she stared at the black-clad figure on the cover. Only minutes ago, she'd thought nothing else could surprise her, but she'd been wrong.

Ty stepped toward her. "Is something wrong?"

Robin sank down onto the sofa. "The man in this picture . . ." She ran her fingers across his image and whispered, "Oh, my God."

Later that night, Robin set aside one library book and started on the next. So far, she hadn't learned any more about Nasty Jack Tucker and his attempted stagecoach robbery. She wasn't sure what the answers she searched for would solve, but she felt compelled to learn if her great-great-grandmother, Hannah Sann, had been on the stage that Nasty Jack had died trying to rob. Uncovering the details of Hannah's demise seemed a step in the right direction. A step toward disproving the curse's existence. After all, the legend had started with her great-great-grandmother's death.

From time to time, Robin reminded herself of her intentions—to invalidate the curse, not break it. She was determined to ignore all the mystical dogma her uncle had spoon-fed her from infancy. While most children were learning to make their beds, she was being warned to climb out on the right side of hers in the morning. The sinister left side would lead to bad luck for the day.

But the mysterious events of late made it more and more difficult to disregard her superstitious education. The string of mind-boggling coincidences in her life grew longer by the day. All the women in her family dying between the ages of twenty-nine and thirty had been odd enough. Now, the sword-wielding gambler of her dreams, a man with curly black hair and intense blue eyes, had come to life in the form of her next-door neighbor—fencing saber and all. To top that off, Alex was reading a book whose main character dressed exactly like the dream-gambler he resembled. Same black Stetson, same black clothing and silver belt buckle complete with engraved stallion, same black mask.

It was too much.

Robin slumped in her chair at the dining room table and flipped to the index of *Stagecoach Robberies of the Old West*. She skimmed her finger down the T's until she came to the name Jack Tucker. Most of what she read on page 253 was repeat information. But when she came to the last two paragraphs, she sat up straight in her chair.

. . . of the five passengers on the stagecoach, one woman was killed when the stage overturned. Two male passengers survived, and a second woman and an infant were never found.

When taken into custody, One-Eyed Wiley Judd, a member of Tucker's gang, confessed they'd been chasing a woman who'd stolen the money from their Springer, New Mexico, bank heist. Accounts differ as to which of the two female passengers on the stage One-Eyed Wiley referred to. Most presume she was the woman who disappeared from the scene of the accident, and that she carried with her not only the baby, but the money, as well. But a few of the captured members of Tucker's gang insisted that Nasty Jack's nemesis died when the stage overturned.

Robin read the passage again, her heart hammering. It wasn't much new information, but it was more than she'd found before. Bit by bit, the puzzle was coming together. The stagecoach passenger who'd died was female, so she could have been Hannah. And a baby had been on board. The child might have been Hannah's daughter—Robin's great-grandmother. But the woman who disappeared baffled her. Who was she? Had she taken Hannah's baby and the money, too?

Weary, Robin pushed the book aside and laid her head on the table. She lifted her right hand and gazed at the antique ring resting on her finger. She wished she could go back and change history . . .

wished she could find a way to keep Hannah from boarding that stage.

The breeze blowing in through the back window held the scent of rain, though the weatherman had predicted this storm would pass by the town. Robin lowered her hand to the table and closed her eyes. She thought she smelled something else in the rain-scented air—the sweet perfume of roses. But that was impossible. Ty and his friend had hauled her bruised and battered bushes away.

Her nose itched. Robin sniffed, then sneezed. Maybe she really was catching a cold, as she'd suggested to Millie on the phone.

Or maybe that pesky butterfly had come back to annoy her.

The first thing Alex noticed when he walked into his bedroom was the blue butterfly perched atop his pillow. He stopped at the side of the bed. "I was worried about you. I thought the tornado might have blown you to your destiny."

Moving slowly and quietly, so as not to frighten it away, he slid open his nightstand drawer and withdrew a magnifying glass.

He was entertaining the most peculiar theory about the butterfly . . . that it had some connection to his recent dreams. No logical reasoning existed to support the supposition, which normally would be more than enough for him to discard it.

Perhaps Ethan Yarborough's superstitiousness

was rubbing off on him. Despite common sense, he couldn't keep his mind from dwelling on the fact that every time the butterfly appeared, he dreamed those odd, vivid dreams. The ones starring himself as Johnny Amigo.

Easing down onto his knees, Alex studied the insect up close through the magnifying glass. He supposed these frequent visits shouldn't surprise him so. With butterflies being the second-largest order in the animal kingdom next to beetles, he was bound to see a few. He just couldn't recall a time when he'd been so aware of them. And why were they always blue and always alone? Groups of butterflies were known to gather in the same place to drink and sleep. Studies showed that some traveled great distances simply to spend the night with others in the same place.

Alex tilted his head and squinted. Perhaps this was an unusually pretty moth rather than a butterfly. Most butterflies flew only during the day, while moths came out at dusk. Holding the glass steady, he zeroed in. No. Definitely a butterfly. A *Myscelia ethusa*, the wings an iridescent blue. But the stripes and apical spots were atypical. Yellow instead of black. Interesting. The body was thin. Moths had plump bodies with pointed, hairy antennae. Bare knobs graced the ends of this creature's antennae, typical of butterflies.

Alex felt a sneeze coming on. He tried to stifle it but failed. The butterfly lifted off the pillow and flew about the room. But the creature didn't leave.

Jennifer Archer

Lowering the magnifying glass to the bed, Alex
reached for a tissue. If he were destined for a
cold, he hoped he could shake it before his classes
started week after next. Nothing like beginning a
new session with a red nose and a mind dulled
by medication.

He walked to the window, opened it, then returned to bed and climbed in, reaching for
Amigo's Gold on the nightstand. Like the previous title, this first book in the trilogy featured a
picture of the story's masked hero on the cover.
Frowning, Alex stared down at the now-familiar
figure. He hated reading the series out of succes-
sion. It disturbed his sense of order, but that
couldn't be helped. At least now he might discover why Johnny wore the mask.

Ty had said Robin acted "funny" when she saw
the novel. Alex wondered if she was one of those
literary snobs who scorned reading material with
a commercial slant. That certainly didn't fit his
impression. More likely, Robin had pegged him
as the snob, and she'd simply been surprised to
discover he could enjoy a purely entertaining
read.

With one last glance at the butterfly, which
now hovered gracefully about the window, Alex
flipped to Chapter One and started to read. He
continued to do so until he dropped off to
sleep. . . .

Chapter Sixteen

Water splashed out of the horse trough. Nasty Jack Tucker jumped up, drew his gun and started toward the corn.

Alex whisked his Colt from the holster. "Head for the road! I'll be right behind you," he hissed at the lady. "Run!"

Her thick-lashed brown eyes widened, but she didn't hesitate. Raising her skirts, she crouched low as she took off ahead of him through the towering rows of corn. The dry stalks scratched Alex's face. He pushed them aside and kept running. A gunshot exploded. Dirt scattered at his feet. He turned and shot back, though he couldn't see a single soul behind them.

The lady stayed one step in front of him. Ahead, he spotted her hat on the ground in a bed of scat-

tered yellow rose petals. Without slowing her pace, she snatched it up.

Another blast sounded from behind. A bullet shattered a corncob at Alex's right.

"You best show your faces!" Nasty Jack bellowed. "Or I'll leave your sorry carcasses in this field for the mice to nibble on!"

Pointing his gun in the direction of Nasty Jack's gritty growl, Alex squeezed off another shot.

"Son of a bitch!" Jack shrieked. "My ear! He nicked my damn ear!"

The red-haired witch's eerie, bell-like laughter floated on the wind, the sound of it more startling than the zing of bullets whizzing past.

Cornstalks snagged the lady's skirt, as if to hold her back. When she stumbled, Alex clasped hold of her arm and helped her along.

As they neared the field's edge, he cut loose a shrill whistle. Thunder's nervous nicker answered the call within seconds.

They cleared the field. The black stallion waited by the side of the road. Grabbing the saddle horn, Alex flew onto the animal's back. He pulled the lady up behind him, and they were off.

The horse's pummeling hoofbeats drowned out the witch's haunted laughter and Jack's shouted curses. Scenery passed by in a blur. Alex spotted a shiny flash of red at the side of the road and knew it must be the lady's abandoned Honda Civic.

Her arms tightened about his waist, her body pressed against him. His pulse raced as fast as the stallion beneath them, steady and fierce, with no sign of slowing.

Soon, buildings appeared on the horizon. Alex glanced over his shoulder to make sure they hadn't been followed. When the dust settled, he saw nothing behind them but miles of desolate prairie. Drawing back on the reins, he eased Thunder to a trot.

He turned slightly in the saddle as they pulled into town. "Where to? Do you have a place to stay?"

She pulled her crumpled hat from between them and slapped it against her leg, sending up a sudden cloud of dust that started them both coughing. "A place?" She scanned the street, the boardwalks at either side of it. "There." Plopping the hat atop her head of tangled auburn hair, the lady pointed.

Frowning, Alex led his mount up to a four-poster brass bed that sat in the middle of the street. "Whoa!" he said quietly, bringing the stallion to a halt. He adjusted his mask. "Surely you don't mean to sleep here, ma'am? You wouldn't get a lick of rest. Not with a bunch of drunk cowhands traipsing in and out of the saloon all night long."

She eyed the sign over the adjacent building's door.

"I rent a room above the Crazy Ace," he said.

257

Jennifer Archer

"You're welcome to share it. Of course, I'll bed down on the floor."

The lady arched a shapely brow, her expression telling him she didn't trust him for a minute.

"If you're concerned about soilin' your reputation, I guess I could sleep in the stables."

After sliding off the back of the horse, she smoothed her dirty, torn skirts. "My reputation might as well match the rest of me."

Her bustle had shifted. Misshapen and lumpy, it sat atop her left hip like an overgrown yellow butternut squash. The lady didn't notice—or didn't care. Lifting her arms overhead, she slowly stretched from left to right at the waist. "I have a few kinks to work out. Just allow me time for a bath, would you, Gambler?"

If his hair hadn't already been curly, her sultry sigh would have done the trick. It sifted over Alex, drifted all the way down to his feet and curled his toes instead. With fumbling fingers, he reached into his pocket, pulled out his key and tossed it to her. "Room three. Top of the stairs." All sorts of erotic images wove their way through his mind. "I'll have a tub and hot water sent up."

Stripped down to her underwear, Robin stood next to the oblong tin tub a couple of men had brought to the gambler's room. Buckets of heated water had followed, two by two, until the tub was three-quarters full. Closing her eyes, she breathed deeply of the lilac-scented steam that filled the room.

Ruby, a painted lady who worked downstairs, had delivered toiletries a few minutes ago and offered to help her undress. The gambler must've paid the woman dearly to do so, for she had no use for Robin's attempt at pleasant conversation, and her eyes slashed like razor blades whenever their gazes met.

With a sigh of pure pleasure, Robin opened her eyes. Twisting her hair into a knot on top of her head, she secured it with a pin Ruby had brought. She reached to unfasten her corset. Freedom from the stiff, torturous contraption would be a relief. The whalebone constricted her waist to the width of a string bean while the gussets lifted and swelled her breasts like over-filled helium balloons. Underneath it all, she'd developed a devil of an itch.

"If you need some help with that, ma'am, I'd be happy to oblige."

The husky drawl came from behind. With a gasp, Robin whirled around. Her hand darted from her corset to cover her throat.

The gambler leaned against the door frame, his arms crossed, his Stetson low over his eyes.

"You frightened me."

His mouth tilted up at one corner. "I thought I sent Ruby to take care of those hooks for you."

"We didn't hit it off."

"Ruby tends to be jealous."

"*Jealous?*" She lifted her chin. "*Why would she be jealous of me?*"

He pushed away from the door, closed it behind him and twisted the lock. Then, he tipped back his hat brim. The slits of his mask exposed blue-gray twinkling eyes. She felt those eyes as they boldly traveled over her, touching the spill of her bosom, her cinched waist, the flare of her hips under the lacy white pantaloons.

His gaze lifted, locked with hers. "Ruby has good reason to be jealous." The gambler's voice flowed smooth and warm as buttered rum.

Her skin all but sizzled beneath the heat his eyes generated. Her body ached in places a proper lady wasn't supposed to dwell on, much less mention.

Robin reached for a towel. She should cover herself. She knew she should. But Lil, the lusty red-haired witch, flashed to mind . . . the way she'd flaunted her body, used it to taunt, torment and entice Jack Tucker. Robin dropped the towel. Why should bad girls have all the fun? She was sick to death of propriety. Tired of being an icy virgin daiquiri—a colorful glass of fluff, all promise, no bite.

Tilting her head to one side, she issued a challenge through the dark fringe of her lashes. "So, Gambler . . . if you thought Ruby helped me disrobe, that must mean you planned to find me naked."

His crooked grin slowly widened. "And what if I did?"

"Find me naked?"

"Plan to."

"Then I can only presume you're disappointed."

The gambler drew his sword. "No, ma'am. Not at all." Extending the weapon toward her, he gently traced the flat side of the blade along her left collarbone, into the hollow of her throat, across to her right collarbone.

The startlingly cool metal raised goose bumps on her flesh. Her heart thumped madly, but Robin didn't flinch.

"How about you, ma'am?" His low voice wrapped around her like a hot caress. "Are you disappointed?"

She drew a steadying breath. "That depends . . . Are you as skilled with that sword as you are with a gun?"

"More so."

She kept her eyes on his. "Prove it."

He clearly understood her dare, her invitation. The cool blade left her skin. A second later, the sword's sharp tip touched the top edge of her corset directly between her breasts. The constraining fabric separated as the tip sliced slowly downward to her hips. Then the corset fell open and dropped to the wood floor.

Robin's heart teetered. She glanced down. The loose bodice of the chemise she wore underneath remained untouched, its fancy embroidery still in perfect condition.

A flush of heat spread across her cheeks as she met the gambler's gaze, but she tried to appear unimpressed. "Not bad." She tossed back her head, loosening her hair from the pin that secured it. "But, if I'm not mistaken, you missed something."

Before she could blink, he made a quick, clean swipe down the front of her chemise. With a stunned intake of breath, Robin glanced at her chest. He had slashed the garment in two, exposing the inner curve of her unbound breasts as well as a bare strip of stomach that stretched all the way to the top of her pantaloons. She looked up again.

"Shall I continue the demonstration?" he asked.

She swallowed. "I think that will do."

Determined not to let the gambler get the best of her, she decided it was her turn to do the shocking. Turning her back to him, Robin let the torn chemise slip from her shoulders, leaving her bare from the waist up. Shoving her pantaloons to her ankles, she kicked them off and stepped into the tub. She lowered herself into the warm, fragrant water, twisting around to face him only after she was completely submerged beneath the bubbles.

The sword slipped from the gambler's fingers and clattered at his feet. Without a word, he crossed the room and stopped at the foot of the tub.

Robin scooted forward and pulled the Colt from his holster, then leaned back in the water and pointed it up at him. "My turn," she said with a wicked smile.

"Let me guess," he drawled. "You're gonna shoot the clothes right off of me."

"No, Gambler. You're going to strip for me nice and slow." She batted her lashes and lowered her gaze to the big silver buckle centered at his waist. "First, the belt, then the shirt."

When he was down to boxers and that silly black mask, she let her eyes trail over six feet of lean, hard muscle and bone. "What's the holdup?" With a kick of her foot, she splashed water at him, then jabbed the gun toward his flat belly. "You seem to be forgetting something again."

Mimicking her earlier actions, he turned his back to finish the deed, allowing her only a view of his derriere. He looked over his shoulder. "Well?"

She narrowed her eyes, slipped the tip of a finger between her teeth, then scrutinized the object under question. "A little pale, but nice. Very nice. Now . . . get in."

"I'm not stepping backward into that tub. I'd fall flat on my face."

She made a tsking sound. "Lest you forget, I've

seen you in action. When under pressure, you're graceful as an acrobat."

"Not when a lady has a gun aimed at my bare ass."

Robin lowered the weapon over the side of the tub and left it there. "Why don't you just turn around, Gambler? Has the West's most notorious ladies' man turned bashful?"

"Just followin' your lead, ma'am." His mouth curved up. "It's only fair."

With a sigh, she scooted around until she sat facing the opposite direction.

Settling his hands on her shoulders, he slid in behind her. Water splashed and bubbles parted as he settled his legs on either side of hers and propped his heels at the foot of the tub. When she inched forward to allow him more room, his fingers tightened and he pulled her to him. His knees pressed against her thighs, his chest against her back. She focused on the two long, masculine feet protruding from the bubbles at the tub's far end.

Robin's pulse stuttered. She closed her eyes. "Since you're buck naked, Gambler," she said, sounding breathless, "I assume that isn't your sword handle this time."

His hands slid down her shoulders, under her arms, around to cup her breasts. Below the surface of the water, he shifted the position of his hips, startling a sharp, quick cry of surprise from her throat.

264

"Does that answer your question, ma'am?" he whispered in her ear. . . .

Robin jerked awake to the sound of Tinker's whining.

Lifting her head from the dining room table, she squinted down at him. "Please, boy . . . can't you wait?" She had to continue that dream. If she fell back to sleep right now, maybe, just maybe, she could take up exactly where she'd left off.

She lowered her head again and squeezed her eyes shut. "Please," she whispered. *Just ten more minutes. No . . . twenty . . . give the gambler twenty. Please let me go back to sleep!*

Tinker barked.

Robin opened one eye. He stared at her, his gray head tilted to one side, his whiskers quivering. Since he had her attention, he stood, trotted over to the blockaded doggy door and barked again.

Robin groaned. "Damn it, Tinker." Shoving a hand through her hair, she fumbled around the book-strewn tabletop until she found her glasses. She'd started wearing the old pair of wire frames again since the storm had ruined her new ones.

"Talk about bad timing," she grumbled. She walked to the back door, unlocked it, then followed the dog outside.

The night was cool and pitch-black due to the cloud-laden sky. A light shone from Alex's house. The thought of him in there awake, just

Jennifer Archer

steps away, gave her pulse a little jolt. While Tinker sniffed out the yard, she kept an eye on him, but ventured an occasional peek at Alex's light.

After a while, Robin realized Tinker was in no hurry. She walked to the oak tree, leaned against the trunk and closed her eyes.

Images wove through her mind, sensations . . . sounds . . . smells. Slick, wet skin, splashing water, steamy lilac-scented air. She sighed.

"Can't sleep?"

Her eyes sprang open. She gave a startled cry. "Alex!"

"Sorry." He stepped closer, one hand outstretched to touch her arm. "I didn't intend to sneak up on you. It's just . . . I saw your light."

She stooped and gathered Tinker into her arms while trying to steady her nerves. "Are you always awake this late?"

He shook his head. "I was sleeping. Something woke me. Too bad, too. I was at the climax of a very interesting dream."

Taken aback by his comment, Robin briefly met his gaze. She felt oddly exposed—as if he'd eavesdropped on her thoughts of a moment before. She glanced away. "You, too?"

He followed her to the house. "Good dreams are a bit of a rarity. I hate it when they're interrupted."

"So do I."

Robin opened the door and faced him. He wore a pair of shorts and a wrinkled shirt that he'd

266

apparently thrown on quickly. He'd skipped the first button, fastened the second one, slipped the third one in the wrong hole and forgotten the rest.

She glanced down. He wasn't wearing shoes. This was the first time she'd seen his bare feet and, for some reason, she couldn't quit staring at them. They looked familiar—exactly as she would have expected his feet to look. For an instant, she pictured them surrounded by bubbles.

The image caused a jittery fluttering in her chest. She tried to swallow, hoping it would ease the feeling, but her mouth was dry so she couldn't. "Unfortunately," she said, "you can't recapture a dream."

For the briefest of moments, she thought he might argue the point. His brows drew together. He stuck his hands in his pockets. His eyes appeared restless and indecisive as they scanned her face.

Behind him, the clouds shifted, revealing a silvery slip of a moon. "Oh, look," Robin said. "The moon is different from last night. We're in for a change of weather. Hopefully, no wind. And some sunshine would be nice. It's been so dreary the last few days."

Alex glanced over his shoulder. "The moon's phases are the same worldwide at precisely the same time. The weather, on the other hand, varies from place to place." He turned and eyed her with thoughtful amusement. "Sorry to disappoint you, but the weather reports say another gusty, overcast day lies ahead."

She smiled. "It's only one of my uncle's superstitions." And hers, she admitted to herself. Scientifically sound or not, they were in for mild breezes and clear, sunny weather. She'd bet her last dollar on it.

Turning her back to Alex, she stepped inside the house. "Well . . . good night." She hated to be abrupt, but if she didn't get away from him she was going to do or say something to embarrass herself. Another second of idle small talk would drive her mad. What she really itched to do was invite him inside so she could have her way with him.

She lowered Tinker to the floor. "I hope you get some sleep."

"You, too. You might try a hot bath."

Robin went still. "What did you say?"

The door closed quietly. She heard it click, but still she couldn't move. Then his arms encircled her waist from behind. She felt his face, his mouth, touch the curve of her neck.

"Robin," Alex whispered. "I've missed you." His breath stroked warmth against her skin. "I'll leave if you want me to."

In his roundabout way, he was asking to stay, asking her to make a decision about their relationship. If she gave him the answer he wanted, it might end up breaking both their hearts—or healing them.

Robin drew a shaky breath. Maybe the only way to stop dwelling on losing her life was to start living it again. It was a risk, but was it one worth taking?

Chapter Seventeen

Alex loosened his hold about Robin's waist after seconds passed and she didn't respond. He started to lift his hands from her stomach, but she stopped him by grasping his fingers.

"Don't." She turned and looked up at him, her eyes shadowed with uncertainty and need. "Don't leave me alone."

His pulse quickened. Backing up to the door, Alex drew her to him and held her tight. He kissed her forehead, her eyelids, then touched his lips to hers . . . briefly . . . tenderly.

That one quick taste was all it took. The desire he'd held in check crashed down around him. Alex covered her mouth with his, forgetting caution and regrets, forgetting pros and cons, forgetting everything but her and his own driving need.

Slowly, he skimmed a hand down her spine, feeling each bump and hollow beneath her thin cotton T-shirt. At the same time, he spread the fingers of his other hand wide as he flattened it against her bottom and pressed her against him.

Just when he started to lift her shirt, a modicum of the discretion he normally prided himself on returned. He stopped kissing her long enough to search her face, to gauge her reaction and make certain he hadn't misinterpreted her request that he stay. For all he knew, while he'd anticipated a mutual seduction, she might have had in mind a little conversation, a late-night snack of crackers and tea.

He found nothing in her expression to indicate he should stop. In fact, the only snack she seemed intent on having was him. With eager fingers, she fumbled to undo the buttons on his shirt, her cheeks flushed pink, her eyes a bit wild and impatient.

Alex smiled. Dizzy with wanting, he slipped his hands beneath her shirt and leaned forward to kiss her neck. While she moved to the next button, he worked his way up to an earlobe, then gave it a gentle nip.

Robin emitted a short cry of surprise that caught Tinker's attention. The dog appeared out of nowhere, growling and snarling at Alex as he darted about their ankles.

Robin nudged the schnauzer with her toe. "Go away, boy . . . please." Tinker paused to whine at her, then resumed his barking. She cast Alex a sheepish look of apology. "If I put him in the guest room upstairs, he'll sneak up on the bed and forget all about us."

That sounded good to Alex. And not only because he was ready to get rid of the bloody mongrel, but because he knew Robin's bedroom was also upstairs.

They climbed the steps blindly, never letting go of each other. Four steps up, Robin managed to get the shirt off his back. It hit the railing and slid to the floor. Three steps later, hers came off. It landed on the living room sofa below.

Apparently not wanting to make the ascent easy for them, Tinker ran up ahead, then back down again, darting about their feet and nipping at Alex's toes. The dog's distressed yelps seemed to come from a great distance away—somewhere far beyond the quick, steady boom of Alex's own heartbeat.

After Tinker was finally stowed away, they ended up next door in Robin's bedroom. Alex stood with his back to the door as she walked to the bed and switched on the lamp beside it. A sudden, muted glow chased away the room's shadows. She turned and met his gaze, and he saw that the shadows in her eyes had also fled. Now, they looked soft and expectant, so sexy and beautiful he almost couldn't breathe.

Without a word, Robin held his gaze as she unzipped her shorts and stepped out of them.

A swift strike of heat fired Alex's blood. Her bra was little more than a thin strip of white lace, her panties, a matching triangle. The ankh amulet she wore about her neck rested between the swell of her breasts. The silver shimmered as it caught and reflected the light.

Though her straightforwardness was more than a bit unexpected, Alex liked it. The fact that she wasn't the least bit timid about showing him her body was a heady and arousing realization. His eyes trailed slowly over her, and he discovered several other things about Robin he liked immensely, too. Just as soon as he could quit gawking and make his way over to the bed, he planned to prove it to her.

"Look at you, you're . . ." He blew out a long, slow breath. "Wow." It was a dreadful understatement, but he couldn't think of any other word that would do her justice. He'd never been more tempted or wanted a woman more than he wanted Robin at that very instant.

"Alex," she said. "Can I be frank?"

"When did you start asking permission?"

"I've been cooped up in this house for a very long time."

He could guess the point she wanted to get across and decided to save her the embarrassment of having to make it. "It won't be easy, mind you, but I won't rush things. We can take our time."

She sighed. "What I'm trying to say is . . . I've been cooped up a long time and, well, I've sort of been fantasizing this scenario between us since the first time I saw you in that ridiculous fencing outfit."

"You have?"

"Yes. So do me a favor. Please . ... just get your butt over here and satisfy my curiosity, would you?"

She didn't have to ask twice. Alex crossed the room in three long strides.

It wasn't in Robin to act coy and flirtatious like she did in her dreams. But she quickly discovered that explicit honesty worked just as well.

She barely had time to slip off her glasses before Alex reached her. In one swift move, he took off his glasses, too, and dropped them beside hers on the nightstand. His hot, hungry mouth crushed down on hers. His fingers slid into her hair. He backed her up until her legs hit the bed, then leaned over her when she fell backward onto it.

Propped slightly up on one elbow, Robin reached between her breasts for her bra clasp.

Alex broke contact with her lips and glanced down. "Let me."

His fingers brushed against her skin as he tried to work the catch free. Each stroke intensified Robin's feeling she'd turned into a giant, exposed nerve-ending that screamed to be touched.

Unlike the gambler, Alex didn't possess the ability to disrobe a woman with one smooth flick of his wrist. And, though he gave it his best effort, he struggled to unhook the clasp. It caught on an edge of scalloped lace and refused to give.

"Bollocks!" His face reddened.

Robin giggled. As far as she was concerned, his eager, impatient attempts were more erotic, more intimate, than slick expertise.

Narrowing his eyes, he glared at her with mock seriousness. "I don't give up easily. Lift your arms."

Lying flat on her back, she did as he ordered.

Alex slipped his fingers beneath the elastic band, pulled the bra over her head and tossed it aside. His gaze settled on her breasts. "My God." He blew out a long, slow breath, then reached for the top of her panties. When she lifted her hips to accommodate him, his Adam's apple bobbed, and he slowly slid the lacy garment down her hips and legs.

Alex looked up. "My God," he whispered again. Keeping his gaze steady on her, he stretched out an arm behind him and groped the table for his glasses.

Having grown up with a sexually liberated mother-figure like Millie, Robin had never learned to be bashful about her body. But when Alex slipped on those glasses, a flush of heat erupted at her scalp and spread like hot lava straight down to the tips of her toes. The gesture was so typically Alex, yet so unforeseen, it caused her pulse to hiccup.

It hiccupped again when he quickly stood and removed the rest of his clothing.

Robin blinked. Resting on her elbows, she looked at him openly, then scooted toward the edge of the bed.

"What's wrong?" His voice sounded hoarse and wary.

Grabbing her wire frames, she shoved them onto her nose.

Alex's grin spread slowly.

For several moments, while her nerves hummed, and her heart banged like a big bass drum in her ears, she simply stared at him, her eyes skimming from his head to his toes and every place in between. He stared back with obvious appreciation, and when he finally reached for her, Robin was long past ready. He gently slipped off her glasses, then reached for his.

She never imagined she could be so thoroughly swept away. His appetite was voracious and all-consuming. It thrilled and stunned her so completely that she just held on, ready to ride the wave of sensation wherever it might take her.

Suddenly, nothing existed but Alex. Alex, filling the dark, empty places in her soul until no room remained for paralyzing anxiety or indecision or caution. Alex, beside her, inside of her, his hands and mouth everywhere . . . bringing her to life again.

Later, she would remember it as a series of sensory flashes. Seductive glimmering visions complete with sounds and scents and textures. Alex's broad shoulders and lean, hard chest above her, against her, hot beneath her fingertips . . . his long, hard thighs . . . the clean, musky smell of his skin . . . quick, sharp gasps and shaky sighs . . . words of pleasure murmured again and again.

Together, they soared, clinging and quivering, their bodies taut and in tune. When they could climb no further, she shuddered beneath him, each spasm of shared pleasure bringing tears of sweet joy to her eyes.

The fall that followed was mind-shattering and delirious, and when she landed, Robin knew she would never be the same.

"Have you ever wondered what it is about sex that makes everyone so crazy for it?" Robin bit into a cookie. "Think about it. I mean, cookies are great, too, but people don't obsess about them. Songs aren't written about them. Movie themes don't center around cookies. Nobody plans a murder or commits suicide over a snickerdoodle."

Alex glanced over at her. She sat on the bed beside him wearing a short silky robe she'd tied loosely about her waist when she went downstairs for the snacks.

He chose a snickerdoodle from the plate sitting on the bed between them and took a bite. "Sex is comfortable."

"Comfortable? My old house shoes are comfortable. Leather car seats are comfortable."

277

"Yes, but they aren't exciting. Sex is comfortable and exciting. Nothing else can make that claim. At least, not that I can think of."

She held up her cookie and frowned at it. "Cookies can be a comfort, I guess," she mumbled, then lowered her hand for another bite. "Sex isn't always comfortable, though. Exciting, either, for that matter. Sometimes it's one or the other. Sometimes it's neither."

Alex's mind skipped to Leigh. Sex with his ex definitely fell into the "neither" category. Leigh turned the pursuit of pleasure into a major production, with her as director and himself an actor who couldn't get the lines right.

He lifted his head from the pillow long enough to lick sugar off Robin's lower lip. "Let me rephrase. Sex is both comfortable and exciting when it's between two people who are not only hot for each other, but who trust and respect each other."

Robin's brows drew together. She lowered her gaze to the bed. "How was it with me?"

"Extremely comfortable." He paused. "And if it had been any more exciting, you'd be peeling me off the ceiling about now."

She grinned. "Really?"

"I'll definitely show up for a repeat performance." He touched her chin. "I trust you, Robin. Other than my sister, you're probably the only woman I've trusted since I was a very young lad."

"In what way?"

"I trust that you're honest with me. That you don't play games. That you accept me for who I am."

She searched his eyes, then turned, took another bite of cookie and stared off into space.

They munched in silence for several minutes.

"What about me?" Alex finally asked, breaking the contemplative mood. "Was I comfortable?"

Leaning over, Robin brushed a kiss across his lips. "Even more than my old house shoes."

"Exciting?"

"Hmmm." She tapped a finger against his chest. "Have you ever ridden a runaway horse?"

He thought of the black stallion in his dreams, then answered, "Never."

"Well, neither have I, but just imagine it." Her brows arched above the rim of her glasses. "Now pretend you're naked and the horse is bareback and running at warp speed."

Alex laughed. "That's quite a picture. And good for my ego, I might add."

Lifting the plate from the bed, Robin set it aside, then stretched out beside him. She propped herself on one elbow and looked down at him, her chin in her hand. The front of the robe fell open, exposing one pale breast.

Alex slipped his hand beneath the silk. "These are spectacular."

She wrinkled her forehead. "They're mediocre at best."

"I'll have you know, I've seen a wide variety,"

Alex said, feigning indignation. "Enough to know what I'm talking about. Are you questioning my expert opinion?"

"All right, you win. As small boobs go, they're okay."

"I've always preferred quality over quantity."

"Since when?" she scoffed, sneering at him.

"Since the other night when the police officer shined his flashlight on your chest, and I got a glimpse of subtle perfection."

"You peeked!" Looking pleased by his compliment, she rolled on top of him and jabbed him in the side.

Alex laughed. "I wasn't the only one."

She grew quiet. The teasing glint in her eyes dimmed as she stroked the hollow beneath his throat.

"Alex," she finally said, "before you decide whether or not we'll have a repeat performance, as you put it, there's something about me you should know."

"The decision's already made." He slid the robe down her shoulder. "I know all I need to know."

She rolled over and sat up. "I'm trying to be the honest woman you believe me to be. If we're going to get involved, it's only fair that you're informed of some of my more peculiar idiosyncracies."

Pulling the sheet to his waist, Alex scooted back against the pillow. "All right. If it will make you feel better. But, I assure you, it won't change anything between us."

Robin drew a noisy breath, then proceeded to tell him a tale that made the hair prickle at the nape of his neck. A story about several generations of women in her family who had died between their twenty-ninth and thirtieth birthdays.

Alex swallowed. "I've heard this before. You were on the radio. Doctor Dave—"

"You're kidding!" She blushed. "How humiliating. I can't believe—"

"Don't be too embarrassed. I was the reason you called in."

Her eyes widened. "That was you? The man who didn't trust women?"

"Yes, ma'am," he said, affecting a Texas drawl. "Pretty doggone pathetic, huh?"

Grabbing a pillow, Robin buried her face in it and laughed for a full minute.

Alex couldn't bring himself to divulge that he'd dreamed of her that night after the radio program. The time wasn't right to share that particular bit of information. He'd yet to figure out how he'd dreamed her appearance so precisely when, at the time, they hadn't set eyes on each other. He suspected that the legacy had been so much a part of Robin's upbringing that a part of her believed the curse was real. If he was to convince her such supernatural conceptions were nonsense, it wouldn't be wise to start off by suggesting he'd first met her in a dream.

"This curse . . ." he said, when she finally stopped laughing and caught her breath, "it's what caused your agoraphobia?"

She nodded. "I've come to realize that it's also the reason I've isolated myself my entire life. Other than Uncle E and Millie, I've never risked becoming too close to anyone. If I didn't marry . . . didn't have children . . . the curse would die with me."

"Curses don't exist, Robin. You're an intelligent woman. I don't need to tell you that."

"Of course you don't."

"Then what are you afraid of? Fairy-tale monsters can't kill you."

"Neither can mice, but I'm afraid of them, too. So are a lot of other people."

Alex studied her. He wondered what he might say to end her unreasonable fear. "What if I told you surveys have shown that approximately twenty-three percent of workers repeatedly suffer on-the-job accidents because they have a fatalistic attitude? They believe they're unlucky, that there's no way to avoid something happening to them."

She looked incredulous. "How do you know these things?"

"I read a lot." He readjusted the pillow behind his shoulders. "The point is, people die each and every year from preventable accidents for no other reason than because they think they're jinxed. Fear does them in, so to speak."

"Are you implying that my great-great-grandmother invited the stage to overturn and kill her? That it's my great-grandmother's fault a bank robber shot her?"

"No. I—"

"Then there's my grandmother. She must've asked that car to jump the curb and run over her. And I suppose you're going to tell me my mother willed the paint can to fall off the ladder and strike her on the head."

Alex chose his words carefully. "I'm saying, because they believed they were cursed, when they found themselves in a tight spot they undoubtedly lost self-confidence, resulting in a lack of coordination and clear thinking."

"Hmmm." She blinked at him. "I know you're right. But the curse . . . it's just one of those crazy ideas that's taken hold of me. I can't shake it."

A month ago, Alex would have said he didn't understand. But a month ago, he hadn't been having dreams that spilled into reality.

Rapid movement beside the lamp shade caught his attention. Alex squinted at the fluttering blue wings.

A month ago, a butterfly hadn't been stalking him.

Chapter Eighteen

The moon didn't lie. As Robin had predicted, the day dawned mild and sunny. At noon, Millie drove over for lunch. They took advantage of the nice weather by eating outside.

Millie leaned back in her lawn chair and sipped her iced tea. "You make the best egg salad."

"Thanks." Robin sneezed into her napkin.

"I hope you're drinking plenty of fluids for that cold."

"I am. I plan to nip it in the bud before it gets any worse." She glanced at her watch. "It's about time for another cold pill."

Robin set her plate on the ground for Tinker to lick.

Millie shuddered. "That's disgusting."

"I wash my dishes."

"I taught you better."

Robin shrugged. "I guess it's another issue I can take up with your friend the clinical psychologist. When can he make a house call?"

Millie seemed to hold her breath, as if afraid one false move might change Robin's mind. "How does tomorrow sound?"

Her cold wasn't the only thing Robin intended to nip in the bud. Thanks to Alex, she was determined to get over her panic attacks, to start living again. Really living. "Tomorrow's great, but isn't that short notice for him?"

"Doctor Lasser owes me. Yesterday, his wife was in the boutique looking for something to wear to one of his shrink functions. I saved her from a major fashion disaster and him from mortal embarrassment." Millie set her tea glass on the ground, then loosened her belt a notch. "You should've seen what that poor, tasteless woman had in mind to wear to a formal dinner."

"Leigh would love you," Robin muttered.

"Who's Leigh?"

"Alex's ex-fiancée."

Millie's eyes widened with interest, but before she could comment, Tinker started a commotion at the side of the house.

A heavy-set man wearing coveralls poked his head around the corner. "I've got a delivery for Robin Wise from Green Thumb Nursery."

Robin stood. "I didn't order anything from the nursery."

"I did," said a voice from behind.

She turned. "Alex?"

Stepping through the space in the hedge, he nodded at the workman. "Bring them back."

Moments later, the man pushed a wheelbarrow full of roses into the yard. A second man pushing another wheelbarrow followed.

"Roses grown in pots require a bit more care," Alex explained as the men unloaded. "But they can be planted all summer long. That's the nice thing about them."

Stunned speechless, Robin watched quietly until the men finished. They left the yard, but returned seconds later with another load. After they'd completed the delivery, Alex signed the invoice and sent them on their way.

The sight of the yellow blossoms all around her tightened Robin's throat. How had Alex known that her roses were more to her than a simple pastime? They had become her fragile link to life, a part of her, a promise. After she died, they would continue to bloom each spring, year after year, proof of her existence.

The tornado had wiped out that illusion. Alex had brought it back.

She faced him, her eyes misting. "I don't know what to say."

"You don't have to say anything. You only have to plant them. I'll help."

She walked over to him, stood on tiptoe and placed her arms around his neck. "Thank you."

Alex turned his head and sneezed. "Be careful. I've caught a bloody head cold."

Robin pecked him on the lips. "Who cares? So have I."

"How interesting . . . you both have colds." Across the way in her lawn chair, Millie looked smug and delighted.

Glancing over her shoulder, Robin lowered her arms and stepped away from Alex.

"Ms. McCutcheon," Alex said, his voice congested. "It's a pleasure to see you again."

Millie grabbed her tea glass off the ground, her plate from her lap and stood. "Believe me, the pleasure's all mine. I can't remember when I've been so pleased." She started for the house. "Unfortunately, I need to get back to work. I'll leave you two to your roses. Robin, I'll make that appointment for you."

Robin asked Alex to wait, then walked Millie through the house to the front door. "You haven't heard from Uncle E, have you? I can't get through to him. And he hasn't returned my calls."

"The chickenshit. No, I haven't heard from him. He's afraid to face me after going against my wishes and giving you your mother's ring early." She lowered her voice to a whisper. "Forget about Ethan. Tell me about Alex."

Lifting her hand, Robin gazed down at the blue topaz ring. "Why would Uncle E avoid me?"

"He'll come around. Are you and Alex—?"

"Good-bye, Millie." Robin opened the door,

then kissed the older woman's cheek. "Thanks for coming by."

With a sigh that lifted her shoulders, Millie stepped outside. "I'll call you later to let you know when Dr. Lasser can see you."

"I'll be ready."

Robin took another cold pill, then returned to the backyard. She found Alex surrounded by shovels and various other gardening tools.

For almost an hour, they dug and prepared holes for the bushes. Robin recalled Alex's description of sex with the right person as being "comfortable" and decided that silence with the right person was also surprisingly easy.

From time to time, she peeked at him sideways from beneath the brim of her straw hat. The long, lean muscles of his upper arms bulged and strained as he worked the shovel. Prominent veins lined his forearms and the backs of his hands. Robin knew the gentleness of those hands and arms, as well as the strength. That realization made her mind a little hazy and caused her own hands to tremble.

Pausing to catch her breath, she took off her hat and lifted her braid so the breeze cooled the back of her neck. "You're not the least bit winded," she said to Alex. "How do you stay in such good shape? I mean, let's face it, teaching school isn't exactly physical labor."

He stooped, lifted a pot and turned it upside down. "I run five miles each morning." Supporting the rose with his hand, he struck the pot's upper rim against the edge of the shovel. "Back home, I assisted in coaching the university's rowing team. Since we're landlocked here, I've had to give that up."

Robin leaned against her shovel and stared down at him. "So, you run now, instead. Anything else?"

He turned the pot upright again, then, lifting out the plant and earth ball, placed them into the hole he'd prepared. "When the weather cooperates, Carin and I try to work in a bit of tennis each week. When it doesn't, there's always racquetball." He stood and shoveled soil into the hole.

Robin laughed as she placed her hat back onto her head. "Let's see . . . canoeing, racquetball, tennis, running, rowing, fencing, tutoring, summer workshops for gifted children, teaching. Oh, and woodworking, too. I'm sure I've forgotten something. Aren't you restoring an old car?"

"Ty and I are doing it together. You forgot guitar. And wrestling. I used to wrestle, though I haven't in some time."

"And I suppose you're good at all of it." She grinned. "Except for the fencing, I mean."

The shovel went still. Alex leaned against it, his face contorting into an affronted look. "I'll have you know, my fencing is improving. I just need a bit more practice."

She laughed again. "That's quite a list of interests for one person, don't you think?"

"I suppose I came by it naturally. My pop was one of those people with a bit of knowledge and skill in a vast number of subjects and activities. I'm afraid that was his downfall."

Robin frowned, then turned her head and sneezed. "In what way?"

With the back of the shovel head, Alex tamped soil down around the bush. "Pop died in a race car crash his first time out on the track in a real competition. I was twelve."

She noticed that the loss still held enough power to dim the light in his eyes. "I'm sorry, Alex. I'd say I know how it feels to lose a parent, but mine disappeared from my life before I really knew them. It must have been harder for you."

"Pop's death definitely changed things. My mum and I have been at odds ever since. It frightens her that I'm so like him. She was afraid I'd ruin my life, the way she thought he had. So, for a time, she tried to rein me in."

"And failed, obviously."

He moved to the next hole and stooped again. "I didn't want to admit she might've been right about him—or about me. So, I decided I'd show her." He grinned. "I'd be the best at everything. That wasn't too difficult as far as my studies were concerned. But when it came to other activities . . ." He looked up at her with a self-derisive gleam in his eyes. "Let's just say I also inherited a bit of Pop's clumsiness. I had to put forth more effort than the other lads, but I didn't care."

Robin kneeled beside him and turned another pot upside down. "Do you still have to be best at everything?"

Alex hesitated, as if considering the question. "Leigh taught me something." He glanced up and grinned. "I have warts. I'm not perfect. I don't even want to be. Not anymore."

She pulled off one gardening glove and touched his cheek. "I happen to like your warts."

He turned his face into her palm and kissed it. "You might want to reserve judgment until you know a bit more about me. You're not the only one with peculiar idiosyncracies."

"Such as?"

He chuckled. "What would you think if I told you I dream I'm the paperback hero I've been reading about?"

Robin felt as if all the blood had drained out of her body. She became so light-headed she almost teetered backward.

Alex took hold of her elbow and helped her stand. "Are you all right?"

She wasn't all right. Not at all. She couldn't share the crazy idea in her mind. By telling Alex about the curse, she'd already revealed far too much of her insecurity, exposed one too many of her oddball beliefs. So far, Alex hadn't flinched. But if he found out she suspected they might be sharing their dreams . . .

"It's just this cold," she said. "Maybe I'd better

take a break . . . get a drink of water."

As she headed for the house, she told herself their dreams were most likely entirely different. By coincidence, only one element seemed similar.

But she didn't believe it. Not for a minute.

After the rosebushes were all planted, Alex brought Sheeba over for her first supervised visit with Tinker. It didn't go well. The cat hissed, and the schnauzer yapped whenever they brought them within three feet of each other. So, he and Robin held them at opposite sides of the room and let them stare. It was a start.

Later, with Sheeba tucked away safely back home, Alex returned. After a bit of enjoyable coaxing on his part, Robin decided that since they both had colds, it would be okay if he spent the night.

In Robin's moonlit bedroom, they blended together like crossing shadows—smoothly, darkly, completely. His need for her was an ache he couldn't soothe, a fever he couldn't break, a hunger he sensed he would never satisfy.

"How did you know?" she whispered. "My roses . . . no one else understands."

"We're connected, Robin." He touched her lips. "Don't you sense it? I know what you think . . . what you feel."

Her eyes gleamed at him through the darkness, watching, waiting. Alex supposed she thought it an odd statement for him to make. He, a man of science, of logical thought. But this thing between them . . . it was something he didn't care to analyze, to pick apart and examine, piece by piece. For the first time in his life, he only wanted to feel, to experience, to accept and surrender.

Alex's mouth replaced his fingers. He kissed her slowly, fully, and then he lost himself. He gave himself to her warmth, her softness, her healing acceptance of all that he was . . . and all that he was not.

Much later, just before he fell asleep, Alex sneezed. "Excuse me."

Like an echo, Robin sneezed, too. "Me, also."

He opened his eyes. In the faint, silvery light streaming through the window, the butterfly floated gracefully, like a bluebonnet blossom suspended in midair. "Look," Alex whispered.

"I know. He's been coming around here a lot lately."

"He frequents my place, too."

"Strange," Robin murmured drowsily.

Alex closed his eyes and drew her closer. Strange, indeed . . .

Alex lay back against the pillows in the four-poster brass bed that sat in the middle of the street. Taking a drag of a thin, black cigar, he glanced beside him at the lady. She wore nothing but her torn chemise, the lacy white bloomers . . . and his Stetson. He passed her the cigar.

She took a puff, tilted back her head, blew

smoke rings into the cloudless sky. "The blue-eyed squaw at the witch's dugout," she said, pausing for another hit. "She's my great-great-grandmother, Hannah Sann."

A cowboy approached on a galloping horse, headed dead-on for the bed. Alex waved his arms to ward him off, but the rider and his mount ran painlessly through them, as if they didn't exist.

Reining to a halt, the cowboy climbed off the roan and tied him to the hitching post. He glanced back toward the bed with unseeing eyes, focused instead on the activity in the street around them. Spurs jingled as he climbed the steps to the Crazy Ace, then pushed through the bat-wing doors. Slick's piano tunes blared then dimmed as the doors swung open, then shut again.

"Nasty Jack doesn't trust her." Alex scanned the street, ever wary of the outlaw and his gang. "You heard what he said . . . he accused her of slinkin' around, spyin' on him. I know Jack Tucker. If he thinks Hannah Sann has got even an inkling of where he hid that stolen loot, her life's in danger. Her baby's, too."

"Which is why I hired you, Gambler. To help me protect her." The lady crossed one leg over her opposite bent knee, then kept time to Slick's music by swinging her foot back and forth through the air. "We'll have to keep a close watch on Hannah. If she knows the whereabouts

of that money, sooner or later she's bound to lead us to it."

A buckboard rambled past. The teamster's whip cracked. Mesmerized by the lady's swaying purple toenails, Alex didn't flinch. "Then what?"

The lady sighed. "Really, Gambler, I'm beginning to wonder why in the world I ever thought I needed your services."

He looked at her through sleepy eyes and flashed her his lopsided grin. "I didn't hear you complainin' upstairs."

She trailed a fingernail down his bare chest to the edge of the sheet and smiled coyly. "At least you're good for something."

Leaning over, he nibbled her ear. "Happy to oblige."

"Later, Gambler," she said huskily, pulling away. "Right now we've important business to discuss. After Hannah leads us to the money, we'll take her and the baby and hide them. The loot, too."

He cocked a brow. "I reckon you're gonna tell me you plan on returning it to the bank in Springer?"

"Of course." Her smile was evasive. She leaned over and kissed his lips. "What else would I possibly do with six thousand dollars?"

Alex's grin widened. He slipped his Stetson off her head. Auburn hair tumbled about her shoulders in wild disarray. Rolling on top of her, he tugged the sheet over their heads.

Nearby, a six-shooter barked. A bullet dinged the brass headboard where the lady's shoulders had rested only moments before. . . .

Alex awoke with his head beneath the covers and his heart in his throat.

"What's wrong?" Robin whispered.

"Did you hear that noise?"

For several seconds she didn't answer. When she did, her voice held an unmistakable tremor. "It sounded like gunfire."

"You did hear it." Alex inched the comforter down to his chin. Robin's bedroom was moonlit and still—the only sound now was the *plop, plop, plop* of the leaky faucet in the adjoining bathroom.

Robin sat up and shoved aside the covers. "It was probably just Tinker. I'll go let him out."

"I'll go with you," Alex said, leery of letting her out of his sight. "I'm thirsty."

While she took the dog out back, he checked the front door lock, then went into the kitchen for a drink of water.

"Can I get you something?" he asked when Robin came back inside holding Tinker.

"Some orange juice would be nice. There's a pitcher in the fridge."

"Go back to bed. I'll bring it to you."

As she climbed the stairs, he opened the cabinet and reached for another glass.

A minute later, he started after her. But before

he reached the stairs, anxiety prickled again. Alex decided to inspect the other downstairs rooms. He made his way to Robin's studio first and flipped on the light.

Alex's gaze settled on the back of the easel, which normally stood by the living room window. Wondering if Robin had moved it in here because she'd finished the painting, he crossed the room to take a look.

The image that confronted him was as startling as a bucket of ice water in the face. On top of the painted bed in the center of the road, Robin had added two things—a yellow rose and a saber. And above the adjacent building's swinging doors, the sign now read "Crazy Ace."

Chapter Nineteen

Alex lowered the glass of orange juice to a work-table behind him, but kept his gaze on the painting.

He drew a steady breath. Robin must have read the Johnny Amigo trilogy, or at least one of the books. That was the obvious explanation. The story had inspired her to paint the Western town, complete with the Crazy Ace saloon Johnny lived above.

But the yellow rose, the sword. They weren't in the books. They were part of a dream—his dream.

Alex's hand trembled as he reached to touch the canvas. Before he made contact, the blue butterfly flew into his field of vision and alighted on the painting, spreading its wings wide.

A shudder rippled through him. Without bothering to turn off the light, Alex strode from the studio and climbed the stairs to Robin's bedroom.

She was sitting up, and her eyes met his when he entered. "What took you so long?" She looked down at his hand. "You forgot my juice."

Alex sat at the edge of the mattress. A logical reason existed for the similarities between his dreams and Robin's painting . . . for the butterfly's regularly scheduled visits before each dream . . . for the fact that he'd met Robin in the first dream before he met her in reality. Somehow, some way, he would uncover that reason.

But he felt he must tread carefully so as not to make Robin aware of his discovery. Earlier, she had indicated she planned to talk to a psychologist about her agoraphobia. She was closing her mind to the possible existence of a curse. Now was not the time to dump all of this craziness into her lap. Not when she had finally summoned the courage to take positive steps toward recovery.

Alex grasped Robin's hand and drew a deep breath. "Robin, I took the liberty of looking at your painting. I hope you don't mind."

She eyed him cautiously. "My usual work isn't quite so . . . bizarre. I can't seem to finish it. Something's missing. I'm not sure what."

"I was wondering . . . how did you come up with such an unusual idea?"

She shifted her gaze to their joined hands. "I'm not really sure. Why do you ask?"

299

"No particular reason." Alex strove to sound casual. "I've been reading a series of Western novels and thought you might've read one of them, too. You probably saw *Amigo's Gold*. Ty came over to fetch it from the sack of books your uncle sent. Your painting perfectly captures the story's setting. It's just as I'd imagined it."

She glanced up, her dark eyes unsettled, perhaps a bit frightened. "No—I don't read Westerns." Turning her back to him, she reclined and pulled the sheet around her shoulders. "It's late, Alex. Let's get some sleep."

Alex switched off the lamp, then slid in beside her. He buried his face in her hair. It smelled so sweet. Her body felt warm and soft. He didn't want to scare her, didn't want to say or do anything to deter her brave efforts to get well. Still, Alex couldn't stop himself from asking one last question.

"You said you've been seeing blue butterflies frequently?"

"Yes?"

"When do they normally visit? At night or in the daytime?"

She stiffened. "I don't know. Both, I think."

Determined not to press her further, Alex wrapped an arm around her waist and pulled her closer.

"Alex," she murmured after a minute, her voice quiet and tense, "this sounds odd, I know, but now that I think about it, the butterfly always seems to show up just when I'm falling asleep."

The first rays of morning sunlight sifted through the bedroom window. Robin pushed up on one elbow and watched Alex sleep. He lay on his side, facing her. Dark hair fell across his high forehead and over one eye. He could use a haircut, but she didn't care. The disorderly style suited him. She wouldn't change it.

Her gaze swept lower. Alex's facial features were slightly out of proportion as far as perfection went. But they were finely chiseled and as distinct as his personality. From his long, straight nose, to his firm, wide mouth, to his strong, angular jaw and squared-off chin, Alex was an original. In a very short time, she had grown to love his unconventional appearance as much as she loved his individualistic personality.

Robin skimmed her knuckles lightly across his cheeks and chin. His beard wasn't heavy, but the previous day's growth had left a shadow.

Alex stirred beneath the movement of her fingers. "I love you," he murmured, drawing her down until her head again rested on the pillow beside his. He nuzzled her neck and whispered again, "I love you."

Robin stilled. "Alex?" she whispered back. When he didn't respond, she realized he was fast asleep.

She wondered if his words were meant for her.

Maybe they were spoken to a woman in his dreams. A lady who looked a lot like her, but who was infinitely more daring and unafraid of anything.

Robin closed her eyes. She loved him. Until this very instant, she hadn't realized it, but now she knew. *She knew.* With every nerve ending in her body, every heartbeat, every breath she drew, she loved Alex Simon.

She blinked back tears. He hadn't balked when faced with all her peculiarities and hang-ups. His patient, methodical way of dealing with questions that seemed unanswerable calmed her. Alex wasn't one to jump to conclusions. She needed his stable rationality.

Robin traced the outline of his ear. She loved the vulnerability in his voice when he spoke of the mother he couldn't seem to please. She loved the admiration she heard when he talked about the fun-loving father he'd lost at age twelve. He had left his lifelong home, his job, his country and moved here because Carin and Ty needed him— and he needed them. Alex was responsible and caring and vulnerable—all more reasons why she loved him.

Once, he had harbored a soft spot for his ex-fiancée's young son, just as he now did for Ty. She figured that was no coincidence. Alex understood all too well how it felt to grow up without a father. He'd wanted to give of himself to both boys—to help fill a void in their lives that he had once felt himself.

Robin sighed. It had been a mistake to allow herself to fall for Alex or to let him fall for her. The timing was wrong. Where falling in love was concerned, for her, no such thing as a right time existed. Now Alex would only get hurt again.

She thought of last night and the questions he'd asked after viewing her painting. The questions frightened her. In her mind, they confirmed the theory she had tried to ignore. Impossible though it seemed, she'd first met Alex in a dream, and they'd been sharing dreams ever since. If that were true, anything was possible. Even a curse.

His words came back to her. *We're connected, Robin. Don't you sense it? I know what you think, what you feel.*

Robin's breath caught. She searched his peaceful face. Could he have meant . . . ? She shook off the thought, refusing to allow herself even to consider it. Alex was not the sort of man to believe in magic. He could not have meant to imply their dreams were connected.

Careful not to wake him, Robin slid from the bed, slipped on her robe and padded, barefoot, downstairs to the kitchen. When she reached the phone, she punched in her uncle's number. She was beginning to think the only way to get through to Ethan was to catch him off-guard, before he was fully awake.

He answered on the third ring, his voice groggy and gruff.

"Uncle E?"

The hint of irritation in his tone abruptly changed to alarm. "Robin? What's wrong?"

"That's what I'd like to know. Why haven't you returned my calls?"

"Sorry, sugar," he said, sounding guilty. "I've just been busy, that's all."

"Did you get my message about searching the microfilm at the library?"

He sighed heavily. "I did. I haven't had time, so I paid one of the college kids who works for me to do it after hours. So far, he hasn't found anything."

"Oh." Disappointed, she held out her hand and studied the topaz stones on her finger. "My mother's ring . . . it's beautiful. But why did you send it with Alex instead of giving it to me yourself?"

"I didn't want to influence you. I wanted you to read my note about your mama's wishes, then decide for yourself whether to go ahead and open it or save it for your birthday."

He wasn't fooling her. Uncle E had hoped she would open it. She lowered her hand. "I should probably warn you. Millie's pissed."

"I figured as much." He made a snorting sound. "It's barely six. Is something else on your mind, sugar?"

"Well . . . yes, as a matter of fact. Remember telling me about butterflies?"

"You mean about them bringing good luck if you trap 'em in your house?"

"No, it was something else. You said something about a person's soul."

Ethan yawned. "Oh, that. Way back when, lots of different cultures believed butterflies could capture wandering souls."

"Hmm. But what would cause a soul to wander?"

He yawned again. "Who knows? Death, maybe. Some ghosts aren't ready to head for the hereafter. They have unfinished business, you see."

"Besides death."

"Well, if you don't cover your mouth when you yawn or sneeze, part of your soul can slip right out of your body. Seems to me if that happened, it might wander about with no place to go."

Considering that outrageous possibility, Robin rubbed her bleary eyes. She and Alex were both fighting colds. They sneezed frequently. And the butterfly always seemed to show up when she was sleepy. She might have yawned in the insect's presence, or sneezed. Robin couldn't recall. Chances were, if she had, she wouldn't have thought to cover her mouth.

"What's this all about, sugar? What's going on?"

"I'm not really sure."

Squinting, she stared out the windows at the silhouette of the oak tree, her apprehension growing. She felt as if she teetered at the edge of a very high cliff. One side promised security, rationality, life. The other . . . a delve into danger, insanity and death.

"What do you know about dreams, Uncle E?"

"In what respect?"

"What are they exactly? Would a person's dreams have any connection to his or her soul?"

"Well, sure they would. Dreams are a soul's whispered secrets."

Robin lost her footing on the cliff. "I was afraid you'd say that."

The fall into darkness was a long one.

The bed shifted. Alex rolled over to find Robin climbing in beside him. A glance at the clock told him it was only six A.M. "What are you doing up so early?"

"Just letting Tinker outside."

He yawned. "I thought I heard you talking to someone. Were you on the phone?" He reached for her. She didn't pull away, but her body felt tense, unyielding.

"You must have been dreaming," she answered, her voice remote. "Go back to sleep. We can catch another hour, at least."

Something about her had changed. Something was wrong. Robin lay right beside him, yet he sensed a distance between them.

She sneezed.

"How's your cold?" Alex asked.

"Still there. You?"

"I'm feeling better."

She stayed quiet for several seconds, then blurted, "You haven't seen any butterflies in here in the last few minutes, have you?"

Alex frowned. "No. But, I haven't been looking. Why?"

"Just wondering."

Disturbed by her question, as well as her sudden aloofness, Alex closed his eyes. . . .

A breeze rustled the cornstalks, and though the night was warm, Alex felt the lady shudder beside him.

She pressed a hand to her hat so it wouldn't blow away. "Something's wrong. We've been out here at least two hours, and I haven't caught one glimpse of Hannah or heard the baby cry."

Alex held his gaze on the dugout's lamp-lit window, kept his ears attuned to the angry, drunken voices inside. "It's dark enough now. I think I can move in closer without bein' seen." He pushed to his feet but stayed low.

"I'll go with you."

He drew his sword with one hand, his Colt with the other. "Stay put. I'll handle this."

The lady issued a noisy sigh. "Really, Gambler. A dead detective is of no use to me. At least leave me a weapon so I can back you up, if nec-

essary." She nudged him in the side with the tip of her parasol. "Or would you prefer that I hold the scoundrels at bay with my frilly umbrella?"

After a moment's hesitation, Alex handed her his sword. "Here. But for your own protection, not mine."

She lifted her gaze to the star-studded sky. "Of course."

Alex crushed her close for a dizzying kiss. "I'll be back for you, ma'am," he said huskily when it ended. Then, he was off.

Crouched low, he hugged the shadows as he dashed toward the witch's meager house. Just short of the front porch, he dropped to his knees and elbows and crawled the rest of the way. The sudden silence set off an alarm in his mind. With his finger poised against the Colt's trigger, he slowly shifted to his feet and lifted his head to the edge of the windowsill.

The dugout's single room was dirty, cluttered . . . and empty.

Confused and filled with dread, Alex turned to start back to the cornfield.

A sudden, sharp blow sliced pain through his skull. Blinded, he dropped to his knees.

Far in the distance, somewhere beyond the ringing in his ears and the searing agony in his brain, he heard the lady cry out.

Gathering his senses, Alex struggled to his feet and staggered toward the cornfield. Halfway there, he fell to the ground and closed his eyes.

He fought to clear his head, to shake off the pain.

When he opened his eyes again, he was back at the side of the dugout where he'd started.

The lady screamed.

"Hold on, ma'am!" he muttered hoarsely, before the pounding in his head overwhelmed him. Then he was sucked away into a whirlpool of silence and darkness. . . .

Chapter Twenty

Two days later, Alex stood in his living room with the telephone receiver pressed to his ear as he waited through the rings. When Carin poked her head through the front door, he motioned her inside.

Ty followed his mother to the couch and slouched down beside her. Looking red-faced and irritable, the lad folded his arms across his middle and scowled at his kneecaps.

"Hello, Robin," Alex said when she finally answered her phone. His pulse kicked up. Telephone conversations were the only contact they'd had since he'd left her house two mornings ago. Whenever he tried to see her, she always made excuses. "How are you feeling?"

"Not good. This cold's hanging on."

He noticed she no longer sounded the least bit congested. "Do you need anything? I'd be happy to run to the market."

"Thanks, but Millie's coming by later to stock my cupboards."

"I have soup. Let me bring you some for lunch."

"I appreciate the offer, but I'm really not hungry."

"You could save it for dinner, then."

"Alex . . . I'm fine. Stay away. You'll just get reinfected."

Alex blew out a long, slow breath. He guessed she didn't mind infecting Millie. Turning his back on Carin's look of pity, he asked, "Are you getting any rest?"

"As a matter of fact, I was dozing when you called."

"Oh . . . I'm sorry I disturbed you."

"You didn't disturb me." Robin's voice softened. "I appreciate your concern, I really do."

Frustrated, he shoved his fingers through his hair. "I'll check on you later. Take care of yourself."

Alex hung up and faced his sister.

"Oh, dear," she said softly, her eyes amused. "You've a bad case of it this time."

He stuck his hands into his pockets. "Robin has a bugger of a head cold."

"If you ask me, you're the one who's ill. You look dreadful."

Jennifer Archer

Leaning a shoulder against the wall, Alex decided he wasn't surprised he looked like hell. Ever since his last dream, he'd suffered a doozy of a headache, as if someone really had struck his skull with the butt of a gun. "I've had a bout of insomnia the past couple of nights." In fact, he thought he might be losing his mind. The more desperate he was to sleep, the more wide awake he became. And, he was slowly coming to realize that rest was not what he was after. If Robin wouldn't see him in person, then he'd see her in his dreams. He was starting to believe it.

Carin shifted her attention to the scatter of books and papers on the floor beside the couch. "What's all this?"

"When I can't sleep, I read."

Leaning down, she picked up one book. "Butterflies?" She exchanged it for another, then glanced up at him. "Dreams?"

Alex shrugged. "Just a bit of research material."

Carin sat back and studied him. "Ty and I are leaving in the morning for the mountains. Are you certain you won't go with us? You look as if you could use a holiday."

"I wish I could." Pulling his hands from his pockets, Alex started across the room toward them. "I'm sure the two of you will have a wonderful time."

Ty's face flushed a deeper shade of red. Alex

312

watched the lad's angry gaze shift sideways toward his mother.

Carin glanced briefly at her son, her eyes tired and troubled.

"So," Alex said, concerned by the tense, wordless exchange. "Are you up for a bit of work on the Mustang today, Ty?"

Ty's brows twitched. His shoulders lifted slightly then fell. "Sure," he answered gruffly, then stood. "I'll see ya out there."

When Ty was safely out of earshot, Carin said, "He isn't happy about the trip." She shook her head. "I don't understand. Ty loves the place. He and Ray used to get so excited the night before we'd go. They'd—" She paused, pressed her lips together. "That's it. How stupid of me."

"Don't be so hard on yourself, Carin. This is a difficult time for you both."

"I guess I should call it off. The trip, I mean."

Recalling a time when he'd been a lad struggling with the loss of his own father, Alex walked over and sat beside her. "I don't think so. It won't be easy for him, but sooner or later he'll have to face the memories."

The doorbell roused Robin from a fitful sleep. A sleep disturbed by flashes of a dream that set her heart racing and covered her skin with sweat. She was being chased through tall ears of corn, but the faster she ran, the farther away the edge of the field seemed to stretch. When she glanced at her feet, she saw that she stood on a treadmill. But she just hiked her petticoats higher and continued her futile race.

Blinking more fully awake, Robin glanced at her watch. She could hardly believe it was already past noon. Thinking Millie must have misplaced her key, she reached toward the coffee table for her glasses, shoved them onto her nose and pushed herself off the couch.

Before she reached the entry hall, the bell rang again. "Hold on, Millie. I'm walking as fast as I can." Twisting the lock, she swung the door wide. "Oh . . ."

"Good afternoon, Robin." Carin's gaze drifted down Robin's body. "I'm sorry if I interrupted your nap."

Heat rushed up Robin's neck. She still wore her cotton pajama pants and shirt. In fact, other than to take a shower, she hadn't been out of them in the past two days. She couldn't seem to get enough sleep. If she slept, she didn't have to think.

Stepping away from the door, she said, "Come in, Carin. It's good to see you again."

Carin walked into the house, waited while Robin closed the door, then followed her into the living room. "We haven't spoken since the tornado hit. I'm relieved your house didn't sustain too much damage."

"I was lucky." Robin motioned Carin toward

the sofa, then sat in a chair across from her. "Alex said you fared pretty well, too."

"Better than those poor souls who live in the trailer park. After seeing the devastation they suffered, I can hardly complain."

For several long seconds, neither woman spoke. Robin cleared her throat while desperately searching her mind for a topic of conversation. She couldn't imagine what brought Alex's sister to her door. "Could I get you something to drink?" she finally asked. "Iced tea? Lemonade? I think I have a couple of soft drinks, too."

"No, thank you. Please don't trouble yourself. Alex tells me you're ill."

Robin felt another blush creep over her. "It's nothing, really. Just a bad case of the sniffles."

She doubted she'd sneezed or sniffed once in the last twenty-four hours, but she wouldn't reveal to Carin that her head cold was simply a convenient excuse to keep Alex away. After their last night together, she realized it would be best for everyone concerned, especially him, if she put an end to their relationship. And though Robin knew she should behave like an adult and be honest with him rather than pretending to be sick, she just wasn't ready to confront him. In truth, she might never be ready.

"Well . . ." Carin set her purse on the sofa at her side and folded her hands in her lap. "Alex might've told you I'm a nurse. If there's anything I can do for you, any medicine you might need—"

"I appreciate that." Robin wondered if Alex had sent his sister by so that Carin might make a professional assessment of her health.

"Alex is very concerned about you. He cares a great deal for you, you know."

"Did he tell you that?"

"He didn't need to tell me. We're close. I can sense when Alex is smitten." She paused. "I also know when he's hurting."

Embarrassed by the prospect of discussing her relationship with Alex with his sister, Robin searched the other woman's eyes. "Carin—"

"I'm not usually one to meddle in my brother's business," Carin interrupted. "But Alex has been through a lot. If he means anything at all to you then, please, don't string him along. Be honest with him, one way or another."

Feeling ashamed, Robin glanced away. Alex's words came back to her in a rush. He said that he trusted her—trusted that she wouldn't play games. Already, she had misplaced that trust. By doing so, she had accomplished the very thing she had hoped to avoid. She had hurt him.

"I'm sorry if I've overstepped my bounds," Carin continued. "Alex would be completely humiliated if he knew about this."

"No." Robin met the other woman's eyes. "You have every right. He's your brother, and you love him. That's obvious." She smiled. "The last thing I want to do is hurt him. He told me about his failed engagement."

"That was a tough one for him. He'd already spent a good many years trying to prove himself to our mum. Then, to fall in with someone like Leigh . . ."

She looked down at her hands, then met Robin's gaze. "Has Alex told you anything about his problems with our mother?"

"A little."

"Alex and I grew up hearing her rebuke our father constantly. According to Mum, Pop was a pathetic amateur who'd never found his niche, a miserable failure who couldn't do anything right, an embarrassment. She couldn't say anything nice about the man. But, as if that weren't enough, Mum also frequently commented that Alex was his father's son."

Robin felt an instant need to defend Alex and, though she didn't know the woman, immediate anger toward his mother.

Carin lifted her chin. "As you undoubtedly know, Alex isn't stupid. At a very young age, he put two and two together and decided that if he was like Pop, then our mother must think him a failure, too. So when Pop died, Alex set out to prove her wrong. He demanded no less than perfection from himself. He couldn't stand to fail."

"I still see that in him."

Carin gathered her purse and stood. "Well . . . now that I've completely embarrassed myself, I'll leave."

Robin stood, too. "I'm glad you stopped by."

She followed Carin to the door, her decision made. Alex's sister was right. He deserved honesty.

The phone rang. "You get that," Carin said. "I'll let myself out."

Robin told Carin good-bye, then made her way into the kitchen to answer the phone.

Her uncle was at the other end of the line, and she instantly sensed his excitement.

"Sugar," he said. "You know that kid I hired to research the old newspapers? You'll never guess what he found."

Millie wrinkled her nose at the plate of enchiladas the waitress set before her on the cracked Formica tabletop. "Really, Ethan." She glanced across to the opposite side of the booth. "Do you serve anything in this dive that isn't floating in grease? My arteries are hardening just smelling this stuff."

"You love my cooking. You're just too snooty to own up to it."

"You didn't cook this."

"No, but it's my recipe." Sticking a toothpick into the corner of his mouth, Ethan leaned back and scowled at her. "Okay, I'm ready."

She picked up her fork. "Ready for what?"

"The ass-chewing you came here to give me for sending Robin her mama's ring early."

Millie took a bite and tried not to sigh from pure bliss. Anything as sinfully delicious as Ethan's enchiladas should be illegal, but she wouldn't give him the satisfaction of knowing it. She patted her mouth with a paper napkin. "Relax. I'm finished wasting my breath trying to change you. You're too old and ornery. I've given up."

Ethan pressed his hands together in front of him, as if in prayer, and lifted his gaze to the ceiling. "Thank you, Lord."

Ignoring him, Millie continued, "Besides, there's something more urgent we need to discuss. I went by Robin's at noon today, and she was still wearing her pajamas. It was obvious she'd been sleeping."

"So? Everybody deserves a lazy day now and then."

"It was the same yesterday. It's as if she's given up. Like she's just waiting for that silly curse to put a whammy on her."

"I talked to her on the phone today." Ethan frowned. "Now that you mention it, she did sound kinda down in the dumps. Can't say as I blame her. We're down to the wire now. Truth is, I'm worried, too."

Millie felt the flare of her anger as surely as if someone had lit a fire in her gut. "If you're going to worry about Robin," she said between clenched teeth, "worry about her state of mind, not some nonexistent voodoo. Robin had agreed to see a psychologist, but after I made the appointment, she insisted I cancel it. She wants me to cancel her birthday party, too."

Ethan's toothpick twitched. His bushy brows wriggled like sparring caterpillars. "Well, damn. What can we do?"

"Check on her every chance we get. I think I'll call Alex Simon, too, and ask that he do the same." She sighed. "I'll be glad when her birthday's come and gone and she sees that she's been worried over nothing."

Rubbing a hand across his balding scalp, Ethan averted his gaze. "Me, too," he muttered. "Me, too."

Chapter Twenty-one

Robin reached to the bedside table and hung up the phone. She had finally summoned the nerve to be honest with Alex. She had told him she loved him but they couldn't continue their relationship. Now only one regret troubled her: the painting. She wished she could figure out what it lacked and finish it.

Rolling to her side, she curled into a ball and hugged a pillow. Alex had said the time was five o'clock in the evening, which meant she had slept all day. But not a sound sleep. Every couple of hours or so, someone called. Alex . . . Millie . . . Uncle E. For the past several days, they'd been relentless. Why couldn't they leave her alone? Let her rest? More than anything, she needed to sleep, to forget.

But everyone wanted to spend time with her, especially tonight. They wanted to celebrate, they said. But she knew they had other motives in mind. Tomorrow was her birthday—or death day, to be more precise. Thirty years ago, she came into the world at seven A.M.

Seven A.M. Fourteen hours from now. If she stayed in bed all that time, what accident could claim her life? Her mind picked over the possibilities. Maybe the ceiling fan over the bed would fall and crush her. Or the house could catch fire. Or maybe the end would present itself in a more freakish way. She'd get tangled up in the covers and smother. Choke on her own saliva.

Robin heard a whimper. She opened her eyes.

Tinker watched her with a doleful expression. He lay beside her, his head cradled on his paws. When she reached out to pet him, he inched closer and licked her face.

"Don't worry, boy," she muttered drowsily. "I'm just tired."

Uncle's E's words, from days ago, haunted her.

"That stage Jack Tucker tried to rob . . . she was on it. According to the newspaper article, your great-great-grandmother, Hannah Sann— my great-grandmother—is the woman who died on that stage."

Why had she wasted anyone's time tracking down that information? For some reason, it had once seemed important. Now, she wondered what good it did her to know.

322

As her eyes drifted shut, Robin glimpsed the blue butterfly above the bed. She refrained from covering her mouth when she yawned. Right now, she didn't care if the insect captured every last breath of her soul. Compared to the other dates with destiny she'd considered, the butterfly seemed a pleasant way to go. She wouldn't mind riding away on its silky blue wings . . . up, up, up into the heavens . . . light as a whisper . . . free as a breeze. . . .

Robin sat in a chair in a hot, stuffy room. Rope bound her wrists behind her. A tightly tied bandanna covered her eyes. They had blindfolded her the moment they caught her. But she didn't need to see her captors to know their identity. She would recognize Nasty Jack Tucker's mean, gravelly voice anywhere, and his companion's seductive, bell-like laughter was far too distinctive to belong to anyone other than Lil, the red-haired sorceress.

Robin didn't have the vaguest idea where they'd brought her. It wasn't Lil's adobe hut, she knew that much. She had traveled at least three miles of rough road on the back of a galloping horse.

Surely, at any second, the gambler would burst through the door, sword swinging, gun blazing. He wouldn't let her down, would he? Not after she'd given him her most precious gift—her highly prized virginity. Over the years, she had refused countless refined gentlemen far more deserving than he. Well-mannered dandies who flattered, pampered and wooed her.

Someone grabbed a fistful of Robin's hair and jerked her head back. "Where's the squaw?"

Tucker's threatening growl didn't faze Robin. Nor did the witch's fresh burst of maniacal glee. But the touch of cold metal against Robin's throat sliced a trail of pure fear all the way down to her toes. "I told you—I don't know!" She had hoped to sound bold in the face of Tucker's torment, but her voice exited her body as little more than a rasp.

Lil began humming an eerie tune as Nasty Jack slid the flat side of the blade up and down Robin's neck. "Try again," he snarled.

"We—we watched the house with the hope of finding Hannah ourselves."

"I ain't buyin' it. That no-account you hired planned to fill me and my men full a lead so's we couldn't go after her."

Tucker's hot breath smelled like sewer water. She gasped for fresh air. "Surely you don't believe the gambler would be foolish enough to ambush your entire gang alone."

"I seen how the man handles a gun. Now . . . are you gonna tell me where that blue-eyed squaw took my money, or am I gonna have to slice up your pretty white neck?"

Gritting her teeth against the burning pain of the rope against her skin, Robin twisted her arms and tried to loosen the knot. She had worked it loose enough to separate her wrists a fraction of an inch.

Lil's humming ceased. "I declare, Jack Tucker! You surely did put the scare in our prissy little gal. She's trembling like a pig before slaughter!"

Nasty Jack chuckled. "You reckon if I poked her she'd squeal?"

"Best not draw blood too soon," Lil warned. "A delicate blossom like this one would wilt right away at the sight of it. We wouldn't want to waste any more precious time tryin' to revive her."

"What do you suggest?" Tucker growled. "She ain't gonna tell us nothin' if we just sit here and ask politely."

"Well, now, let me see. I believe I have just the thing to coax Miss Priss to talk. A truth potion. I'll mix the brew right up. Meanwhile, you run check on the boys. Make sure that detective didn't somehow slip past them."

The blade left Robin's throat.

A string of muttered curses followed Tucker across the room. "Don't get any fool ideas, shrew. I won't be gone long."

A door creaked open, then slammed.

"Well, well," Lil crooned. "Alone at last."

Robin sensed that the woman circled her chair.

"Such pretty clothes you wear. Back home in Georgia, I wore pretty things, too . . . gifts from my many suitors. Why, I had hats with more ribbons than you could count. And parasols by the *dozen, far fancier than this." She laughed. "What a head-turner I was. Other women's husbands brought me French champagne . . . chocolates wrapped in shiny gold foil."*

Suddenly, the tone of her voice changed from wistful delight to haughty disdain. "I'd have put you to shame!" she snapped. "You look like a two-dollar floozy compared to me."

Robin sat taller and forced a smile. "My parasol . . . my hat! Take them! They're yours. Please. I'd like you to have them."

"Foolish girl!" She slapped Robin across the cheek with the palm of her hand. "I don't want your tawdry hand-me-downs! I want the bank money. And I don't intend to share it with that smelly pip-squeak, Jack Tucker, either."

Lil pulled off Robin's blindfold, then stooped in front of her.

A riotous cloud of gray-streaked red hair framed the woman's pallid face. A smudged ring of black surrounded her translucent, pale green eyes. Robin blinked as a spasm of dread shook her to the core. Staring into those eyes was like peering through colored glass straight into madness.

Where was the gambler? What was taking him so long? Surely Tucker's gang of misfits were no match for the best detective this side of the North Atlantic!

She struggled with the rope and scanned the dark, dirty room. It appeared they had brought her to a one-room shack. An empty one, at that. Less than five feet away, a telephone sat on a makeshift table—the only furniture in the place. Somehow, she must get to it . . . call 911.

Forget the gambler—she would help herself. Maybe the sheriff was right about him. He was nothing more than a rascal—a ladies' man. After coaxing her into his bed, he now had no use for her. Robin bit her lower lip. What a fool she had been! With one crooked grin, the rogue had charmed the pantaloons right off of her!

"I have the sight, you know," Lil whispered. "You share the squaw's blood." She closed her eyes and breathed deeply. "I smell it in you. Take me to her before it's too late. Only I can save your great-great-grandmother from her fate." Her laugh rippled the air.

Behind Robin's back, the knot in the rope slipped another half-inch. "You'd save Hannah from Nasty Jack?"

"Not from him! From the curse." Lil arched her painted brows, lifted her cleft chin. "The blue-eyed squaw . . . when Jack and the boys aren't around she talks to me. I declare, that girl can talk a blue streak! She had her eye on my topaz ring—a gift from the mayor back home. Said she'd never owned anything half as pretty. If I'd give it to her for her thirtieth birthday tomorrow, she'd tell me where Jack hid the money. We'd split it fair and square."

"So you gave Hannah the ring?"

"I told her I would, soon as she showed me Jack's stash." Lil leaned closer. Her mouth touched Robin's ear. "Later, I cast a spell on that ring that the blue-eyed squaw will never live to see thirty," she whispered. "Nor will anyone else who wears it."

"But, why?" Robin gasped. "Hannah said she'd take you to the money."

"That's right." Lil stood and twirled across the floor. "Then she'd die, and I'd keep it all for myself." She stopped twirling suddenly, her face contorting with rage. "The squaw . . . she slipped sleeping herbs into my food and stole my ring. Jack's money, too. She took her baby and vanished."

Her mouth twisted into a grotesque grin. "The joke's on her," she hissed. "What use is money to a dead woman?"

Across the room, the phone began to ring. The witch took no notice. She laughed and danced and twirled while it rang and rang and rang. . . .

Alex tried to concentrate on the Mustang's undercarriage instead of his earlier conversation with Robin. By tinkering with the automobile, he had hoped to forget that she'd given him the brush-off. The diversion wasn't working.

She loved him, but she didn't want to continue their relationship.

"Ridiculous," Alex muttered.

Quite certain he would never understand

women, he fumbled around on the garage floor for the wrench he had previously set aside. Perhaps he should quit feeling sorry for himself and pay her a visit. Force her to say it to his face. Could he really stand to lose Robin without a fight? No woman had ever affected him on such a gut-deep level. Not Leigh, not anyone. With Robin, he felt completely free to be himself . . . no need to prove anything, no reason to apologize for any shortcomings, real or imagined.

Robin was afraid, that was the problem. Alex suspected that by refusing to see him, she was trying to protect him from that bloody curse she feared. She had allowed superstitious nonsense to cloud her judgment, to control every decision, to manipulate her emotions.

Millie and Ethan had both contacted him, worried about Robin's withdrawal. Alex was more than a bit concerned himself, which was exactly why he should be at her door, demanding to work this out, rather than flat on his back on a dolly beneath a car.

"Bloody coward," Alex mumbled, disgusted with himself. Robin wasn't the only one with fears. She feared a curse. He feared failure. What if he couldn't get through to her?

Alex worked to dismantle the linkage from the gearbox. As soon as he summoned the proper words, a magic phrase that would bring Robin to her senses, he would march his bum right over to her house.

Squinting above at the job he'd started, Alex cursed. He wished Ty were available to hand him tools and move the light when he needed it in a different position. Seeing clearly was difficult beneath the vehicle. The Mustang's front end was propped up on a couple of old tire ramps the house's previous owners had left behind. He had a small space to move about, but Alex had quickly discovered that do-it-yourself removal of a transmission at home was a two-man job. Especially since this was his first attempt at such a task.

When his cordless phone rang, Alex left the wrench attached to the transmission casing, rolled around until he lay lengthwise beneath the car, then felt alongside it on the floor for the phone.

"Alex?" His sister spoke before he could say "hello."

"Carin! How are the mountains?"

"Ty's gone, Alex—"

"What?" On instinct, he lifted his head. It struck the Mustang's undercarriage.

"I walked down the road to the lake. Ty didn't want to go." Carin's voice cracked with emotion. "He—he's hardly spoken two words since we left on this trip."

Alex rubbed the rising knot beneath his scalp. "Slow down, Carin. Tell me what happened."

"I stayed at least two hours at the lake. I took a book along, read a bit. When I returned to the cabin, the car was gone. So was Ty."

330

"How long since you discovered him missing?"

"About three hours. I didn't know what to do. Ty knows he's not allowed to drive, but I hoped . . . prayed, he'd simply gone cruising. The couple at the cabin nearest ours drove me around to look for him. Then, we went into town to talk to the police."

Alex was determined not to let his own alarm increase his sister's. Before speaking, he drew a deep breath to steady his voice. "If Ty took off shortly after you left for the lake, he could be close to home by now."

"I suppose he might have started in that direction."

Even in daylight, Alex didn't like the idea of Ty driving by himself on the two-lane highway between here and the Spanish Peaks of Colorado. The thought of his fifteen-year-old nephew attempting it in the dark sent a shudder through him. But he much preferred that scenario to the idea that the lad was lost on a mountain road in the middle of nowhere.

He felt more than a bit guilty for encouraging his sister to take the trip against Ty's wishes. "We knew he was upset. More than likely, he's on his way here, Carin. He'll arrive any minute, safe and sound and horrified about what he's done."

"I hope so. Would you go by the house? I'll try to call, but even if Ty's there, I'm afraid he won't answer."

"Of course. I'll leave right away."

"If he doesn't show up, check with the Cooleys. Their son Derek is a close friend of Ty's. They live—"

"I've been to the Cooleys' house with Ty. I remember where it is."

"Thank you." She paused. "I've never been so frightened."

The worry in her voice made him wince. "I hate that you're alone, Carin. I wish—"

"I know," she said. "I need Ray terribly."

He closed his eyes. "The minute I know anything, I'll ring."

"There's no phone at our cabin. And you can't call my cell phone—I'm out of range. I'm at the neighbor's. Ring me here." She recited the number. "If I'm not available, they'll get a message to me."

Alex repeated the number, committing it to memory until he could jot it down on paper. "Don't be alarmed if you don't hear from me right away. I want to give Ty plenty of time. And I'll drive around town to see if I can spot your car."

"If I have any news here, I'll let you know."

He forced himself to relax his grip on the phone. "Leave a message on my machine if I'm not home."

Alex broke the connection, then lowered the phone to the garage floor beside him. With his thoughts on Ty, he lifted his head and tugged on the wrench he had left attached to the car.

The wrench fell free. But, a second later, before he could react, the driver's side of the car came down, too. On instinct, Alex threw out his hands and jerked back. "Bloody—!" His head made a cracking sound as it struck the concrete. The car settled hard against his right shoulder and chest, knocking the wind from his lungs and pinning him to the floor.

Alex tried to clear the haziness in his throbbing head.

Pain gnawed at his shoulder. He'd been prying . . . jerking on the transmission. *Bloody stupid idiot! Should've placed jack stands under—*

The labored breath he drew stabbed pain through his right side. His chest felt heavy.

Chapter Twenty-two

Millie paced across her antique Persian rug. Back and forth, back and forth in front of the sofa on which Ethan sat. His head rested against the cushions and, though his eyes were closed, she could see the strain in his face. Beethoven's "Concerto in D Major," one of Ethan's favorites, played on the stereo.

"I thought she would never answer the phone," Millie said anxiously.

Ethan didn't move. "But she did."

"I woke her. Eight o'clock in the evening, and I woke Robin up. All this sleep is a symptom of depression. We should go over there. One or both of us should spend the night with her."

He opened his eyes. "Now, Mil, Robin said she doesn't want company. What could we do, anyhow? She's down for the night. And I've already taken every safeguard I know to take. The garlic's on the mantel. She's wearing the ankh. I've—"

Millie stopped in front of him. "Don't start."

"Okay. Forget that last part. Robin's asleep in her own bed. I can't think of a safer place for her to be."

"But her state of mind . . . What if she does something desperate?"

Ethan took her hand, drew her down beside him. "You know Robin better than that. We'll check on her in the morning. Eight o'clock. We'll take breakfast. What do you say?"

"I told her seven."

"Seven's even better." He stared past her. "Robin was born at seven."

Millie started to scold him again for dwelling on the curse, but when he put his arm around her, she settled her head on his shoulder instead. "I won't get a wink of sleep."

"Me, neither. I'm damned worried about her."

Twisting around to look up at him, Millie sighed. "But not for the same reasons I am."

"No use hashing that out again. We've just about gnawed the issue to a nub."

He lifted his hands to her shoulders, started massaging the tense muscles there.

"Ethan?"

"Hmmm?"

"I'm glad you're here with me tonight."

"That makes two of us."

335

She smiled to herself. "Any ideas how we might pass the time?"

His fingers stilled momentarily, then slowly resumed their massage. "Oh, I bet I can come up with a thing or two."

Alex gathered his wits enough to take stock of his situation. He'd been correct. The left tire ramp had collapsed. No wonder the house's prior owners had left the ramps behind. They must be defective or too old to use safely. When the Mustang had come down, it had settled on one side of his chest, pinning him.

Every breath hurt. He had a bugger of a headache. But he didn't think his injuries were life-threatening. At worst, he might have a mild concussion, a cracked rib or two.

But the prognosis might be grim. Now the vehicle was supported by only one ramp. If only he could manage to push himself out.

With his one free hand, Alex pressed against the automobile's undercarriage. Pain shot through his chest. Something creaked—the car, the ramp, he wasn't sure which. He stilled. Any movement on his part might weaken the support of the other ramp. Then he'd really be in trouble. Without help, he wasn't going anywhere.

The phone. Without moving too much, Alex patted around on the floor beside him with his palm. Nothing. Had he knocked it away when the car shifted?

His fingers brushed against cold metal. The wrench. Lifting it, he dinged it against the Mustang. "Help!" The weak sound of his voice surprised and frightened him. He guessed he'd been trapped for close to twenty minutes, but he felt as if the breath had been jarred from his lungs only moments ago.

A breeze sifted beneath the car and over him. Earlier, he'd cracked the garage door for air. *Should have opened the bloody thing completely. Better chance for someone to hear. . . .*

Alex continued striking the wrench against the car and calling out. Grogginess came over him. He decided either the past several nights without sleep had finally caught up to him, or he really had suffered a concussion. More than once, he dozed, then woke and started banging again. Time passed in a hazy blur. The air coming in beneath the garage door grew colder. His thoughts faded in and out as he tried not to dwell on his pain or worry about the car crashing down all the way.

Sometime during the night, the phone rang. Alex tried again to locate it. But after only a few seconds, he gave up. He was so weak . . . so fatigued. Between each ring, Alex heard Sheeba's mew from inside the door to the house. Noises seemed garbled, as though they originated from the bottom of a deep, hollow well. He knew Sheeba probably needed to go outside, knew Carin was probably ringing to ask for news of Ty.

Hours ticked by. He dozed fitfully. Restless snatches of sleep in which his mind drifted from his nephew to his cat to his own precarious state. His heavy eyelids opened, drooped closed, then opened again. Alex thought he spotted the blue butterfly in his peripheral vision. *Must be hallucinating . . . dreaming . . .*

Dreaming. Abruptly, he opened his eyes, shifted his gaze in all directions. Where was the bloody pest when he needed it? The tiny blue messenger might be his only hope. If he couldn't get through to anyone in reality, perhaps he could reach Robin in sleep.

Alex laughed aloud at his own foolish reasoning. He must be going into shock. But a tickling sensation against his cheek captured his attention. His heart leaped. Alex slowly turned his head. The butterfly sat on his shoulder.

A strange sense of relief swept through him. As the last of his energy trickled away, he closed his eyes. "Robin," he whispered. "I need you. Help me. . . ."

Sapped of all energy from struggling with the ropes that bound her wrists, Robin slumped in the chair. The potion's hypnotic fumes swirled throughout the room, making her drunk . . . drowsy . . . disoriented.

The witch seemed unaffected. She hummed a haunting tune as she stirred her boiling brew.

Robin could no longer hold up her heavy head.

Her chin drooped to her chest. She closed her eyes.

"Robin . . . I need you. Help me. . . ."

She sat up, came fully awake in one split second. "Who was that?" *Robin scanned the dingy, barren room.* "Did you hear it? My name. Someone whispered my name."

Lil's humming ceased. She looked away from her pot. "There's only you and me in this room, Miss Priss. And, if a spirit were present, I'd be the first to know."

Robin fought to bring Lil's blurry, distorted image into focus. "But someone called to me for help."

No longer melodious, Lil's laughter twanged like an out-of-tune guitar. "Calling to you, is he? Poor, poor Gambler. Jack and the boys aren't as soft-hearted as me. Torture's their method of choice when it comes to forcin' prisoners to spill the beans."

Had the gambler summoned her? Robin wasn't certain. The words she heard had been whispered too softly to distinguish the speaker's identity.

She strained against the ropes, cried out as the cord cut into the delicate skin at her wrists.

"No use fightin'. You're mine to treat as I wish 'til I have a mind to set you free." *Lifting the ladle close to her face, the witch smelled the potion, then shifted her wild eyes to Robin.* "There, there. Don't cry, now," *she taunted.* "Just tell me the whereabouts of your great-great-grandmother, *and I'll loosen those ropes easy as you please."*

Frustrated by her helplessness, Robin squeezed her eyes shut, tried to dam the steady stream of her tears. But the whisper came again, filling her head with its desperate urgency.

"I need you. . . . Help me."

The tears flowed faster, hot, salty streaks of futility. Blinking to clear her vision, she scanned the room for a possible means of escape. But, suddenly, everything changed. She no longer sat in a ramshackle shack, but in her own living room . . . on her own sofa.

Across the way, the witch stood beside Robin's kitchen stove, her glassy green eyes glimmering with malice. "You can't help the gambler," *she hissed.* "You're a prisoner inside your own home."

"Robin . . ." *The ardent entreaty filled her mind like a prayer.* "Robin . . . help me . . . help me . . . help . . ."

"Who are you?" *she cried, ignoring Lil's mocking chuckle.* "Gambler . . . is it you? Hanna?"

Her eyelids grew heavy again as the cloyingly sweet scent of the potion wrapped around her. Sounds twisted and twirled, blared then receded, as if caught up in a cyclone. The lilting melody of the witch's eerie song . . . a cat's nervous screech . . . the desperately murmured plea . . .

With every ounce of her strength, Robin tugged her wrists apart. The knot slipped free. The rope fell to the floor. She reached between her breasts, into her cleavage, pulled out her can of Mace and lunged at Lil. Aiming the spray at the witch's pale face, Robin pressed the button.

Lil's unearthly scream prickled goose bumps across Robin's skin.

The witch covered her eyes with one hand, grabbed blindly for Robin with the other.

Robin dodged. She reached for the pot on the stove. Grabbing the handle, she swung. The steaming, boiling brew splashed onto her captor.

A horrible wail filled the room. Robin covered her ears to muffle the sound. She ran from the house, across her yard, down a dusty road. Scenery passed by in a blur: her garden of yellow roses, the cornfield, her red Honda Civic nose-down in a ditch.

When she came into town, a stagecoach was pulling away from the Crazy Ace. "Driver!" Robin pushed her endurance to the limit until she caught up. "Driver! Have you room for me?"

The burly man tugged on the reins, halting his team. "If you got the price of a ticket, lady, climb aboard."

Robin tossed him a coin. She lifted her skirts and climbed into the coach.

The stage took off again.

Four other passengers sat inside. Robin settled on the bench next to a portly gentleman wearing round, wire-framed spectacles. She nodded at the elderly man across from her, but couldn't catch the eye of the pretty woman beside him. The young blonde clutched an infant girl with one arm, a fat, black satchel with the other. The baby contented herself by twisting the ring on her mother's finger—a gold filigreed bauble with three blue topaz stones.

Gunshots blasted behind them.

The rotund gentleman next to Robin gripped the edge of the seat. "What was that?"

She poked her head out the tiny side window. Far in the distance, a gang of riders approached. Ducking back inside, Robin stared across at the young woman's startled blue eyes. "Hannah? Hannah Sann?"

Hannah drew her daughter closer and met Robin's gaze. "How do you know my name?"

"Hannah . . . listen to me. You have to get rid of that ring you're wearing."

Another distant round of gunshots disturbed the air. "Hold on!" the driver shouted. The stage moved faster, bumping and jostling Robin and the other passengers.

Hannah glanced down at her finger then up again, her eyes frightened. "It's mine. It was a birthday gift."

"Trust me . . . please. I'm trying to save your life. Your baby's, too." Robin reached across for her great-great-grandmother's hand, but it was too late.

The stage tilted sharply to one side, then rolled.

Bodies collided. Screams and cries echoed. Doors banged. Wood creaked and groaned.

When they finally skidded to a stop, the stage lay on its side. Robin lifted her head, breathed in a cloud of dust. Only the baby cried. All else was quiet. Frantically, she searched the coach's interior. The two male passengers had either passed out or died. Hannah was gone.

Robin's head ached. She felt dizzy, dazed. It would be so easy to just lie down, give up. She was too tired to fight Nasty Jack . . . too tired . . .

"Robin . . ." The whisper sailed through her mind. "Help me! Help me!"

Coughing, Robin summoned her strength. She had come too far to give up. She must find Hannah . . . save her. She kicked the door open, then pulled the baby from the floor beneath the bench. Cradling the child with one arm and grabbing Hannah's satchel with the other, she climbed outside.

The approaching horses' hoofbeats pounded the earth like thunder.

Hannah's broken, lifeless body lay at the base of a nearby mesquite tree. Heartsick, Robin stooped and twisted the topaz gem off her great-great-grandmother's finger. Choking back tears, she turned and threw the cursed ring as hard as she could out across the rugged countryside toward town.

As Nasty Jack and his gang galloped up alongside the overturned stage, Robin crouched low and covered the baby's mouth to silence her cries. With Hannah's satchel in tow, she ducked into a dried-up riverbed where she fell to the ground to catch her breath.

"Robin . . ." *came the whisper.* "I'm in danger. Please, hurry . . . !"

She jumped. Her great-great-grandmother was dead. The plea for help could not have come from Hannah. This time, the words had not been whispered. The voice was the gambler's, but his Texas drawl was gone. His accent was clipped, British. Robin drew a startled breath. He sounded like . . .

"Alex!" Robin sat straight up in bed, shivering and cold, though her skin was coated with perspiration. She grabbed the telephone receiver from the bedside table, then punched in Alex's number. It rang ten times before she finally hung up.

She was out of her bedroom in less than five seconds, bolting downstairs with Tinker at her heels. Alex was in trouble. He needed her help. She had never been more sure of anything.

Robin threw open the living room door and ran, barefoot, into the backyard. The first blush of morning stained the horizon with a soft pink glow. *Sunrise.* The time must be nearing seven o'clock. Only minutes left until . . .

As she approached the hedge separating her yard from Alex's, an all-too-familiar wave of anxiety welled up in her chest. She could call 911 . . .

or a neighbor . . . or wait for Millie and Uncle E.

She paused at the gap in the hedge—the space she had feared to cross—a scant few inches that, for her, might as well be the Grand Canyon. What if Alex didn't have another minute to spare? What if . . . ?

"Alex!" she screamed. "Alex! Where are you?" She scanned his yard, the dark windows of his house. A cool morning breeze carried birdsong to her ears . . . and something else . . . a sharp, distant ring, much like a dinner bell.

"Alex!" she yelled again. She picked up Tinker to quiet his barking, then listened more closely. After a moment, another clang sounded. And then she heard a voice. Her name. He called her name.

Drawn by Alex's cries, Robin inched forward. She blocked out everything else but the sound of his voice. The distinct ring of metal against metal. She stepped across the hedge . . . passed through his yard . . . around to the front of the house. Each step she took was faster than the one before. Finally, she was running, her heartbeat chaotic, her mind wild with fear. Fear for Alex, not for herself. Fear that she might lose him. That she wouldn't reach him in time.

His garage door was partially open. The space beneath would be just large enough for her to squeeze through on her stomach. Robin lowered Tinker to the driveway, then sprawled beside him, facedown. The clanging inside the garage resumed. So did Tinker's barking.

"Alex!" Robin yelled.

"I'm here. Under the car."

Robin poked her head beneath the door. The overhead light was on. Another light, strung by a cord, dangled beside an old red Mustang.

"Oh, my God. Alex! Are you okay?" Robin scrambled all the way into the garage.

"Don't touch the car! Don't let that bloody dog near it!"

Robin grabbed Tinker as he dashed in beside her. "What happened?"

"The ramp . . . the other one might go, too . . . any minute." His voice sounded strained, listless.

"Are you hurt?"

"The phone—my cordless. Do you see it somewhere on the floor?"

She scanned the area. "Yes. Here it is. Against the wall. I'll call 911." She hurried over, picked it up.

"The number . . ." Alex mumbled. "Carin . . . I can't remember the number."

"But—"

"Ty . . . I need to find him. He could be lost . . . hurt."

Robin crouched beside the car. Alex sounded half out of his mind. "What happened to Ty? Where's Carin?"

He drew a noisy breath. "Before the car fell. He left the cabin. . . . Carin called the police. Ty's confused, that's all. I should have seen it. . . . I should have seen it coming . . . should've talked . . . he's a good lad. He needs—"

"Alex—" Robin didn't even try to make sense of his fragmented sentences. Obviously, his nephew was in some kind of trouble. But right now, Alex was her first concern. "Let me put Tinker inside your house, and I'll get you out of there."

He didn't seem to hear. "The phone. I heard it. Carin . . . she must have tried to reach me. Inside . . . inside the house . . . my messages."

Robin sensed the effort it took for Alex to speak. Worried about his injuries, she opened the door leading into his kitchen and set Tinker inside. She closed the door again. A second later, she heard Sheeba's hiss and Tinker's answering growl.

"You can't help Ty stuck beneath that car. What should we do?"

"The jack. In the storage closet. Against the back wall. Do you know how to use one?"

She hadn't lived thirty years as a single woman without learning to change a tire. Rounding the car, Robin headed for the storage closet. She opened the door, set the phone on the floor and rummaged through the mess inside. Obviously, Alex hadn't organized the space since moving in. "Where? I don't see it."

"It's there. Look—"

"Here it is!" She tucked the jack under her arm, then picked up the phone and punched in 911. As she stepped back into the garage, the tire squeaked against the standing ramp like rubber-soled tennis shoes skidding against pavement. Robin's breath caught.

"Hurry," Alex said.

Chapter Twenty-three

Ethan swerved to the side of the road and stopped so an ambulance could pass. "You'd think you could afford a decent alarm clock." He glanced across at Millie. "It's almost seven-thirty. We should've been at Robin's house half an hour ago."

The ambulance's wailing siren and flashing lights shot a tremor of pure panic through Millie. Robin hadn't answered her phone when they'd called to tell her they'd be late. "Oh, God, Ethan. Look! They're turning onto Robin's street!"

She swallowed down a knot of fear and glanced across at him. Ethan's normally ruddy face was blanched and taut with stress. "Don't just sit there," Millie snapped. "Follow them! Hurry!"

Tires squealed against pavement. Ethan didn't even slow down to turn the corner. "That's Alex Simon's place they're stopping at, not Robin's." He pulled to the curb in front of Alex's house.

Before the truck came to a complete stop, Millie was out the door. She ran across the yard toward the ambulance in the driveway.

Inside the garage, two paramedics were helping Alex onto a stretcher.

"Is this really necessary?" Alex asked, sounding embarrassed. "I'm fine, really. Just a bit sore."

One of the paramedics offered him an apologetic smile. "Your wife insisted."

"My—?" Alex stopped talking and turned toward the door into his house when it swung open.

Robin hurried out. She wore her pajamas. Her feet were bare. She didn't appear to notice Millie standing just outside.

"Ty's okay," she said, her voice enthusiastic, encouraging. She took Alex's hand when she stopped alongside the stretcher. "Carin left several messages on your recorder. She found Ty last night. He's fine. They're heading home today."

From behind, Millie felt Ethan's hands grip her shoulders. Her eyes filled with tears. "Look at her," she whispered. "Oh, Ethan . . . look. She's out of her house . . . her yard."

"Thank God she's safe." Ethan's voice was quiet, gruff with emotion.

"Not only that, she's in *Alex's garage*. And

350

wearing her pajamas." Millie faced him. "Do you know what that might mean?"

"Oh . . . !" Robin said. "Millie, Uncle E. I'm glad you're here."

Turning, Millie watched, amazed, as Robin walked toward them.

"Alex got stuck under his car. A tire ramp collapsed while he was working under it. He was trapped all night, but he's going to be okay. He—"

"—So are you, sweetie." Millie grabbed her, pulled her close, wrapped both arms around her. "You're going to be okay." She stepped back and smiled through her tears. "You're going to be okay!"

"You did it, sugar," Ethan said. "You know what time it is?"

Robin's eyes widened. She glanced from Ethan to Millie, then back again. "Oh . . . I forgot. Is it—?"

"Seven's come and gone." Ethan chuckled. "You broke the curse."

Robin clapped her hands and squealed, causing the two paramedics to exchange a puzzled glance.

"Thank goodness." Millie crossed her arms. "Maybe we can finally hear the end of that bunk once and for all.

Holding her right hand out, Robin stared down at it. "The topaz ring . . . it's gone. No . . ." She shook her head. "Surely . . ."

Ethan frowned. "Your mama's ring?"

351

"I threw it away," Robin whispered.

Millie couldn't believe what she was hearing. "You threw your mother's ring away? Why on earth?"

"It was cursed. So I threw it away after the stagecoach wreck."

"For goodness' sake. Stagecoach?" Baffled, Millie shook her head. "What stagecoach?"

"The stagecoach my great-great-grandmother died on." Robin turned to Alex. "In my dream."

He smiled at her. "You saved me," he said as the paramedics lifted the stretcher. "You faced your worst fear to save my life."

"When I heard you calling me, I forgot everything else."

Dreams? Stagecoaches? Millie exchanged glances with Ethan. "Robin, do you actually mean to tell us you could hear Alex's cries from inside your house?"

"No." Robin walked over and took Alex's hand. "In my dream. He called to me in my dream."

Alex looked up at her. "You said your mother's ring held the curse?"

"Yes, the witch hexed it."

"Lil?" Alex asked.

Robin nodded. "I was too late to save Hannah, but I took the cursed ring off her finger and threw it away."

Alex looked skeptical. "And now you can't find it?"

"Nope." Robin grinned. "But it was on my finger when I went to sleep."

"It slipped off," he insisted. "It's in your room somewhere. It must be."

Robin raised her brows. "Oh, must it, now? You believed in magic just long enough to save yourself, is that it?"

Frowning, Alex adjusted his glasses. "It was a dream, Robin. None of it truly happened. There was never a curse or a witch named Lil or a Nasty Jack Tucker or any of that. Getting rid of the ring in your dream had nothing to do with your finding the courage to come over here. You did it all yourself."

With a sigh, Robin said, "After everything that's happened, you're still the logical scientist. Why don't you explain to me how you know who Lil is? And how do you know about Nasty Jack? I didn't mention him."

Millie was afraid the paramedics might drop the stretcher with Alex on it, but they seemed too intrigued by the strange conversation to leave. She opened her mouth to interrupt, but when she witnessed the look that passed between Robin and Alex, she refrained. Robin could babble nonsense from now until dusk if she wanted. In Millie's vast experience, women in love often did.

She grinned up at Ethan. He grinned back. Their little girl was going to be fine. That was all that really mattered.

* * *

Expectant whispers, muffled sobs, and romantic sighs filtered through the Crazy Ace Saloon. On the piano in one corner of the big, crowded room, Slick played "We've Only Just Begun" by The Carpenters. Behind the bar, Ruby dabbed her eyes, but failed to restrain the teardrops that plopped onto the red satin stretched across her quivering bosom.

As the judge rambled on, Alex kept his eyes focused on the vision across from him. She wore frilly white from the top of her tilted hat, to the tip of her purple toenails. In one hand she held a bouquet of yellow roses, in the other, her closed parasol.

"You can kiss the bride now," the judge slurred.

Alex blinked. Reluctantly, he tore his gaze from the lady's long-lashed brown eyes to look at the shriveled old man in front of them. "What did you say?"

The judge reeked of whiskey. His bloodshot gaze shifted from the bottle on the bar back to Alex. "I said you're hitched now, Gambler. Lay one on her and be done with it."

The music stopped. A hush fell over the room. Slowly, Alex turned to the lady at his side . . . his wife.

She dipped her chin, lifted only her eyes to look up at him. "Well, Gambler," she said in a husky voice that instantly slid Alex's thoughts south of his belt buckle. "What are you waiting for?"

In one swift move, he swept her off her feet and started for the staircase leading to his room. He'd be damned if their first kiss as husband and wife would take place in front of a bunch of ogling cowhands and jealous painted ladies. Their first kiss would take place on satin sheets, surrounded by scented candles and strains of Barry White.

Halfway up the stairs a blue butterfly flitted past. Mesmerized by the insect's graceful dance, Alex paused. The lady loved him. There was no more need to pretend. Nothing left to prove.

When his wife tossed her bouquet of yellow roses over the banister, Alex could no longer wait. He pulled off his mask and sent it flying, too.

She studied his face, then smiled coyly. "I knew it was you all along. You never needed to hide from me."

Amidst whistles and cheers, the lady opened her parasol, blocking their faces from view of the crowd below.

"Good idea," Alex whispered. Starting today, his crooked grin was for her and her alone. He lowered his lips to his wife's mouth . . . and kissed her thoroughly. . . .

Alex awoke in the lawn chair to the sound of chirping crickets and the enthusiastic voice of Doctor Dave on the radio at his side. It was dark out now. He'd slept right through sunset.

At his feet, Sheeba and Tinker slept on the

ground, curled up side by side. Sometime during their confinement together in his house while Robin pried the Mustang off him, the animals had made peace with each other. The truce had not come easy. Like him, they were both a bit battered and sore, but nothing critical.

Alex's mild concussion, bruised lung and two bruised ribs had cost him a couple of uncomfortable days and one miserable night, but he wasn't complaining. His situation could have been worse. Much worse. He had not even had to spend a night in the hospital. They'd treated him in the emergency room, then released him.

"What's on your mind this evening?" Doctor Dave asked. "Give me a call at 800-555-6676, and we'll talk about it."

Alex decided to go inside. He reached to switch the radio off, but a light came on in Robin's bedroom across the way, making him hesitate.

After the ambulance had taken him away, she had not met him at the emergency room like she'd said she would. Her uncle had showed up instead. Ethan had conveyed her apologies, but he didn't need to explain. Alex had suspected Robin might experience a backlash of her agoraphobia after all the excitement died down.

Since coming home yesterday morning, he had talked to her several times on the phone, but they hadn't seen each other. Carin and Ty had arrived shortly after his return. They'd stayed at his house all day while he slept and had even spent last night.

Robin had insisted on allowing the three of them time alone together without her "interference"—her word, not his. At first, Alex had scoffed at the suggestion. Now he thought she knew best. He and his sister and his nephew had talked well into the night. A river of tears was shed. There was a bit of shouting—a lot of hugging. They had a long road ahead of them, but they were a family. Alex was convinced that, together, they would be all right. Ty would get through this tough time, and he would go on.

Well over an hour ago, Carin and Ty had left after making Alex's dinner and leaving it in the refrigerator. He'd yet to eat it, and his stomach wasn't happy about that fact.

Nevertheless, things other than food occupied Alex's mind. Tonight, as usual, Robin's blinds weren't drawn. He watched her stretch and yawn. She switched on the radio at her bedside, then stepped onto the treadmill and began a brisk walk, her dark braid swaying from side to side.

Alex changed his mind about going in. He left the radio on and reached, instead, for his cordless phone. After punching in Doctor Dave's number, he waited for the operator to put him through.

"Welcome to the program! This is Doctor Dave. Who's speaking?"

Alex turned down his radio so there'd be no

feedback. He wanted everyone listening to hear him loud and clear.

Robin had accelerated her pace from a walk to a jog. Her braid bounced against her shoulders with each steady stride.

He settled his gaze on her lovely bum and cleared his throat. "Hello, Doctor Dave," he drawled, using his butchered Texas twang. "You can just call me Gambler."

Robin stumbled, grabbed hold of the treadmill's side bars. Her head shifted quickly toward the radio on her nightstand.

Alex smiled.

"Okay, Gambler." The doctor chuckled. "You're my first caller, so you get to set the program's tone this evening. What would you like to talk about?"

"I have a dream lover," Alex drawled.

"I see," Doctor Dave said slowly. "You suffer from obsessive fantasies?"

"You might say that. I'd like to ask her a question."

The doctor hesitated. "You, uh, you want to ask a fantasy lover—a person who doesn't really exist—a question over the airwaves?"

"That's right. If I'm not mistaken, I believe she might be listening, and I'm sure she'll understand."

Robin stopped running. She stepped off the treadmill, moved slowly toward the radio beside her bed.

"I don't know." Doctor Dave sounded wary. "This is rather unorthodox. We don't usually—"

"There was a time," Alex continued, ignoring the doctor and losing his feigned Texas accent, "when I didn't believe in magic. Well, I was wrong. Magic exists, but only if you believe. The magic I believe in is love. It's the strongest magic of all, and it can work miracles. It can conquer fears. It can even save lives."

The doctor coughed. "Go on."

Robin turned and walked toward the window, her eyes wide and stunned, the fingers of her right hand pressed to her lips. Though Alex knew she couldn't see him in the darkness, she stared toward his yard. Slowly, she moved her fingers away from her mouth and touched the window.

"I had a dream this evening," Alex continued, his eyes focused on Robin. "I'd like for the two of us, the lady in my dream and I, to do what we did in the saloon in our dream. Only, this time, I want to do it for real. I'm wondering if she's willing."

The doctor started talking but Alex didn't hear what he said. He was watching Robin . . . watching her turn her back to the window . . . watching her run across the room until she disappeared from view.

Ignoring his aches and pains, Alex dropped the phone and started toward the hedge that separated their yards. He stopped just short of the gap that she'd only found the courage to pass through to save his life. He stood there and waited. And while he waited, he prayed—prayed that she'd save him again.

Moments passed, and then she was there, crossing that final barrier without hesitation, flying into his yard . . . into his arms. The impact of her body against his jarred Alex's bruised ribs, but he didn't complain. Why would he when her hands were in his hair, her legs wrapped around his waist? Crying and laughing all at once, she covered his face with kisses.

"I know it's a bit soon," Alex said as his lips skimmed across her mouth. "We haven't known each other long, but I know without a doubt that I love you, Robin. I feel—"

"Yes," she said. "The answer to your question is yes. But we'll do it in my rose garden instead of a saloon. Deal?"

"Deal." He'd never heard a sweeter proposition. "But we'll have to spray. I won't tolerate any black spot at my wedding."

She stood on her own and kissed him again, not stopping as she took his hand and led him, stumbling, toward her house. "There's something you need to see," she murmured against his lips. "Something that can't wait."

Holding on and kissing her back, Alex followed Robin blindly across her yard and into her living room. When she flipped on the light, he stepped back.

Immediately, he noticed the easel had been returned to its usual place by the window.

Robin led him to it. "I finished the painting."

Alex glanced across at the canvas. His gaze skimmed over the image of the west Texas town at sunset, the cornfield off in the distance. He eyed the Crazy Ace saloon, the four-poster brass bed in the middle of the road. He studied the yellow rose . . . the gambler's saber. Nothing seemed changed since the last time he looked. "I'm sorry," he said. "I don't—"

"Look closer," Robin said softly. "I found the ring."

Squinting, Alex leaned forward . . . and then he saw it. Three blue stones on a filigreed gold band encircled the rose's stem.

Alex smiled. "It's perfect. Perfect."

"I thought you'd say that."

Lifting her right hand, he glanced down. The identical ring encircled her third finger.

"I'm starting a new tradition, just in case," Robin said. "If we have a daughter, I won't give her the ring until *after* her thirtieth birthday."

Alex looked into her eyes and smiled. Logical or not, it was a decision even he wouldn't question.

He took her in his arms, held her for a long time while they stared at the image of their shared dream. Finally, he couldn't resist asking the outrageous question that preyed on his mind. "Nasty Jack's money . . . what happened to it?"

Robin glanced up. "Maybe we'll find out tonight. Look."

He followed her gaze overhead. A blue butterfly hovered above them, then flew over to the canvas. Perching on one of the bedposts in the painting, it spread its wings wide.

Alex winked at the insect, then whispered, "Thanks."

As it lifted off, he and Robin followed it to the open door and watched it fly away . . . across the yard . . . past Robin's moon-kissed roses . . . into the shadowed branches of the old oak tree.

Archer's Crossing — Jean Barrett

Crossing Archer Owen seems like the last thing anybody would want to do, or so Margaret Sheridan thinks. Bringing dinner to the convicted murderer is terrifying—for though he is nothing like her affluent fiancé, he stirs a hunger in her she has never known. Then the condemned prisoner uses her to make his getaway. In the clutches of the handsome felon, Margaret races into the untamed West—chasing a man Owen claims could clear his name. Margaret wonders if there is anything Archer won't do. And then he kisses her, and she prays there isn't. For if this bitter steamboat captain is half the man she suspects, she'd ride to Hell itself to clear his name and win his captive heart.

___4502-8 $5.99 US/$6.99 CAN

LOVING CHARITY CATHERINE ARCHIBALD

Vengeance is Jason Wade's only purpose; the Boston lawyer has sworn to avenge his wife's death. Tracking her suspected killer to Wisconsin, he knows that to entertain a flirtation with the lovely Charity Applegate is to court disaster. But her smile weakens his resolve and her honesty breaks down his defenses until Jason wonders if the path to salvation lies not in retribution, but in loving Charity.

On the eve of the Civil War, Charity Applegate accepts the risks involved in following one's heart. Her Quaker family aids the underground railroad, and the arrival of Jason Wade could expose them all. But caught in his passionate embrace, Charity realizes he challenges the strength of her courage even further—by daring her to trust him. And she knows she will have to make a great leap of faith for the best reward for all: love.

___4704-7 $4.99 US/$5.99 CAN

Dorchester Publishing Co., Inc.
P.O. Box 6640
Wayne, PA 19087-8640

Please add $1.75 for shipping and handling for the first book and $.50 for each book thereafter. NY, NYC, and PA residents, please add appropriate sales tax. No cash, stamps, or C.O.D.s. All orders shipped within 6 weeks via postal service book rate. Canadian orders require $2.00 extra postage and must be paid in U.S. dollars through a U.S. banking facility.

Name_____
Address_____
City_____State_____Zip_____
I have enclosed $_____ in payment for the checked book(s).
Payment <u>must</u> accompany all orders. ☐ Please send a free catalog.

Spell Weaver — Roxi Ashe

Lady Taras seeks to create a philter of love but instead her subject becomes a frog. Then, summoned by her king to help defeat a Viking horde, Taras is told that only her potion can make things right. A Viking warrior is wreaking havoc on English troops, and legend claims the man cannot be killed. England has one chance: Turn the warlord into a toad. A frog prince? The handsome raider is anything but. If Taras thinks Cynewulf wreaks havoc on English men, it is nothing compared to what the sight of his well-muscled form does to her. The forceful Dane conquers land as if he's been born to the task and he wins her heart with equal ease. How can she subdue this giant when her potion is a sham? She'll have to rely on a separate sorcery than that she's brewed—and the only magic she knows is woven by love.

___4649-0 $5.50 US/$6.50 CAN

Dorchester Publishing Co., Inc.
P.O. Box 6640
Wayne, PA 19087-8640

Please add $1.75 for shipping and handling for the first book and $.50 for each book thereafter. NY, NYC, and PA residents, please add appropriate sales tax. No cash, stamps, or C.O.D.s. All orders shipped within 6 weeks via postal service book rate. Canadian orders require $2.00 extra postage and must be paid in U.S. dollars through a U.S. banking facility.

Name_____
Address_____
City_____ State_____ Zip_____
I have enclosed $_____ in payment for the checked book(s).
Payment <u>must</u> accompany all orders. ❑ Please send a free catalog.
CHECK OUT OUR WEBSITE! www.dorchesterpub.com

BODY & SOUL
JENNIFER ARCHER

Overworked, underappreciated housewife and mother Lisa O'Conner gazes at the young driver in the red car next to her. Tory Beecham's manicured nails keep time with the radio and her smile radiates youthful vitality. For a moment, Lisa imagines switching places with the carefree college student. But when Lisa looks in the rearview mirror and sees Tory's hazel eyes peering back at her, she discovers her daydream has become astonishing reality. Fortune has granted Lisa every woman's fantasy. But as the goggle-eyed, would-be young suitors line up at Lisa's door, only one man piques her interest. But he is married—to her, or rather, the woman she used to be. And he seems intent on being faithful. Unsure how to woo her husband, Lisa knows one thing: No matter what else comes of the madcap, mix-matched mayhem, she will be reunited body and soul with her only true love.

___52334-5 $5.50 US/$6.50 CAN

Dorchester Publishing Co., Inc.
P.O. Box 6640
Wayne, PA 19087-8640

Please add $1.75 for shipping and handling for the first book a$.50 for each book thereafter. NY, NYC, and PA reside please add appropriate sales tax. No cash, stamps, or C.O.D.s. A orders shipped within 6 weeks via postal service book rate. Canadian orders require $2.00 extra postage and must be paid in U.S. dollars through a U.S. banking facility.

Name_____
Address_____
City_____ State_____ Zip_____
I have enclosed $_____ in payment for the checked book(s).
Payment <u>must</u> accompany all orders. ❏ Please send a free catalog.
CHECK OUT OUR WEBSITE! www.dorchesterpub.com

New Year's Babies

EUGENIA RILEY, JENNIFER ARCHER, KIMBERLY RAYE

As the countdown to first night begins, three couples will have more to toast than just a change in the calendar . . .

"The Confused Stork" In his dotage, the disoriented bird has delivered Emma Fairchild's baby to Victorian England where she finds her precious package in the arms of a dashing earl.

"Blame It on the Baby" Tory gains a closer understanding of her husband, and he of her, when they switch places, literally. But it will take the miracle of new life for them to realize where their hearts truly lie.

"A Little Bit of Magic" When a baby doll is transformed into a real life bundle of joy, Samantha relies on her handsome neighbor, who knows his way around a nursery and, as it turns out, her heart.

. . . and one thing is certain in a world gone slightly askew: Not only will the new year be rung in with cries of babies, but with declarations of love.

___52345-0 $5.99 US/$6.99 CAN

ATTENTION ROMANCE CUSTOMERS!

SPECIAL TOLL-FREE NUMBER
1-800-481-9191

Call Monday through Friday
10 a.m. to 9 p.m.
Eastern Time
*Get a free catalogue,
join the Romance Book Club,
and order books using your
Visa, MasterCard,
or Discover®*

Leisure
Books